"You really do [...]
everyone in this town, [...]

"My family has lived here as long as any other."

"Be careful," he said. "You're revealing personal information that I might be able to use to track you down in the future."

"This is Haven," she reminded him. "If you ever came back and wanted to find me, it wouldn't be difficult."

"When I come back, I'll definitely find you," he promised.

As much as Sarah wanted to believe he meant it, she wasn't going to let herself hope that it might ever happen. Because in her experience, expectations only led to disappointment.

And so instead of wondering what might or might not happen in the future, she decided to enjoy this moment right now.

But he'd picked up the thread of their conversation again and was talking about other places he'd visited in Nevada and around the country and how some of them weren't places he'd feel compelled to revisit while others he could return to again and again.

"You're not listening to me, are you?" he asked.

"I'm sorry," Sarah said. "My mind was wandering."

"What were you thinking about?"

She lifted her gaze to his. "Truthfully...I was wondering if you were ever going to stop talking and kiss me."

He stopped talking and kissed her.

Dear Reader,

Welcome back to Haven! A lot of years have passed since I first introduced this northern Nevada town, and writing those words now, for (probably) the last time, has put me in a nostalgic mood.

While the historic feud between the Blakes and the Gilmores was (mostly) resolved as a consequence of Brielle and Caleb's reunion in *One Night with the Cowboy*, there's been plenty of other stuff happening in town to keep the rumor mill churning. Not to mention all the weddings and babies!

Current speculation is that Sarah Stafford, recently returned to her ranching roots, is sweet on Andrew Morrow, new owner of the town's beloved bakery. Anyone who has seen them together can attest to their obvious chemistry, but each has secrets yet to be revealed...

Whether this is your first visit to Haven or your eighteenth (or some number in between), I hope you enjoy this "Match Made in Haven" and that you'll come with me to Whispering Canyon, Wyoming, in the very near future to meet some new cowboys— and the women who lasso their hearts.

Happy reading!

xo *Brenda*

A RANCHER OF HIS OWN

BRENDA HARLEN

SPECIAL EDITION

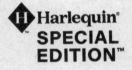

H Harlequin®
SPECIAL EDITION™

Recycling programs
for this product may
not exist in your area.

ISBN-13: 978-1-335-40224-0

A Rancher of His Own

Copyright © 2025 by Brenda Harlen

Harlequin Enterprises ULC
22 Adelaide St. West, 41st Floor
Toronto, Ontario M5H 4E3, Canada
www.Harlequin.com

Printed in U.S.A.

Brenda Harlen is a former attorney who once had the privilege of appearing before the Supreme Court of Canada. The practice of law taught her a lot about the world and reinforced her determination to become a writer—because in fiction, she could promise a happy ending! Now she is an award-winning, RITA® Award–nominated, nationally bestselling author of more than sixty titles for Harlequin. You can keep up-to-date with Brenda on Facebook and X, or through her website, brendaharlen.com.

Visit the Author Profile page
at Harlequin.com for more titles.

For Kelly and Julie, who were integral to so many of my childhood memories. Though our paths diverged as we grew older, it has been a sincere pleasure to reconnect in recent years, not just as family but as friends, and to know that you're each the kick-ass heroine of your own story. xoxo

Chapter One

Since her graduation from college, Sarah Stafford's life had proceeded according to plan. Unfortunately, it took ten years for her to realize that it wasn't *her* plan but one that her parents had mapped out for her. And so today she'd doused that plan in gasoline and dropped a lighted match on it.

Metaphorically speaking, of course.

Though apparently the explosion had been heard in the farthest corners of the executive offices of Blake Mining.

As she'd walked out of the building, she'd been shaking inside. Not that anyone would know it. Sarah had a lot of practice hiding her feelings and showing the world—or at least her family—only what she wanted them to see.

The one person she'd never been able to fool was Claire Blake, formerly Lamontagne.

It was her childhood BFF who'd sensed Sarah's discontent and told her that if she wasn't happy with her life, she should do something about it. As Claire herself had done three years earlier when she left her controlling fiancé in Austin, Texas, and returned to Haven, Nevada.

Though inspired by her friend's actions and advice, Sarah had been hesitant to upset the status quo. Because even if walking into her office didn't fill her heart with joy, she hadn't exactly been *un*happy as the associate director of occupational health and safety at Blake Mining.

It was more that she'd felt…superfluous.

And indulged.

True, she'd worked hard to get her business degree from UT Austin, but almost immediately after graduation, she'd walked into an executive position that she'd done nothing to deserve. Or at least nothing aside from being born into the Blake family.

Her manicured hands wrapped around the steering wheel of her hybrid SUV as she exited through the gates of the company founded by her great-grandfather. Starting tomorrow, she was going to get those same hands dirty in her new job—and not just metaphorically speaking this time—and she was a little surprised to realize how much she was looking forward to it.

Driving into town—such as it was—she found a vacant spot in the parking lot behind Diggers' Bar & Grill and turned off the engine, then remained behind the wheel for another minute to focus on breathing in and out, waiting for the anxiety to hit.

But the familiar tightness in her chest wasn't there.

She actually felt…not quite happy, at least not yet, but definitely lighter. No longer weighed down by the expectations of her family.

Poor little rich girl.

The familiar taunt echoed in the back of her mind, but she shoved it aside in favor of her new mantra: *I am a strong, independent woman in control of my own destiny.*

And if she ended up regretting the choice she'd made—as both her parents had assured her that she would do—at least she'd know it had been *her* choice.

So resolved, she pulled out her phone and sent a text message to her BFF.

Can you meet me at Diggers'?

Almost immediately, three little dots appeared on her screen, indicating that Claire was responding.

Are we celebrating?

We are.

Her friend answered that with a trio of happy faces, followed by:

Be there in 30.
Order food before drinks!

Smiling now, Sarah climbed out of her vehicle and made her way around the back to open the hatch.

She'd done the hard part already; the next step was merely symbolic. But it was an important step to her—tangible evidence that she was shedding her old life and embracing the new.

Without hesitation—though with a silent apology to Michael Kors—she unbuttoned the crepe blazer that she wore over her sheath-style dress and tossed it into the back of her car. Then she toed off the three-inch heels she was wearing—sorry, Jimmy Choo—and discarded them, too. Now she was standing on cold (and undoubtedly filthy) asphalt in stocking feet, but she wasn't quite done yet. She reached up to pluck the bobby pins out of her hair, dismantling the knot that she habitually wore into the office so that her hair fell freely over her shoulders.

"Do you want some music?"

She jolted at the question and, with her heart pounding, pivoted to face the speaker—a tall, broad-shouldered stranger who was as distinctly masculine and undeniably sexy as his voice. Six feet, she guessed, tousled brown hair, square jaw sporting two or three days' growth and eyes the color of dark chocolate.

Her fight-or-flight response took its sweet time considering those options. On the one hand, she was a woman alone with a strange man in a parking lot. On the other hand, it was broad daylight, and this was Haven.

"Music?" she echoed, still undecided about her next move.

She caught a quick glimpse of even white teeth as he grinned.

"To accompany your striptease," he said.

Despite the heat that rushed into her cheeks, Sarah managed to respond coolly, "I'm not sure if I should be flattered or insulted, but I assure you, nothing else is coming off."

"I'm sure I'm disappointed," he said, following his remark with a playful wink that suggested he was flirting with her.

Or maybe that was wishful thinking on her part, because the man was seriously hot.

But she wasn't the least bit interested in getting burned.

Okay, maybe she was just the teeniest bit interested, but she had to trust that she was smart enough to ignore the interest that was suddenly humming in her veins. Because once bitten, twice shy—and she'd been bitten more than once.

And while her heart was still pounding a little too fast, she suspected that fear was no longer the cause—and that gave her even more reason to be wary. Because she had a history of being attracted to men who were all kinds of wrong for her and not recognizing that truth until she was left broken-hearted.

"You should know that I've got pepper spray," she told him, because she'd always subscribed to the theory that the best defense was a good offense and a woman finding herself alone with a strange man had to be ready to defend herself. (Actually, what she had was hairspray, but she'd heard that a travel-size can could be as effective as pepper spray to ward off an attacker.)

The stranger looked pointedly at her empty hands. "And where are you hiding that?"

In her purse.

Which she'd tossed, along with her jacket, into the back of the car.

Dammit.

"I've also got a black belt in karate."

That was a total lie, but she lifted her chin in the hope that her bravado would sell it.

He didn't appear the least bit intimidated.

If anything, the glint in his eye and the hint of a smile tugging at one corner of his mouth suggested that he was… amused.

"I might have been more inclined to believe you if you'd claimed to have a green—or even a brown—belt," he told her. "Do you have any idea how many hours of training are required to get a black belt?"

"As a matter of fact, I do," she responded flippantly.

Another lie.

Apparently the new Sarah Stafford wasn't exactly honest or forthcoming.

On the other hand, she didn't figure she owed a stranger in a parking lot any truths about her life.

"Please, continue with your…not stripping," he said.

She removed a pair of old cowboy boots from the back of her car and shoved her feet into the soft, worn leather. Then she grabbed the faded denim jacket—"borrowed" from Zack Kruger when they'd dated back in high school—and shoved her arms through the sleeves.

And yes, Zack was one of those guys who'd been all wrong for her—and she'd been even more wrong for him. A fact that she regretted to this day, even if he didn't seem to be holding a grudge.

"From cool business executive to sexy cowgirl in half a minute."

The stranger's quiet musing yanked Sarah back to the present; the blatant appreciation in his gaze made her blood heat in her veins.

And because she was obviously attracted to this man and didn't want to be, her response came out uncharacteristically sharp. "Why are you still here?"

"Because that—" he gestured to the vehicle parked beside hers, apparently unperturbed by her sharp tone "—is my car."

"I'm hardly blocking your path," she pointed out.

"No," he acknowledged. "But I'm wary of your black belt. And your pepper spray."

She had to press her lips together to prevent them from curving. Because the man was good-looking *and* effortlessly charming—and she really didn't want to be charmed.

She grabbed her purse and closed the hatch. "Drive safely."

"I'll be fine," he assured her, and winked again. "Yours are the most dangerous curves I've seen in this town."

The stunningly sexy brunette rolled deep blue eyes before walking away, and Andrew Morrow could hardly fault her dismissive response. His parting remark had been ridiculously cheesy—proof that he'd been out of the game too long and was trying too hard.

He was also late, he realized, as he pulled out of the parking lot.

And Kyle Landry knew it, too, as evidenced by his pointed look at his watch when Andrew walked into his kitchen.

"I got caught in traffic," he said by way of explanation.

His friend chuckled at that. "At least you brought your sense of humor."

"So why did you want to meet here instead of at Diggers'?"

Here was The Home Station, where Kyle was the executive chef. Before the restaurant opened, residents of the northern Nevada town had to venture beyond its borders in pursuit of upscale dining. Now people came from Battle Mountain and

Elko and even farther to eat at The Home Station. As a result, reservations were typically booked weeks—and sometimes months—in advance.

"The bok choy in our produce shipment was subpar, requiring me to make some last-minute tweaks to tonight's menu," Kyle explained.

Andrew didn't need to ask what constituted subpar, because he was undoubtedly as particular as his friend when it came to the ingredients he used in his recipes. In fact, on one memorable occasion, he'd sent an assistant out for Madagascan vanilla beans and she returned with Tahitian. According to other members of the staff, Andrew had gone on a rant not unlike those seen on so many cooking shows on reality TV.

"Let's chat in my office," Kyle said, leading the way through a kitchen already bustling with activity.

He poured them each a mug of coffee from the pot behind his desk and waited for Andrew to settle in the chair across from him before he asked, "Did you and Caroline finalize terms?"

Caroline Bennett was the namesake and daughter of the original owner of Sweet Caroline's, reputed to be northern Nevada's favorite bakery.

Andrew nodded. "We did."

Kyle grinned and lifted his mug. "To new beginnings."

Andrew drank. "I'd be lying if I said I didn't have reservations, but I'm going to do it, anyway."

When he graduated from Escoffier's Austin campus of the Texas Culinary Academy—where he'd met Kyle—he'd dreamed of someday owning his own bakery. But he knew that he was going to need a lot more experience—and a significant nest egg—before pursuing that dream, and so he'd taken a job as an assistant pastry chef at Divine, a popular French restaurant in Beaumont, Texas.

Divine was a good place to work, and he was mostly given

free rein when it came to the creation of his desserts. Three years later, just when he was starting to think it might be time to pursue other opportunities, Miranda Ross started to work at the restaurant. The new sommelier was knowledgeable, experienced and passionate—and not only about wine. Two years after that, they were married, and Andrew had shelved his dreams in favor of keeping the job that paid their rent.

But he and Miranda were divorced now, and when she'd moved to Napa Valley with her winemaking boyfriend, Andrew had realized there was nothing keeping him in Beaumont. And then Kyle had told him that there was a prime opportunity in Haven, if he was willing to take it.

"Of course you have reservations," his friend said to him now. "Running your own business is a lot different than making desserts for someone else's customers, but I have no doubt that you'll succeed."

Andrew appreciated the other man's confidence. Because he'd done the research, he knew that any new business was a risky venture. But he wasn't really starting a new business. Rather he was taking over a well-established one, making some minor renovations to the property, giving it a new name and updating the menu.

Still, it was those planned changes that increased the risk. People were generally creatures of habit, opting for what was familiar over trying something new. But Caroline had assured him that so long as he continued to offer her famous chocolate peanut butter banana croissants and the wildly popular raspberry bliss bars—the proprietary recipes being included as part of their deal—the local residents would overlook all else.

"Were you nervous when you took the reins here?" Andrew asked his friend.

"Sure," Kyle agreed. "At the same time, knowing that there would always be a job for me in the kitchen at Jo's was something of a safety net—albeit one I wasn't entirely convinced my mom wouldn't strangle me with."

Andrew chuckled. Though he'd only met Jolene Landry a couple times, the proprietor of the local pizzeria had made an impression. And so did her pizza, which was why her revered establishment was almost a place of worship more than a restaurant.

"Plus it wasn't my money I had to worry about losing," his friend acknowledged. "Liam Gilmore owns the inn and the restaurant, so he's the one who has to reconcile the income and expenses—I just cook."

"That makes me feel so much better," Andrew said dryly.

"You want to feel better? You should try some of the desserts left over from last night's menu."

"I'm not sure how that's going to help."

"Trust me," Kyle said, already halfway out the door.

He returned a few minutes later with a square plate upon which samples of three desserts had been arranged.

"New York–style cheesecake with macerated strawberry topping, lemon crème brûlée with fresh blackberries and a chocolate hazelnut éclair topped with chocolate ganache and toasted crushed hazelnuts."

"You can't honestly expect me to eat all of this."

"Just try a bite of each," Kyle urged.

Because it seemed important to his friend—and because each of the desserts looked delicious—Andrew did so. And then went back for a second taste.

"I have to offer kudos to your pastry chef," he said, when he finally set down his fork.

"We don't have a pastry chef," Kyle told him. "For as long as The Home Station has been in operation, Sweet Caroline's has supplied our desserts."

"What are you going to do when Sweet Caroline's closes its doors?" Andrew asked curiously.

"I was hoping to enter into the same arrangement with the bakery's new owner—which is why I'm happy to know it's going to be you."

"It's going to take me some time to pack up my life in Texas and make the move," he felt compelled to warn his friend.

"In the meantime, I think I've convinced Bonnie, who's been Caroline's right hand for more than a dozen years, to continue making the desserts for us."

"If she's that good, why don't you hire her to work here?" Andrew wondered aloud.

"She's that good," Kyle confirmed. "But we don't have the space for a pastry chef. Besides, I've heard that she's polishing up her résumé for the new owner of Sweet Caroline's."

Before Andrew could respond to that, a knock sounded on the door.

"Chef?"

"Perfect timing," Kyle said to Andrew, before issuing an invitation to his visitor to "Come in."

The door opened and a sixty-something woman with blunt-cut gray hair and sharp blue eyes entered. Over jeans and a T-shirt, she wore a long white apron with Sweet Caroline's logo embroidered in pink on the front and pink Crocs on her feet.

She offered the white bakery box that she carried to Kyle. "Per your request."

"Thank you," he said, already opening the lid to peer inside.

"Tonight's offerings," he explained to Andrew, showing him the contents. "Hummingbird cake with cream cheese frosting, bourbon chocolate mousse garnished with freshly whipped cream and dark chocolate shavings and an apple toffee tart, which will be served warm with a scoop of freshly spun cinnamon ice cream."

"I'll bring that over later this afternoon," the woman promised.

"I'm tempted to pick up my fork again and dig in," Andrew said, and it wasn't an exaggeration.

Kyle grinned. "Bonnie, this is Andrew Morrow—the soon-to-be new owner of Sweet Caroline's."

"It's a pleasure to meet you," Bonnie said politely.

"Did you make these?" Andrew asked.

"I did," she confirmed.

"Do you know how to make those banana peanut butter croissants that everyone is talking about?"

"Chocolate peanut butter banana croissants," she said. "And yes, I do. As well as the raspberry bliss bars."

Andrew wasn't usually impulsive, but he did trust his instincts—and his instincts were telling him that this was an opportunity he shouldn't let slip away. "I hear you might be looking for a job when Caroline closes the doors of her shop."

"I might be," she allowed.

"How much does Caroline pay you?"

"Not nearly enough," she told him. Then she shrugged. "Lucky for you, my husband retired half a dozen years ago with a really good pension and, as much as I love him, I need a reason to get out of the house for a few hours every morning, so I'm willing to continue working for not nearly enough."

Andrew grinned. "In that case, you're hired."

Chapter Two

"I don't see any food," Claire noted, sliding into the booth that Sarah had claimed on the "bar" side of Diggers' Bar & Grill.

"I didn't know what you wanted to eat."

"I've been up since six and I worked through lunch—I want food."

Sarah had also skipped lunch, too nervous about The Big Confrontation with her parents to even consider putting anything in her knotted stomach. But those knots had since loosened enough to allow her to realize she was hungry.

Claire lifted her hand to snag the attention of their server.

"What can I get for you?" Alexa asked.

"We're going to start with the appetizer platter. And I'll have a glass of—" she looked at Sarah "—what are you drinking?"

"It's a cab-merlot blend from Washington State."

"That sounds good, too," Claire decided.

"If you're both drinking the same, do you want a carafe?" Alexa asked.

"I can walk home from here," Sarah noted.

"And Devin's picking me up later, so I don't have to worry about driving," Claire chimed in.

"I'd say that's a 'yes' on the carafe," Sarah told their server.

"I'll put your order in and be right back with that wine," Alexa promised.

While they waited for their food, Sarah told her friend about the meeting with her parents during which she'd shared her decision to leave Blake Mining to work with Claire at Twilight Valley.

"Were they supportive of your plans?" Claire asked cautiously.

Sarah snorted. "My dad accused me of going through another rebellious phase." She lifted her glass to sip her wine. "They've never considered the possibility that I might want something different than what they want for me, and I've finally stopped expecting that they ever will."

"I'm sorry."

She shrugged. "Oh, and when I gave the hard copy of my resignation to my mom, she asked for my access card."

"You're kidding."

Now Sarah shook her head. "I'm being punished for wanting to do my own thing, which is ridiculous, because I wasn't even a cog in the wheel of Blake Mining. I was more like a foreign-language sticker slapped on the outside of the machine—necessary but not particularly useful."

"But as long as you were working in the family business, they felt as if they had some degree of control over you," Claire noted.

"Maybe."

"Trust me," her friend said. "I have some experience with controlling parents—and a former fiancé who wanted to pick right up where they left off. Now you're getting the benefit of thousands of dollars of therapy for free."

"You didn't need the therapy," Sarah said. "You just needed to come back to Haven and find your own place and purpose at Twilight Valley. Although falling in love with my cousin might have also played a part in your newfound bliss."

A smile spread across Claire's face. "The icing on the cake. And that's what we need to celebrate," she decided. "Cake."

"Let's see if we can get through the appetizers first," Sarah said, when Alexa set the platter in the middle of the table.

"Speaking of cake," Claire said, reaching for a potato skin filled with bacon and cheese. "Sweet Caroline's is officially closing its doors in two weeks."

"Are you sure?" Sarah asked. "The rumors about a sale have been circulating for so long, I stopped paying attention."

"I'm sure," her friend confirmed.

"And then the era of the chocolate peanut butter banana croissant will officially come to an end," she lamented.

"I'm *not* so sure about that," Claire said. "Apparently the new owner has already hired Bonnie Reidel to work with him."

"How is it that you've been at the ranch all day and yet you still know all the latest gossip?" Sarah wondered aloud.

"Actually, me and Devin had an appointment at the bank this afternoon, after which we stopped at The Daily Grind where we heard Madison Russell dishing the details to Julie Keswick."

"How would Madison Russell know?"

"Her sister works in the kitchen at The Home Station."

"Which doesn't at all help connect the dots," Sarah told her friend.

"You're right," Claire acknowledged. "All I know is that Madison sounded as if she knew what she was talking about."

"So why did you have an appointment at the bank?" Sarah asked, circling back to pick up that thread of their conversation.

"I need a loan to build another barn at Twilight Valley."

"Your husband hasn't offered to pay for it?"

"He has," Claire admitted. "But I don't want his business propping up my business."

"You know he's got more money than he could ever spend in his lifetime—even after paying for a dozen new barns."

Because Devin wasn't just family money rich; he'd made his own, equally impressive, fortune developing mobile apps.

"Well, I don't need a dozen barns," Claire said. "I only need one more. And while I might stubbornly refuse to take his money—his words—I'm also smart enough to know that having him with me when I met with the loan officer would make it next to impossible for the bank to turn down my request."

"Then you were already in town when I texted you," Sarah realized.

Claire nodded.

"So why did it take you half an hour to get here?"

Her friend lifted her wineglass to hide the smile that curved her lips.

"Forget I asked," Sarah said. "But now I know why Devin has yet to put his house on the market, more than two years after moving out to Twilight Valley. It's so that you have a convenient love nest whenever you're in town."

"We don't stop by the house every time we're in town."

"I don't need to know. And I don't want to know that you were having sex in the middle of the afternoon when I haven't had sex at any time of the day in…a very long time."

"You could end that drought anytime you want," Claire said. "Any guy in this bar would be happy to go home with you. All you have to do is communicate interest with a crook of your finger."

"Unfortunately I've known most of the guys in this bar my whole life, and I am *not* interested."

"How are we doing here?" Alexa asked, as she removed the empty platter from the table.

"Good," Sarah said.

"Still hungry," Claire countered. "We need nachos."

"Chicken or beef?"

"Chicken. With extra salsa and sour cream."

"I can't believe you're still hungry," Sarah said, reaching for the carafe to top off their wineglasses as Alexa walked away.

Claire winked. "I worked up an appetite today."

"Don't want to know," Sarah reminded her friend.

But maybe it was time to take the initiative to end the drought.

"Do you think I could borrow Eduardo this weekend?" she asked, referring to the German shepherd/collie cross that her friend had taken home from the local shelter a few years earlier.

"You want to use my dog to pick up men?" Claire guessed.

"Jenna met Harrison at the dog park," she pointed out to her friend.

And while Sarah was happy that her sister had found "the one," Jenna's new romance seemed to shine a harsh spotlight on Sarah's solitary status.

"And they've got a great meet-cute story," Claire agreed. "But it's *their* story. Instead of trying to replicate it, you need to be open to writing your own."

"I'm open," Sarah insisted.

"With guards at the gate."

She frowned as she considered her friend's claim.

"And I know that there are reasons for the guards," Claire said, not unsympathetically. "But if you really want to meet someone, you're going to have to tell the guards to stand down."

"Actually I did meet someone today. Sort of."

"How do you 'sort of' meet someone?" her friend asked, her interest piqued.

"We chatted for a few minutes but went our separate ways without introductions."

"Obviously he made an impression or you wouldn't be telling me about him now."

Sarah sipped her wine. "He thought I was a stripper."

Claire hooted with laughter. "Ohmygod—you have to tell me more."

"I threatened him with pepper spray."

"The guards were clearly on duty," her friend noted.

"Today is the day I started living the life I want," she reminded Claire. "And I don't want any more casual hookups."

"How about orgasms?" her friend asked. "Don't you want more of those?"

"I'm not sure I remember what an orgasm is."

"That's just sad."

Sarah had to smile, because while her lack of a love life *was* sad, being with her BFF made her happy. And this—hanging out with Claire and drinking wine—was exactly what she needed today.

Her smile slipped along with her foot when Claire kicked her under the table. "Serious hottie at nine o'clock."

"Is it nine o'clock already?"

Her friend laughed. "How many glasses of wine have you had?"

She stared at the garnet-colored liquid in her glass. "I think this is three."

"He's at the bar now," Claire said, her gaze focused in that direction.

"Who?"

"The tall, dark and very sexy stranger."

"You're married to my cousin," Sarah reminded her friend.

"And very happily," Claire acknowledged. "But my marital status has absolutely no bearing on his hotness."

"I'm not turning around, because Ellis Hagen's sitting at the bar, and every time he catches my eye, he thinks I'm flirting with him."

Her friend chuckled at that.

"He's chatting with Duke but scoping out the room, almost as if he's looking for someone. Not Ellis, Hottie," she clarified before Sarah could ask. "And you don't have to turn around, because he's got a mug of beer in hand now and is heading in this direction."

Sarah sipped her wine, her eyes widening as the man who'd snagged her friend's attention stepped into view. "I know him."

"Do you?" Claire sounded intrigued.

"Well, no. Not really." Before she could look away, his gaze snagged hers and he smiled in a way that made her feel tingly inside. Or maybe that was the third glass of wine. "But our paths crossed earlier today."

Claire's lips curved as he made his way toward their table. "He's the one who thought you were a stripper?"

"He's the one," Sarah confirmed.

"It was an honest mistake," Hottie said, inserting himself into their conversation. "Based on the fact that she was taking her clothes off—"

"My jacket," Sarah interrupted indignantly. "I was taking off my jacket."

"And your Jimmy Choos," he noted.

"That's where your assumption proves faulty," she retorted. "Because strippers never take off their shoes."

Claire's eyes narrowed on the stranger. "And how did you know they were Jimmy Choos?"

His brows lifted. "A man can't know shoes?"

"Not a lot of straight unmarried men do."

"How about a straight, unmarried man who grew up with a sister obsessed with designer footwear?" he suggested.

"A possibility," Claire agreed with a nod, her face lighting up when she saw another man walk into the bar. "And there's *my* hottie—I mean *husband*."

"This was supposed to be girls' night," Sarah reminded her.

"It was—and it was fun," her friend said, already sliding out of her seat. "But now I'm going to go home with my hottie husband to have a different kind of fun."

If they'd still been alone, Sarah might have reminded Claire that she'd already had fun with her husband that day. Instead, she glanced at her watch and said, "I should probably be heading home, too."

"No." Claire held up a hand. "Stay. Finish your wine." She nudged the stranger toward the seat she'd vacated. "Hottie here will keep you company."

"But—"

"No *buts*." Claire leaned down to brush a kiss to her friend's cheek, whispering in her ear as she did so. "Tell the guards to stand down and have fun."

"Hottie?" he said quizzically, when he and Sarah were alone.

"You'll have to forgive Claire. The filter between her brain and her mouth sometimes gets washed away by alcohol," Sarah told him. "Whereas I generally just say what I'm thinking even when I'm stone-cold sober."

"So now I have to ask—do *you* think I'm a hottie?"

She held his gaze for a minute before responding. "I wouldn't disagree with Claire's assessment, but I'd also deduct points for the fact that you've got no game."

"True fact," he said with a nod. "I'm seriously out of practice when it comes to flirting with pretty women."

"Acknowledging that you have a problem is the first step toward solving it."

"And the second step?"

She gestured to the bench Claire had vacated. "Practice."

He slid into the booth with his beer. "Are you inviting me to practice on you?"

"I'm inviting you to share the nachos that Claire obviously forgot she ordered," Sarah said, as Alexa delivered the platter of chips covered in shredded chicken and melted cheese to the table.

Besides, she could use the practice, too, and what was the

harm in flirting with a stranger she was unlikely to ever see again?

"I won't say *no* to that," Hottie said.

"Well, dig in," she urged.

When they'd made a dent in the mountain of chips, she finally ventured to ask, "Are you new in town or just passing through?"

"Is there a right answer to that question?" he wondered aloud.

Sarah shook her head. "Either way, I'm not going home with you."

His sigh sounded sincerely regretful. "It was the dangerous curves line, wasn't it? I totally blew any chance with you with that line."

"You never had any chance with me," she said, dipping a chip into the sour cream.

"Ouch."

She grimaced. "I didn't mean it like that."

"How did you mean it?"

"This is the new me," she'd said, gesturing to the denim jacket she'd donned over her designer dress. "And the new me doesn't sleep with men she just met."

He swallowed a mouthful of beer. "Any chance we can go back in time and introduce me to the old you?"

That surprised a laugh out of her. "A tempting thought."

"Obviously not tempting enough."

She wiped her fingers on a paper napkin. "I spent the first seventeen years of my life flouting expectations and the next fifteen trying to make up for all the mistakes I made," she confided. "Finally, today, I'm starting to live the life that *I* want to live."

"And you don't want to explore this chemistry between us?" he guessed.

"I want—*I need*—to remember that every action has consequences."

"I'm sure I saw a condom dispenser when I was in the men's room earlier."

Apparently the man had more game than she'd given him credit for, because their playful banter was seriously turning her on. Or maybe it was the chemistry he'd mentioned, because the air was fairly crackling with electricity.

"Not the consequences I was thinking about, but good to know."

"So tell me what the life you want to live looks like," he suggested.

"I'm still figuring that out," she admitted. "But I can tell you that it doesn't look like a nine-to-five office job that bores me to tears.

"Although I did like the wardrobe. And the paycheck that allowed me to afford the designer labels."

"I like the denim jacket and cowboy boots," he said. "Even if the jacket's a little big, because it suggests that you've got a sentimental streak."

She scoffed. "Which only proves that you don't know me at all."

"You kept your ex-boyfriend's jacket for...how many years?"

"How can you be sure that it doesn't belong to a current boyfriend?" she asked him.

"Because if you had a current boyfriend, you wouldn't be sitting here with me. And you would have threatened me with his existence rather than nonexistent pepper spray in the parking lot."

"I do have pepper spray," she said, reaching into her purse for the travel-size can to prove it.

His brows lifted. "That looks like hairspray."

"Have you ever got hairspray in your eyes?" she challenged.

"I can't say that I have," he acknowledged. "I'm usually careful to avoid such mishaps when I'm styling my hair."

She'd always appreciated a man who could make a joke at his own expense, and a reluctant smile curved her lips now. "Well, if you had, you'd know that it would effectively repel an attacker."

"Though probably not as effectively as a black belt," he noted.

"Which you've already surmised that I don't have. Not a brown or green one, either," she confided.

"And the jacket?" he prompted.

"You're right about that, too," she finally said, her thumb rubbing over one of the metal buttons. "It belongs to an ex-boyfriend."

"Recent ex or long-ago ex?"

"Both."

He considered that for a minute. "Any chance he'll be coming back for it?"

She shook her head. "He lives in Seattle now."

"Seattle isn't so far," he pointed out.

"With his new girlfriend," she told him.

"Ah."

Somehow the single syllable managed to communicate a whole lot of understanding.

But she shrugged off his sympathy. "It was time for both of us to let go and move on. Zack just realized it before I did."

He swallowed another mouthful of beer. "Do you miss him?"

"No." She abandoned the button on her jacket to reach for her wineglass again. "But I do miss the possibility of a future with him. Or at least the possibility of a future with *someone*."

"You're only thirty-two years old," he noted. "You've still got plenty of time to build a future with someone."

Her gaze narrowed. "How do you know how old I am?"

"Math," he said simply. "Seventeen plus fifteen."

"So you were paying attention when I was talking," she mused.

"In the desperate hope that my attentiveness might somehow compensate for my lack of game."

"I think you've got more game than either of us gave you credit for." She pushed aside her still half-full glass. "Or I've had too much wine."

"How much is too much?" he asked.

"Enough to know I'm at risk of doing something stupid."

"Are you talking about me? Because I'm absolutely willing to overlook the insult if I'm the something stupid you want to do."

She laughed again, but rather than answering his question, she asked her own. "So how long are you going to be in town?"

"I'm headed to the airport in the morning," he admitted.

"Flying back to… Texas?" she deduced, hearing just a hint of the trademark Southern accent with a twist.

"Good guess," he said.

"Well, I hope you got to see some of the sights while you were here."

"There are sights?"

"Ouch," she said, feigning insult on behalf of her hometown. "We might not have the Alamo or a space center, but we've got some sights—that may or may not be of interest to anyone who doesn't live here."

"Since my time in Haven is nearing its end, I guess I'll have to take your word for it."

"Finish your beer, Tex," she said. "I've got a better idea."

Chapter Three

"That's not actually my name, you know. My name's—"

"Don't tell me!"

Andrew was surprised by her vehement interjection. "You don't want to know my name?"

"If I don't know, I won't be tempted to try to look you up after you've gone back to Texas," she explained.

"Do you think you might be tempted?" he asked curiously.

She shrugged, as if reluctant to reveal too much. "It's a possibility."

He was surprised by the admission and pleased to know that the pull he was feeling wasn't entirely one-sided.

"Well, Texas is a big state," he pointed out. "And I might have a common name...like John Smith."

"Is your name John Smith?"

"No," he admitted.

"And that's why I'm going to stick with calling you Tex," she said. "It rolls off the tongue much easier than Not-John-Smith."

"And what should I call you? Parking Lot Peeler? Pepper Spray Wielder?"

She was obviously unimpressed with both of those monikers.

"Friend of Claire?" he suggested as an alternative.

"That one works," she decided, flagging the server to ask

for the check only to learn that her friend had paid the tab before leaving the restaurant.

"Except that Friend of Claire doesn't exactly roll off the tongue," he noted. "How about F-O-C? Or FOC?"

She slid him a look. "No. For obvious reasons."

"Okay, Friend of Claire," he relented. "What's the plan?"

"We're going to start with the Main Street walking tour," she told him.

"It's a little chilly for a stroll, don't you think?" he asked, when she took a minute to fasten the buttons that ran down the front of her jacket before they exited the building.

"You have to walk to appreciate the atmosphere of Main Street." She stuffed her hands in her pockets. "Plus I've had three glasses of wine, so I don't think I should be driving."

"I've had one beer," he told her. "I could drive."

"Then you can take us to Crooked Creek Ranch after the walking tour."

Which turned out to be exactly that—a casual stroll down the primary route through the center of town. Both sides of the street were lined with buildings that housed shops or businesses, not unlike any other small town in America. What made Haven different, or at least this tour of it, was that his guide had a personal anecdote to share about each one.

"We'll start here," she said, gesturing to the doors of the restaurant through which they'd just exited. "Diggers' Bar & Grill, a landmark in Haven and favorite local eating establishment."

"I can vouch for the nachos—and the beer," he said.

"Duke, the owner and sometimes bartender, takes pride in his menu—and he doesn't tolerate fighting in his bar. The punishment for anyone who breaks the rule is banishment from the premises for a full year, which is probably why no one has dared to throw a punch inside since Doug Holland gave Jerry Tate a black eye six or seven years ago.

"More recently, however, there was a stabbing in the back parking lot. A group of out-of-towners, already drunk, stopped in for a drink. Duke refused to serve them and kicked them out of the bar, and when they started fighting among themselves, one of the guys pulled a knife."

"I understand now why you were a little apprehensive when I showed up in the parking lot."

"You caught me by surprise," she admitted. "And I'm not a fan of surprises."

"Then I'll apologize," he said. "Though I'm not sorry I got to see you taking your clothes off."

She huffed out an exasperated breath. "It was only my jacket."

He grinned. "I know, I just like seeing you blush."

"I don't blush."

"Since I'm the one looking at the pretty pink color in your cheeks, I'm going to have to disagree."

"Continuing the tour," she said, stepping away from the streetlight that illuminated her face to cross the road.

He followed.

"The hardware store." Easily identified by the sign as well as the displays in the windows.

"A staple in any community," he noted.

"This one is owned by Glenn Davis," Friend of Claire told him. "He was called out to change the locks at Frieda Zimmerman's house three times in as many months before he took the hint and asked the widow to have dinner with him. They've been almost inseparable since that first date, proving that people in their seventies can find love, too."

"Good to know I've still got more than three decades to figure things out," he noted.

"Obviously you're a glass-half-full person," she remarked, as she started walking again. "My takeaway from that story is that I've only got three and a half decades left."

"Half-full or half-empty, the important thing is that the glass is refillable," he quipped.

"A true optimist," she mused, pausing in front of The Trading Post next. "Several years ago, a young clerk was shot during an armed robbery here, setting up a conflict between local defense attorney Katelyn Gilmore and her new husband, Sheriff Reid Davidson."

"Who won?" he asked, curious about the outcome despite not knowing any of the characters.

"The client ended up pleading guilty, and Katelyn and Reid recently celebrated their seventh anniversary."

"A happy ending."

She nodded. "For Sierra Hart and Deacon Parrish, too, who battled over the last box of Frosted Flakes in the cereal aisle before falling in love."

"Apparently your grocery store is a real meet market. M-E-E-T," he was quick to clarify when she slid him a look.

"It's also where Haylee Gilmore met her future mother-in-law for the first time—when she was four months pregnant."

"Who was pregnant? Haylee or her mother-in-law?"

Friend of Claire rolled her eyes. "Haylee. With twins."

"How do you know all this stuff?" he wondered aloud.

"I get my coffee at The Daily Grind every morning."

Before he could ask her to explain that cryptic response, she gestured to Anthology Books. "Do you know who Quinn Ellison is?"

"The mystery writer?"

She nodded. "Every time Quinn launches a new book, she kicks off her tour at this bookstore."

He was a fan of the author's work and knew that her tours took her to major cities around the country. "I wonder what brings a bestselling novelist to a small town in northern Nevada."

"She lives in Cooper's Corners, about fifteen miles from here," Friend of Claire told him.

"No kidding?"

"No kidding," she confirmed. "She's also a very big fan of Sweet Caroline's chocolate peanut butter banana croissants."

"You're not the first person who's mentioned those croissants to me today," he remarked.

"I don't know what time your flight is, but if you can get to the bakery early in the morning and get your hands on one, you won't regret it," she told him.

"They're really that good?"

"Better," she said. "And possibly only available for a limited time, if it turns out that the rumors about Caroline's plans to sell the bakery are true."

It was the perfect opportunity for Andrew to confess, to tell her that he knew for a fact that Caroline *was* selling the bakery—because she was selling it *to him*.

But Friend of Claire had already moved on to Granny's Attic, a secondhand store, and the opportunity slipped away. Next up after that was Fur, Feathers and Fins for pet supplies, followed by Footloose, a shoe store.

"Across the street is our local second-run movie theater—and it looks like tonight's movie just let out," she said, as the doors opened and a stream—or at least a trickle—of people spilled out onto the sidewalk. "In the summer, the theater offers early and late screenings and sometimes weekend matinees, but during the offseason, there's only one screening—and only Wednesday through Saturday."

She was quiet for a minute, watching the moviegoers disperse. Most of them were teenagers, he guessed, hanging in groups with a few couples paired off and holding hands.

"I had my first date official date with Zack Kruger in that theater," she confided to him now. "A long, long time ago."

"The original owner of the denim jacket?" he guessed.

She nodded and smiled, a little wistfully, he thought.

"He was the first boy I ever kissed. The first boy I ever loved. But that night, our first date, we saw *Mission: Impossible III* and then went to Jo's for pizza." She gestured toward a group heading away from the theater. "Which is probably where they're going now. Jo's is famous for its pie and a popular hangout for local teens."

"Is there anything else to do for fun in Haven?" he asked, belatedly realizing that was something he should have considered before signing on the dotted line.

"There's a bowling alley on Station Street and the community center has a library, gymnasium, ice rink and swimming pool. But the most popular destination is Adventure Village, a family-friendly recreation park. It has paintball fields, a rock-climbing wall, laser tag, go-karts, mini-putt and an arcade."

"Did you have a first date with anyone there?" he asked curiously.

"No, but my cousin Jason did. And three months later, he and Alyssa were engaged for real."

"As opposed to…fake engaged?"

"Yeah. It's a long story," she said, crossing the street again and turning back toward Diggers'.

"This is The Daily Grind—formerly Cal's Coffee Shop."

"Where you get your coffee in the mornings," he recalled. "And apparently the hottest gossip, too."

She nodded. "And where Hope Bradford was enjoying a latte when she was reunited with Michael Gilmore, her high school sweetheart, ten years after leaving town and breaking his heart."

"Am I supposed to know who that is?"

She seemed surprised by his question.

"Lainey Howard from *Rockwood Ridge*," she clarified.

"That's a… TV show?" he guessed.

She shook her head. "I can't believe you've never seen *Rockwood Ridge*."

"Apparently a popular TV show," he realized.

"Very popular," she said. "And Hope was a semi-famous actor who gave up her Hollywood career to marry MG, a local rancher, and teach drama at Westmount High School."

"So you have sights *and* celebrities in Haven, apparently."

"We do," she confirmed.

As they'd wandered up and down Main Street, he'd found himself enjoying her company so much that he'd almost managed to forget the air temperature was barely forty-six degrees. But now that they were standing outside a coffee shop, the prospect of a hot drink was decidedly appealing.

"Since we're here, do you want to grab a cup of coffee?"

"I wouldn't mind a latte," Friend of Claire said. "But we can't walk in there together."

"Why not?"

"Did you not hear what I said about The Daily Grind being the source of all the hottest gossip?"

Of course he'd heard, but he'd been certain she was exaggerating, at least a little.

"Do you really think that if you walk in there with me, people will start talking?"

"You sat at my table at Diggers'—I guarantee that people are already talking," she told him.

He was surprised—but not bothered—by the idea that people might be talking about him in conjunction with Friend of Claire. Although maybe that was because he didn't actually live in this town.

Not yet, anyway.

But apparently she *was* bothered by the idea, so he said, "Do you want to wait out here while I go in to get the drinks, then?"

"If you order two coffees, Madison—the barista working

tonight—is going to crane her neck peering out the window, trying to see who the second one is for," she warned.

"Paranoid much?" he asked, amused rather than concerned.

"Trust me, I'm doing you a favor. *You* wait out here, *I'll* get the drinks."

"Madison won't crane her neck peering out the window to see who's with *you*?" he challenged.

"Sure, but she doesn't know you, so her efforts won't gain any traction."

"Okay, I'll wait here," he relented. "Just regular coffee, black."

"Got it." She nudged him back a few steps, away from the coffee shop windows, and winked at him. "Might as well make Madison work for it."

A few minutes later, they continued on their way with paper cups in hand.

"The Stagecoach Inn—which is probably where you're staying because it's the only decent hotel in town," she noted, pausing on the sidewalk in front of the boutique hotel. "In fact, the only other option for short-term rental accommodations is the Dusty Boots Motel, out by the highway."

"I can neither confirm nor deny in an effort to minimize the risk of revealing information you don't want to know about me."

She chuckled softly. "Okay, so I'll pretend that you didn't hear the history of the inn when you checked in and tell you that the original building dates back to actual stagecoach days. Sadly, it was quickly forgotten when rail travel became more popular and, by the time Hershel Livingston bought it some fifteen years ago, it was falling apart."

"Now *that* name sounds familiar," he said. "Didn't he make his fortune in casinos and brothels?"

"Ironic, don't you think, that he planned to settle in Haven, one of only a few places in Nevada where gambling and prostitution are illegal?"

Apparently it was a rhetorical question, because before he had a chance to respond, she continued, "Anyway, Hershel spent millions on the rehab of the building, then abandoned the project just as it was nearing completion."

"Why would he do that?"

"No one knows for sure," she told him. "One theory is that his Las Vegas bride visited Haven during the renovation process and immediately hated it here. Another is that she caught the billionaire dallying with a local woman—or wo*men*."

"That would explain why she wasn't fond of the town," Andrew surmised.

"Whatever the reason, Hershel abruptly ordered his crew to vacate the property and put it up for sale. Eventually Liam Gilmore decided to finish the renovations and reopen it as a boutique hotel."

"There seem to be a lot of people in this town named Gilmore," he noted.

She nodded. "I probably should have started the tour with the fact that the Blakes and the Gilmores were two of the founding families of Haven more than one hundred and fifty years ago. Samuel Blake was a down-on-his-luck businessman from Omaha, Nebraska, and Everett Gilmore was a struggling farmer in nearby Plattsmouth. Both came to Haven after purchasing a parcel of land from a developer, only to discover, when they arrived in Nevada with their respective families and worldly possessions, that they'd purchased the same parcel of land.

"Both title deeds were stamped with the same date, making it impossible to know who had the legitimate claim to the property, so they agreed to share it, using the natural divide of Eighteen Mile Creek—more commonly known as Crooked Creek—as the boundary between their lands."

"At least they were able to come to a peaceful resolution," Andrew remarked.

Friend of Claire smiled wryly. "Except that it wasn't. Because the Gilmores arrived first and had already started to build their home in the valley on the west side of the creek, the Blakes had to build in the rocky hills on the east side. The Gilmores' cattle immediately benefited from grazing on more hospitable terrain, while the Blakes struggled from year to year to keep their herd viable. Then they discovered silver and gold in their hills and gave up ranching in favor of mining.

"Now we're back to where we started," she noted, pausing in front of the bar and grill to drop her empty cup in a trash can.

"And now I have to admit that you were right—Haven has some sights."

And he was staring at the most beautiful one of all, though he managed to keep *that* thought to himself this time for fear that she would roll her eyes and walk away again.

"Are you still good to drive?" she asked, when they'd made their way around to the parking lot at the back of the restaurant.

He nodded.

"Then I feel confident in saying, you ain't seen nothing yet."

Chapter Four

Andrew was surprised when Friend of Claire pulled out her own keys, but she only unlocked her vehicle to retrieve a blanket before climbing into the passenger seat of his rental car.

She'd said that they were going to Crooked Creek Ranch, but she hadn't given him a street name and number to punch into his navigation app.

"The address will take us to the main house, and that's not where we want to go," she'd said, when he asked.

Which left him entirely dependent on her directions. Not that he was worried she might lead him astray, just that he liked knowing where he was going. After about twenty minutes and several turns, he discovered that they'd abandoned asphalt streets in favor of gravel roads.

As his midsize sedan bumped along over the ruts, he cringed at the sound of the stones kicked up by the tires pinging against the undercarriage.

"I'm not sure the rental company is going to appreciate me taking this vehicle off-road."

"We're not off-road," she denied. "We're just on a private—and rarely used—road."

He jolted as the front driver's side wheel dropped into a pothole—or maybe it was a sinkhole—and again at the scraping sound when it managed to crawl out again.

"And now I know why there are so many trucks in this

town," he noted, grateful that he'd paid for the extra insurance when he rented the vehicle.

"City boy," she said, sounding amused.

"Guilty," he agreed.

They drove for another five minutes or so along the rutted surface. There were no streetlights out here; no signs of any civilization.

"You can stop here," she told him.

He pressed on the brake and leaned forward to peer out the windshield. "Right here? In the middle of nowhere?"

"Sure," she agreed.

"I thought you said we were going to Crooked Creek Ranch."

"This is it," she said.

All he could see was…nothing.

And when he shifted into Park and turned off the engine, killing the lights, nothing but dark.

"I expected a ranch would have buildings. And cows."

"We're near the northern boundary of the property," she said. "Far away from the house and the barns and the cows—though sometimes the small herd is brought up here for grazing later in the season."

"Are you sure we won't get arrested for trespassing?"

"I'm sure," she said. "Jesse Blake might come around with his shotgun if he thinks strangers are nosing around on his property, but he won't call the sheriff."

"Am I supposed to feel reassured that we won't get arrested but we might get shot?"

She chuckled as she tucked the blanket under her arm and opened the door. "We're not going to get arrested *or* shot, I promise."

Though still wary, when she reached for his hand, he knew that he'd willingly follow wherever she led.

But she didn't lead him anywhere just yet.

"Give your eyes a few minutes to adjust," she told him.

"Adjust to what?"

"You'll see."

"I don't think I'm going to see anything in the pitch-dark," he countered.

But after those few minutes, he realized that it wasn't pitch-dark.

And while they were definitely in the middle of nowhere, with no streetlights or other artificial light sources to illuminate their journey, there was a narrow sliver of moon shining bright in a sky filled with more stars than he'd ever seen.

She tugged on his hand then and guided him away from the car. He stepped cautiously, aware that the terrain here was likely even rougher than the supposed road they'd driven in on and that falling and breaking his leg was not how he wanted this evening to end.

"This spot looks good," she said, stopping in the middle of the field. He could see the dark outline of trees in the distance and, beyond the trees, the peaks of the mountains spearing up to the sky.

She started to unfold the blanket and he took the opposite end to help her spread it over the grass.

Because apparently forty degrees (he was certain the temperature had dropped since they'd left town) was ideal weather to sit outside.

Or lie down, as she was now doing, stretched out on the blanket, her boot-clad feet crossed at the ankles and her hands clasped behind her head, her gaze focused on the sky.

When in Rome, he thought, and dropped to the blanket beside her, mirroring her pose.

"What do you think, Tex?" Her voice was little more than a whisper in the dark, her reverent tone not unlike that used to communicate in church.

"I think… I've never seen anything like this," he confided in a similar whisper.

He didn't consider himself a particularly religious man, but staring up at the stars, he felt certain that God did exist, and the certainty filled him with peace.

And that was before she reached her hand out to link her fingers with his again.

When tomorrow came, he'd have to focus on his future plans and other priorities, but for tonight, he was going to enjoy the company of this fascinating and beautiful woman.

And while he was admittedly a little disappointed that she'd nixed the idea of sleeping with him, the truth was, he wasn't that man anymore, either. Casual hookups and dead-end relationships had been left far in his past, even if spending time with Friend of Claire tempted him to wish things were different.

"I hear water," he realized, after several minutes had passed in companionable silence.

"That's the creek," she told him. "It always gurgles in the spring, fed by the snowmelt from the mountains. Later in the summer, the flow will be little more than a trickle, almost inaudible."

"Have you always lived in Haven?" he asked her now.

"Always—aside from four years at college," she confirmed. "I was so excited to go away to school, to be anywhere but here. And then, when I was gone, I couldn't wait to come home.

"Because the big cities might have more in the way of amenities and opportunities, but they don't offer a view of the stars that can compare to this."

"It's truly spectacular," he agreed.

The sound of howling in the distance made them both still.

"What was that?" Andrew whispered.

"Sounded like a coyote," she said. "They tend to hunt between dusk and dawn."

"And we're stretched out on this blanket like a picnic spread," he realized.

"It's not interested in us."

"It? Or they?" he wondered aloud. "Don't they travel in packs?"

"Coyotes live in family groups but generally hunt alone or in pairs. Wolves travel—and hunt—in packs, but Nevada doesn't have an established wolf population," she told him. "We do see foxes and bobcats and even the occasional mountain lion out here, though."

"And now I'm ready to head back into town," he said.

She chuckled softly.

They were silent for several minutes, looking at the sky and listening to the quiet murmur of the creek—and the occasional howl of a coyote in the distance.

"I'm glad you brought me out here," he said. "I'm freezing my ass off, but I'm glad."

"You drove," she reminded him. "So technically, you brought me out here. And it's not *that* cold."

"You're a northern Nevada resident. I'm from southern Texas," he felt compelled to point out.

"You can go back to the car if it's too cold for you out here," she said. "Or…we could move a little closer together to conserve body heat."

"I choose option B," he immediately replied.

She laughed softly as she shifted to his side of the blanket. He put his arm around her, holding her close.

"Better?" she asked.

"So much better," he confirmed.

And it really was.

In fact, now that her body was aligned with his, he wasn't just feeling warmer but in danger of overheating.

"Can I ask you a question?"

"Sure," she agreed. "But I'm not promising to answer."

"I got the impression you wrote me off after our brief interaction in the parking lot earlier today, but when I came back to Diggers' later, you invited me to sit down with you. Why?"

It was a good question, Sarah acknowledged, and not one to which she was entirely sure of the answer. Or maybe she didn't want to admit—even to herself—that she'd found herself immediately and intensely attracted to the man now stretched out on the blanket beside her.

"As I said at the time, I knew Claire's nachos were coming and there was no way I was going to be able to eat them all myself."

"And then you took me on a walking tour of Main Street."

She shrugged. "I didn't have anything else to do."

"And then you brought me out here—or at least gave me the directions so that I could bring you out here," he clarified.

"That surprised me, too," she admitted softly.

Tex shifted so that he was propped up on an elbow, looking at Sarah as she continued to look up at the stars. "What do you mean?"

"This is one of my favorite places in the whole world—and where I come when I want to be alone. Aside from Claire, I've never brought anyone here."

"So why me? Why tonight?"

"Three glasses of wine?" she suggested lightly.

And could immediately tell by the flatness of his gaze that her response had disappointed him.

"Or maybe I realized that I've spent a lot of years keeping people at a distance and I decided it was time to let someone in."

"And so you chose someone who won't be in town long enough to expect more than you're willing to give," he guessed.

"That's a distinct possibility," she allowed. "It's also possible that I realized you're charming and funny and, for some inexplicable reason, you seemed to like me without knowing anything about me."

"I'm not opposed to knowing about you," he said. "But you won't even tell me your name."

"People often make assumptions about others on the basis of their name."

"Are you someone famous? Were you on that TV show with Hope Bradley?"

"Hope Bradford," she corrected. "And no, I'm not famous. Infamous, perhaps, but not famous."

"Sounds like there's a story there."

"More like lots of stories. You could ask anyone in town, and they'd have a story about me."

"About Friend of Claire?"

She smiled. "That would be a dead giveaway, because she was my partner in crime most of the time."

"What if I don't want to hear the stories that everyone knows? What if I want to know something that no one else does?"

"I'm not sure that's possible," she said lightly. "Because Claire knows everything."

"Okay, tell me something that only a handful of close friends know," he suggested.

"Hmm." She took a minute to consider his request before responding, "I have a tattoo."

"Do you?"

"I do," she confirmed.

"Where is it?"

"That's something even fewer people know," she told him.

"Shoulder blade?"

She scowled. "Why was that your first guess?"

"Shoulders, ankles and wrists are the most common places that women choose to get ink."

"How do you know that?"

He shrugged. "I know a lot of useless information."

"Well, if I'd known that, I might have opted to be inked somewhere else," she confided. "I hate being predictable."

"So what is it? A heart? Flower? Butterfly?"

"For your information, it's a lion."

"Not so predictable, then," he mused.

"I wanted something that symbolized strength and courage."

"I suspect you have plenty of both."

She felt her cheeks flush with pleasure at the unexpected compliment. And while she didn't often feel strong or courageous, she was aspiring to be both.

"Now it's your turn," she said.

"Sorry, no tattoos," he told her.

"Tell me something that only a handful of close friends know."

"Hmm…" he said, echoing her quiet musing.

Or maybe he really couldn't think of anything he wanted to share.

But after another minute, he finally replied, "When I was a kid, I wanted to be a rodeo star."

Which was when she realized that she had no idea what kind of job he had, though considering the taut muscles she could feel pressed against her, she wouldn't have been surprised to learn that he'd followed that dream.

"Saddle bronc? Steer wrestling? Bull riding?" she asked, naming the events that immediately came to mind.

He shook his head. "I can't tell you anything more specific than that. You'll laugh."

"I won't laugh," she promised.

"Rodeo clown."

She laughed.

He gave her a look.

"I'm sorry," she said, not sounding sorry at all.

"For your information, the job of a rodeo clown is physically demanding—and incredibly dangerous."

"I know," she agreed. "That's why, in the business, they're actually considered bullfighters rather than rodeo clowns."

"Apparently you know stuff, too," he mused.

"So what derailed your rodeo clown aspirations?"

"My parents took me to the LRCA Rodeo and I realized that bulls are huge—and terrifying."

She laughed again. "I'm tempted to ask what career path you decided to follow instead, but I'm afraid that would violate our rule about revealing potentially identifying personal information."

"It was your rule, not mine," he reminded her. "So it's your call."

She hesitated, considering, then shook her head. "Instead I'll tell you that Spencer Channing, two-time PBR and PRCA bull riding champion, now raises and trains horses right here at Crooked Creek."

"No kidding?"

"No kidding," she confirmed.

"You really do know something about everyone in this town," he mused.

"My family has lived here as long as any other."

"Be careful," he said. "You're revealing personal information that I might be able to use to track you down in the future."

"This is Haven," she reminded him. "It's next to impossible to remain anonymous here. If you ever came back and wanted to find me, it wouldn't be difficult."

"When I come back, I'll definitely find you," he promised.

As much as Sarah wanted to believe he meant it, she wasn't going to let herself hope that it might ever happen. Because in her experience, expectations only led to disappointment.

And so instead of wondering what might or might not happen in the future, she decided to enjoy this moment right now.

But he'd picked up the thread of their conversation again and was talking about other places he'd visited in Nevada and around the country.

"You're not listening to me, are you?" Tex realized.

"I'm sorry," she said. "My mind was wandering."

"What were you thinking about?"

She lifted her gaze to his. "Truthfully... I was wondering if you were ever going to stop talking and kiss me."

He stopped talking and kissed her.

Chapter Five

Six weeks later

Sarah had never been a morning person. But her habits quickly changed when she started working at Twilight Valley Equine Rehabilitation and Retirement Facility with Claire and discovered that being at the horse rescue early meant having time to indulge in a morning ride. And so those rides became part of her new routine, serving the dual purposes of exercising the horses who lived at the ranch and giving her some one-on-one time with her friend. Because working together didn't actually afford much of that as Claire spent most of her time outside with the horses while Sarah was usually in the office, focused on fundraising initiatives for the not-for-profit facility and handling other administrative tasks that her friend had been only too happy to abdicate to her.

They weren't the only two people who worked at Twilight Valley, but they were the only ones who were there every day. Claire's husband, Devin, helped out when he could, but his work as a security systems analyst and his hobby as an app designer kept him busy. There was also a handful of local residents who volunteered on a regular basis and a greater number who showed up on a less frequent schedule. Weekends and the summer months inevitably brought more help to the ranch, including high school students in need of volunteer hours.

This morning, they'd headed to Eagle Rock, one of the highest points on the property. Claire, riding Mystic—a now nine-year-old gelding who'd come to Twilight Valley in its first year of operation—stopped at the top of the ridge to watch the sun rising over the mountains in the distance. Sarah, on the back of a twenty-two-year-old retired broodmare named Jezebel, took a few minutes to catch up with her friend. When she did, she exhaled softly, her breath stolen by the view.

"Missing your office job yet?" Claire asked her friend.

Sarah continued to gaze out on the horizon, truly awed by the beauty of the land around her, backdropped by the majesty of the Silver Ridge Mountains and an impossibly blue sky.

"The day I walked out of Blake Mining was the second-best day of my life."

"What was the best?"

Sarah shifted her attention to her friend now and grinned. "The day I met you."

"Aww," Claire said, her eyes misty. "That was one of the best days of my life, too."

"Only one of?" she said teasingly.

"The day I married Devin bumped it out of the top spot."

"But only because we're now cousins by marriage in addition to being BFFs, right?"

Claire laughed. "A definite bonus."

It filled Sarah's heart with joy to know that Claire and Devin had each found their perfect match in the other, even as she wondered if she'd ever be so lucky.

But she was focused on other priorities right now. After too many years going through the motions, she'd finally realized that she needed to be happy with her life before she'd want to share it with anyone else. Besides, the options in Haven were limited, and every time she met a great guy, it turned out he was from somewhere else. California or Washington or… Texas.

She shoved the memories of Tex to the back of her mind. She'd only spent a handful of hours with the man, but he'd obviously made an impression because, six weeks later, thoughts of him continued to pop into her mind during the day and hijack her dreams at night.

And anyway, she was happy right now working alongside her best friend in a job that gave her a feeling of purpose and a sense of satisfaction.

I am a strong, independent woman.

"Did you say something?"

"Just reminding myself that I don't need a man to make my life meaningful."

"Any particular man you don't need?" Claire wondered.

"Nope," she answered quickly.

Too quickly.

Her friend tipped up the brim of her cowboy hat to show Sarah her narrowed gaze. But Sarah kept her mouth firmly closed, and Claire didn't press her to expand on her response.

And really, there was nothing more to say.

The day after she'd met Tex—the day he'd left Haven—Claire had wanted to know what happened between her friend and the hottie from the Lone Star State, and Sarah had told her.

Almost everything.

"Any plans for the weekend?" she asked Claire, deliberately steering the conversation away from her solitary life as they began to walk the horses back to the barn, the slower gait serving the dual purposes of cooling the horses down and allowing for easier conversation.

"We're going to my parents' house for dinner tomorrow night."

"I'm sorry," Sarah said, understanding that family gettogethers were always a source of stress for her friend.

Growing up, Sarah had pulled out all the stops to get the attention of parents who were so preoccupied with the family business they had little time for their family. Claire, on the other hand, had done everything she could to fly beneath her parents' radar. Not an easy task when Paul and Elsa Lamontagne monitored every aspect of her life, from the amount of time she spent in front of the TV to the programs she watched, from the books she read and the clothes she wore to the friends she spent time with.

It was hardly a surprise that the preacher's daughter rebelled against her controlling parents. And Sarah had been right there with her, every step of the way. They'd truly been partners in crime—or at least accomplices in misbehaving.

"My mom expects me to bring dessert, because I always do, but the bakery's still closed."

"The grand reopening is the twenty-eighth," Sarah said. "I stopped at The Daily Grind to grab a latte on my way home yesterday and got the latest."

"And what is the latest?" her friend asked.

"According to Jana Beatty and Harper Langdon, the new owner is making big changes to the menu to put her own stamp on things."

"Change is good for everyone—and long overdue in this sleepy town," Claire said. "But apparently you didn't get all the latest news, because the new owner isn't a *she*—*his* name is Andrew Morrow."

"How do *you* know that?"

"I ran into Laurel Walsh at the grocery store earlier in the week," Claire confided, naming a mutual friend who worked at Jo's Pizza. "She said that the new owner has been into the restaurant a couple times already and is *very* handsome."

"Did Laurel know anything else about him?"

Now Claire shook her head. "Apparently all her efforts at conversation were politely rebuffed, but she did tell me that he always ordered a large pie, so she assumed he had someone to share it with."

"Or he wanted leftovers for the next day," Sarah suggested.

"That's what I figured, too. Oh, and according to Ayesha Dhawan, he stops by The Daily Grind for a coffee sometime between two and three p.m. every day, which is usually when she's there for her afternoon pick-me-up."

"Sounds like everyone has something to say about this guy."

"Everyone always wants to play with the shiny new toy," Claire noted.

Sarah choked on a laugh.

"It's true," her friend said. "And when I saw Beverly Clayton at the bookstore, she told me to tell you to elbow your way to the front of the line."

Now Sarah snorted. "Last time I saw Beverly Clayton, pushing her youngest grandbaby in a stroller through Prospect Park, she told me that even though I was looking at thirty in the rearview mirror, I shouldn't give up all hope that I might someday meet a nice man with whom to settle down."

"The words were obviously poorly chosen but you know her intentions were good," Claire said.

"I know. And there are days that I think I wouldn't mind settling down, but I don't want to settle."

"And you shouldn't," her friend agreed. "But maybe you should at least take a stroll by the bakery to check out this new guy before someone else calls dibs."

"I have," Sarah admitted. "Not because I wanted a glimpse of the new owner but because I wanted to see what was happening inside. Unfortunately, the windows are covered in paper."

"Then I guess you're going to have to walk over to The Daily Grind and linger over a latte one afternoon."

"No doubt, if his habits are known—as they apparently are—the coffee shop is packed between two and three. And obviously that explains why I had to wait twenty minutes for my coffee when I was there yesterday afternoon," she realized.

"But no sightings of handsome strangers?"

"No," Sarah confirmed. "But I wasn't looking, either. I just ordered my drink and, when it was finally ready, walked out the door with it."

"You need to always be looking," Claire told her. "Because the pickings in this town are slim, especially for those of us who grew up here and have known most of the local guys all of our lives."

"And yet you managed to find someone."

"With a little help from my friend."

"A *lot* of help from your friend," Sarah said immodestly. "In fact, I'm thinking if this job doesn't work out, I might offer my services as a matchmaker."

"You better hope this job works out," Claire teased, as she hoisted herself out of the saddle and dropped to the ground. "Because no one wants a matchmaker whose love life is a mess."

"My love life is *not* a mess," Sarah denied, following her friend's lead in dismounting. "It's simply nonexistent."

"Definitely put that on your business cards."

"Shut up, Claire."

Claire shut up—but she was grinning widely as she began to untack her mount.

They worked side by side in companionable silence, grooming the horses. When they were done, Claire wrapped her arms around Mystic's neck and hugged the gelding for a long minute.

"You're in a melancholic mood this morning," Sarah noted.

"I guess I just realized how much I'm going to miss him when he goes to his new home."

"Of course you'll miss him," she agreed. "But he's not leaving until the fifteenth of June."

"Which is Sunday," Claire informed her.

"Apparently time really does fly when you're having fun,"

Sarah remarked, startled to discover that the month was al-most half over already—which meant that it was almost her friend's birthday.

And now she had an even bigger incentive to meet the bak-ery's new owner.

Five minutes.

After working practically from sunup till sundown for the past few weeks, all Andrew Morrow wanted was five minutes to enjoy a cup of coffee that didn't need to be reheated half a dozen times before he swallowed the last mouthful.

So when another customer paused near his table at The Daily Grind, he didn't look up. Instead, he kept his attention focused on the screen of his phone, as if he was unaware of her presence.

And even without looking up, he knew it was a woman. And while it would be polite to invite her to sit down—be-cause it turned out that the afternoon was a busy time at the local coffee shop and vacant chairs were in limited supply—he wasn't in the mood to be polite. Because he'd learned that being polite led to meaningless chitchat, which often took a turn in the direction of more pointed inquiries.

Some of the women—and it was almost always women—wanted to know about his plans for the bakery. Some made discreet inquiries about his sexual orientation and relationship status; others were less discreet in their offers to set him up with a daughter or a niece or a neighbor.

Maybe he was being rude, but he wasn't in the mood for any of it today. He had no interest in being set up and no time for any kind of romantic entanglements right now.

And yet, thoughts of Friend of Claire had intruded on his mind every day—and night—since he'd left Haven, and now that he was back, those thoughts came even more frequently. She'd assured him that he wouldn't have any trouble finding her if he wanted to, and Andrew definitely wanted to. But there were only so many hours in the day and there was so much that he had to do before the bakery's grand opening at the end of the month that he'd decided to wait before doing so.

Of course, the simplest solution to avoiding unnecessary attention would be to take his coffee back to the bakery where he could lock the door—and lock out his intrusive neighbors. But he was trying to remember that those same intrusive neighbors would hopefully become paying customers when he opened for business. Not to mention that when he was at the bakery, there was always one task or another that required his attention, leading to his coffee being abandoned and growing cold.

Over the scents of freshly ground beans and yeasty doughnuts and toasted bread, he caught a whiff of perfume. Something subtly fruity with warm undertones. Sexy…and somehow familiar.

His chin jerked upward and his gaze locked with Friend of Claire's.

She was wearing a long-sleeved Henley-style top tucked into dark jeans that hugged her narrow hips and long legs today, with her long dark hair in a ponytail and her face bare of makeup. Still, she looked every bit as stunning as the day they'd first met—and just as surprised to see him as he was to see her.

Her blue eyes went wide. "Ohmygod… *Tex?*"

Andrew had known it was only a matter of time before he crossed paths with her again, and he'd been looking forward to that eventual meeting. But it hadn't occurred to him that she might find him before he was ready to be found.

"I've relocated, so maybe you should call me Nevada now," he said, in a deliberately casual tone. "Or you could use my actual name, which is Andrew. Andrew Morrow."

She blew out a breath. "You're the new owner of Sweet Caroline's?"

"I am," he confirmed.

"I came in here looking for you. For Andrew Morrow, I mean. I didn't know... I'm going to need a minute," she said. "My head is spinning."

And though he hadn't done anything wrong, he felt a ridiculous need to apologize, because it was obvious that she was as blindsided by his presence as he was by hers. Maybe more so.

"Why don't you sit?" He gestured to the vacant seat across from him.

She set her cup down, then pulled the chair away from the table and sank into it.

After she'd taken the minute, she lifted her gaze to meet his again. "I never would have guessed... You don't look like a baker."

"What does a baker look like?" he asked curiously.

She shrugged. "A chef's hat and neckerchief and a round belly that makes him giggle when it's poked."

A smile tugged at his lips as he realized she was describing the Pillsbury doughboy. "How do you know I don't giggle when you poke my belly?"

"I guess I don't," she said lightly.

"So what can I do for you, Friend of Claire?"

Her cheeks colored. "My name's Sarah. Sarah Stafford."

He shook her proffered hand and experienced the same jolt of awareness he'd felt when she took his hand at Crooked Creek Ranch. And when her eyes lifted to his again, he knew that she'd felt it, too.

"It's nice to meet you, Sarah Stafford."

She looked away first and pulled her hand back.

"You said you were looking for me," he reminded her.

"Right." She wrapped her hands around her cup. "Well, not you you—because I didn't know you were you—but the new owner of the bakery."

"Because?" he prompted.

"Because I need a cupcake."

"*A* cupcake?" he echoed, certain he hadn't heard her correctly.

She nodded.

"Singular? As in one?"

She sipped her coffee, then responded with another nod. "For June fifteenth."

"The bakery doesn't open until June twenty-eighth. I'd be happy to talk cupcakes with you anytime after that, but until then, I can't help you."

"But I need a cupcake for June fifteenth."

"I'm sure there's somewhere else that you can get a cupcake," he said reasonably.

"It can't be from anywhere else," she told him. "It has to be from Sweet Caroline's."

"Then you should have bought it four weeks ago," he pointed out to her.

"If I had, it would be stale by now."

"Most cupcakes freeze pretty well," he said.

"That advice doesn't do me much good at this late date."

"Well—" he picked up his mug again "—that's all I've got for you."

She pursed her lips while he sipped his coffee.

"You do know how to make cupcakes, don't you?" she finally asked.

"I've made a few in my time," he acknowledged in a dry tone.

"Then you can no doubt handle my request for a chocolate cupcake with caramel and walnuts and chocolate chips inside, topped with chocolate frosting drizzled with caramel sauce."

"Sounds like something you should be able to figure out how to make yourself."

"You'd think so," she agreed. "But while I'm a fairly decent cook, baking is not my thing."

"And I've got too much to do before the grand opening without adding one more thing to the list."

She rearranged the sugar packets in the caddy in the center of the table, so they were all facing the same way. "What if I offered to buy a whole dozen cupcakes?"

"Same answer," he told her.

"What if I bought a dozen *and*—" she plucked a paper napkin out of the dispenser and used it to wipe a drop of coffee off the table "—made dinner for you?"

His brows lifted at that. "Like a date?"

"No!" Her cheeks immediately flushed with color. "Like a meal that isn't pizza."

"Apparently my visits to Jo's have not gone unnoticed," he remarked.

"Not just your visits to the pizzeria," she told him. "Your trips to the grocery store and your afternoon coffee breaks have been the subject of much speculation."

"Speculation about what?" he wondered.

"Where you came from. How you ended up here." Now she scrubbed at an imaginary spot with the napkin. "If you're single or married."

"I told you I wasn't married."

"Actually what you said was that an unmarried man could know something about women's shoes."

"And you suspect that was a clever way of hiding my true marital status?"

She shrugged. "A lot of guys are less than forthcoming about their relationships. And the absence of a ring isn't definitive proof of anything."

"Do you have a theory about where this wife has been hiding while I've been out and about around town?" he asked curiously.

"She could be unpacking and settling in at home. Or maybe

you keep her tied up in the attic. All those old houses on Morningstar Road have fabulous attics."

His brows lifted. "How do you know I live on Morningstar Road?"

"Small town," she said again.

"Well, you have a creative mind, Sarah Stafford," he mused, not sure if he was amused or insulted by her outrageous speculation.

"I watch a lot of crime shows," she confided. "And somehow, we've gotten way off topic."

"What was the topic?"

"My cupcake request."

"Which now comes with an offer to make dinner for me?" She nodded.

"You must think your cooking's pretty good," he mused.

"My chicken marsala is legendary," she assured him.

He'd been eating a lot of sandwiches lately—and pizza from Jo's, and the promise of a real home-cooked meal was undeniably appealing. The prospect of spending more time with Sarah was even more so.

"So—do we have a deal?" she asked.

"I guess we do," he finally agreed.

She smiled. "If I could pick up the cupcakes on Saturday, that would be great."

"Saturday being…tomorrow?"

Now she nodded.

"Custom orders usually require forty-eight hours' notice."

"I'll keep that in mind for next time," she said lightly. "When do you want your chicken marsala?"

"Why don't we say Saturday for that, too? You can pick up your cupcakes when you deliver my food."

She swiped across the screen of her phone, opening her calendar app. "What time?"

"Six o'clock?"

She added that information into her phone. "Address?"

"I thought you knew where I lived."

"The rumor mill only gave me the street name, not the actual house number."

"Twenty-seven," he told her, holding out his hand for her phone. "To give you my phone number, so you can contact me if anything changes."

She gave him her phone. He added his contact information, then sent himself an empty text message so that he had her information, too.

"Can you make enough chicken for two?"

She lifted a brow.

"Even my rumored wife deserves to be fed, don't you think?" he said.

"You said you weren't married."

"But you're still not entirely sure you believe me, are you?"

"Well, in case you're not joking, you should know that I have a brother and several cousins who are ranchers, and all of them will be made aware of my plans so that they know where to start looking if I go missing."

"Tempted to renege on our bargain now?" he asked, fighting against the smile that wanted to curve his lips.

"No," she decided, after an almost imperceptible hesitation. "I need that cupcake."

"Cupcake*s*," he reminded her, emphasizing the plural. "You said you'd buy the whole dozen."

"Right." She pushed her chair away from the table and stood up. "So I guess I'll see you at six o'clock tomorrow."

He nodded again, already looking forward to it.

Chapter Six

Sarah left the coffee shop feeling as if she'd made a deal with the devil. And perhaps she had. Lord knows, Andrew Morrow tempted her more than any man had in a very long time.

After the night they'd gone to Crooked Creek Ranch, she'd tried to forget about him, certain she'd never see "Tex" again.

Relieved to know she'd never see him again.

Just one more mistake to be left in the past as she moved forward with her life.

Except that he was suddenly back in Haven—to stay this time!—and whatever spark had ignited between them that first night at Diggers' continued to crackle six weeks later.

Which should have been all the proof she needed that he was completely wrong for her, because she'd only ever been attracted to men destined to break (or at least dent) her heart.

But they'd struck a bargain, and so, twenty-seven hours after leaving the coffee shop, Sarah found herself headed to Andrew's house with a pan of chicken marsala.

Obviously taste was the most critical factor, but offering a dish that looked and smelled appealing heightened anticipation. So she sprinkled fresh parsley over the chicken, dusted the potatoes with paprika and glazed the baby carrots with brown butter.

When she was satisfied with the appearance of the meal, she turned her attention to herself. She brushed out her hair, dabbed some mascara on her lashes and some gloss on her lips, then dressed in a pair of dark blue jeans with a loose-knit short-sleeve sweater on top and leather sandals on her feet.

Not that she was trying to impress him or anything. But before she'd tracked him down at The Daily Grind, she'd stopped home for a quick shower after leaving Twilight Valley so she wouldn't approach him smelling like hay and horses. Aware of her time constraints—needing to be at the coffee shop between 2:00 and 3:00 p.m. in the hope of crossing paths with him—she hadn't taken the time to put on any makeup or do anything more than towel-dry her hair before pulling it into a ponytail.

And maybe she'd wanted to make it clear to him—and everyone else at the coffee shop—that she wasn't trying to impress the new owner of the bakery.

She wasn't trying to impress him tonight, either, but she did want to remind him that she was capable of looking better than a freshly scrubbed stable hand. And the appreciative look in his eyes as they skimmed over her when he opened the door confirmed her efforts had not gone unnoticed.

Then he spotted the faux fur bear paw oven mitts on her hands, and his lips twitched, as if he was fighting against a smile.

"The pan's hot," she said, by way of explanation.

"As you can see, I've held up my end of the bargain."

"All I can see is a baking pan covered in foil," he pointed out.

"Maybe you could invite me to come in so I can put the pan down?" she suggested.

He stepped away from the door so that she could enter.

"Kitchen's this way," he said.

He looked good, too, she noted, as she followed him down the hall to the back of the house. He was casually dressed in jeans and a T-shirt, the former hugging his really great butt and the latter showing off his strong arms.

In the kitchen, she saw that two places had been set on the island, complete with a bottle of wine, uncorked, and two glasses waiting to be filled.

She set the pan on top of the stove and removed the bear paw mitts. "The chicken can be kept warm in the oven at three hundred and twenty-five degrees while you wait for your dinner guest."

"My dinner guest is here," he said.

"Oh. Okay, then. I'll just take my cupcakes and get out of your way."

He smiled, and *damn* if her knees didn't turn to jelly.

"You're my guest, Sarah."

"Oh."

"Assuming you don't have other plans," he added.

"No. No other plans. Not tonight," she said, which she knew suggested that she had plans on other nights but was preferable to admitting that her social life was pretty much nonexistent these days.

"Does that mean you'll stay and have dinner with me?" he prompted.

"On one condition."

"What's that?"

"I get a tour of the house before we eat."

He grinned. "Absolutely. Although there's not a lot to see. I mean, it's a big house, but it's mostly empty right now."

First, though, he programmed the temperature she'd suggested, then picked up the oven mitts she'd set on the counter to slide the hot pan into the oven to keep it warm until they were ready to eat.

"Let's start at the top," he suggested, leading her to the staircase.

She followed, enjoying the view.

"Isn't there a saying—something about not trusting a skinny chef?"

He glanced over his shoulder. "Are you checking me out?"

She shrugged. "It occurred to me that a man who makes his living baking sweet treats should be a little soft around the middle from sampling his own product."

"The key is to sample," he told her, when they reached the top of the first flight of stairs. "To taste a little bit of filling or nibble on a bite of pastry rather than consuming a whole beignet or croissant."

She followed as he turned and started up the second flight, thinking that she wouldn't mind nibbling on her tour guide. She pushed the thought aside, asking instead, "And that's enough to prevent the carbs from taking up residence in your midsection?"

"That and the fact that I'm on my feet—measuring and mixing and kneading and rolling—for most of the day."

"I guess that would do it," she acknowledged, walking through the door he opened at the top. "I've only been working at the ranch six weeks, and already I can feel the difference in muscles that only ever got a workout at the gym—and not very regularly at that."

He gave her a minute to inspect the room, which was more time than she needed as the space was surprisingly—and perhaps disappointingly—empty. There was no antique furniture draped with dust cloths, no hope chests—or even cardboard boxes—filled with mementos of times past, not even a lost button or dropped hairpin.

"You're disappointed?" he guessed.

"Maybe. A little."

"The previous owners did a very thorough cleaning job before they moved out."

"I can see that." But she could also see wear marks and scratches on the old random-width plank flooring that attested to the home's age and history. She crossed that floor to look out the tall narrow windows at the opposite end of the room. "But at least the floor creaks."

"I don't think a creaky floor is a selling feature."

"That depends on your buyer," she acknowledged. "To me, it's a testament to the history of the building."

"And you said you weren't sentimental," he reminded her.

She shrugged. "I like old houses. They have stories to tell."

She thought of her parents' three-story mansion on Miners' Pass and how, when she looked at it, the only thing she saw was how much money they had. She didn't begrudge them their lavish style of living, and she couldn't deny that they put a lot of money back into the community, but apparently she still had some unresolved issues when it came to their prioritization of the business over all else.

"Let's see what the next level tells you," he suggested.

She took a cursory peek in each of the first three bedrooms. Each had obviously been freshly painted—probably before the house was put on the market, though the color choices (pale lavender, powder pink and steel blue) were a departure from the neutral tones that real estate agents usually recommended for optimal buyer appeal—and were empty of furniture. The lavender and pink bedrooms shared a bathroom with two sinks and a tub-and-shower combo, and the third—the smallest of the three—had its own (much smaller) en suite with pedestal sink and corner shower.

The fourth bedroom was obviously the master and gorgeously furnished with dark raw wood furniture, including floating nightstands that flanked a queen-size bed and two tall dressers on the opposite wall. The simple linen drapes hung on a wrought iron rail over the window coordinated with the duvet cover and pillowcases. A Kindle sat on top of one of the bedside tables, a pair of dark-rimmed reading glasses beside it.

"Why do I feel as if I've seen this furniture before?"

"Do you ever go shopping in Battle Mountain?"

"The front window display of Garrett Furniture," she realized.

He nodded.

She was pretty sure the woven rug on the floor and the earthenware vase with the branches on his windowsill had been part of the showcase, too.

"I'm extremely detail-oriented in the kitchen," he confided. "Not so much in other aspects of my life. So when I found something I liked, the simplest solution seemed to be to buy all of it."

"Was the Kindle part of the display, too?"

"No. But I think there was a Quinn Ellison book on the nightstand—which happens to be what I'm reading on my Kindle right now. And the glasses are mine."

She could picture him in them and found the image incredibly appealing. "I'll bet you look cute in the glasses."

"Cute?" he echoed dubiously.

"What's wrong with cute?"

"Nothing, I guess. It just seems like a significant demotion from hot."

And suddenly she knew that they were both thinking about the night they met.

Or maybe those thoughts had been lingering in the background all along. But now they were front and center—as obvious as the big bed in the middle of his room.

"Not necessarily," she decided, forcing her attention back to their conversation. "I think it's more a matter of context."

"The context being that you'd drunk three glasses of wine that night?" he guessed.

She should have agreed, dismissing her attraction to him as something induced by alcohol. Instead, she shook her head. "I thought you were a hottie when I first saw you in the parking lot, before I'd had any wine."

"So what's different now?" he asked her.

"The difference is that you're no longer a stranger I'll never see again—now you're someone I'm likely to cross paths with on a regular basis."

"Which would make it a lot easier to meet for coffee or dinner or…whatever," he noted.

"I'm on a dating hiatus," she told him, as she moved deeper into the room to check out the en suite. "There will be no meeting for coffee or dinner or…whatever."

The bathroom boasted a simple wood counter with a square vessel sink on top and open shelves beneath, a glass-walled walk-in shower easily big enough for two and a separate free-standing bathtub.

"I would have bought this house for the bathroom alone," she told him.

"I don't see myself ever using the tub," he admitted. "But the shower is great."

And suddenly her very active imagination was painting a picture of him in that tub, and the graphic image was causing the blood to heat inside her veins.

She cleared her throat. "We should finish the tour before the chicken gets cold."

"I put it in the oven, per your instructions," he reminded her.

"Oh. Right."

But he took the hint and led her back down the stairs to the main level.

At the front of the house was the living room—which she'd caught a quick glimpse of on her way to the kitchen. A closer perusal revealed that she hadn't missed much as it was furnished with a couple of folding lawn chairs and a huge flat-screen TV mounted to the wall. Across the hall from the living room was a home office/den with built-in bookcases, currently empty, and a Murphy bed that allowed space to do double duty as a guest room.

"Because the three guest rooms upstairs aren't enough?" she couldn't resist teasing.

"They don't come with beds," he said, pulling down the wall panel to reveal the double mattress hidden inside.

"This is a really great house," Sarah said, as they moved from the den to the dining room—also empty of furniture. "The previous owner obviously put some money into renovating and upgrading but without destroying its individuality and charm."

"That was one of the things that most appealed to me," he told her.

"I looked at a house down the street before I bought mine on Fieldstone," she confided. "But as much as I loved it, it just seemed like too much house for one person."

"Yeah, I'm probably going to question my choices when I have to pay the heating bill in the winter, but the proximity to the bakery was really what sold me on this place. That and the fact that it was available for immediate occupancy."

"You might want to go back to Garrett Furniture before then," she said, "Unless you don't mind watching TV from the questionable comfort of a metal frame covered with plastic webbing."

"Most of my stuff is being shipped from Texas," he told her. "It should arrive early next week. In the meantime, the lawn chair works. And I haven't had much time to sit around watching TV, anyway."

He retrieved the plates from the island to dish up the meal she'd prepared.

"Do you want me to do that?" she offered.

"I think I can handle the serving," he told her. "Why don't you pour the wine?"

So she poured the wine. When he carried the plates back to the island, she was sampling the pinot noir he'd chosen.

"I went with the red, because I remembered that's what you were drinking at Diggers'."

"You really are a man who pays attention," she mused.

He pulled out a stool and gestured for her to sit. "Is that such a rarity?"

"As much as a unicorn galloping over a rainbow."

"How is the wine?" he asked, as he took his seat beside her.

"It's nice," she said.

He picked up his glass and sampled, then nodded to indicate his agreement.

"So tell me about your new ranch job," he said, as he cut into his chicken.

"That question came from out of the blue," she remarked.

"You mentioned it when I was giving you the tour of the house. I figured my follow-up questions were better left until we were sitting down to eat."

She stabbed a baby carrot with her fork. "It's an equine retirement and rehabilitation facility or, as most people around here refer to it, a horse rescue."

"And how did you end up there?" he asked curiously.

"I'm still not entirely sure," she admitted. "But I suspect that Claire started to recruit me—subtly but relentlessly—when the doors of the rescue opened three years ago."

"Your friend Claire works there, too?"

"It's her ranch," Sarah told him. "Formerly her aunt and uncle's spread. But they raised cattle and saving horses is Claire's passion.

"For several years, she volunteered at a horse rescue in Austin that rehabilitated and rehomed horses that had been injured, abused or neglected. When she came back to Haven, she wanted to continue that work here."

"The two of you have been friends for a long time?"

She nodded. "Since grade school. We were pretty much inseparable growing up. I used to love going to Claire's house, where her mom always had homemade cookies for us to snack on while we did homework. Claire preferred hanging out at my place, because there we were pretty much free to do whatever we wanted without anyone reminding us to do homework first."

"The grass is always greener," he mused.

"Apparently," she agreed. "Anyway, after high school, we both chose to go to UT Austin to study business, because neither of us could imagine going away without the other. But after graduation, I came back to Haven and Claire, believing herself to be in love with a guy she met in our final year, opted to stay in Texas."

"I'm getting the impression you weren't too fond of the guy," he noted.

"He wasn't right for Claire," she said. "Thankfully she realized it, too, before she walked down the aisle. And now she's married to my cousin, so we're not just best friends, we're family, which is why I was so desperate for the cupcake."

"The cupcake is for Claire?" he said, seeming surprised by this revelation.

"Didn't I tell you that?"

He shook his head.

"It's been our tradition since eighth grade, when I found out her family never had a cake for her birthday."

"You can't celebrate a birthday without cake." Andrew sounded scandalized.

"Which was my thought," she agreed with a smile. "But at fourteen, I couldn't afford a whole cake, so I bought her a cupcake. A chocolate caramel nut cupcake from Sweet Caroline's, because it was her favorite. And every birthday since, I've bought her the same."

"You were so desperate for the cupcake, I wondered if it was for a boyfriend," Andrew confided now.

She shook her head. "No man is worth that much effort."

"Ouch."

"Sorry," she said, aware that she didn't sound the least bit remorseful. "I haven't had the best of luck in the romance department and it's possible that experience has colored by opinion."

"Possible, huh?" He studied her for a long minute, obviously hoping for more details than what she'd already given him.

She just shrugged and nibbled on another bite of chicken.

"So how long have you been on this dating hiatus?"

"Eight months," she told him. "With only one little blip."

The corners of his mouth twitched. "Is that what that night was—a blip?"

"Whatever it was, it's not going to happen again," she assured him.

He didn't argue the point, instead asking, "So what did you do before you started working on your friend's ranch?"

"I worked at Blake Mining," she told him. Which was the truth, if not the whole truth.

"And what prompted your career change?"

So many things.

But none that she wanted to get into with him now.

"Maybe I got tired of being paid too much money for doing too little work," she responded lightly.

"Said nobody ever," he assured her.

"My job mostly entailed research, assessments, reports and meetings," she told him. "To sum up, it was pretty boring—and still, sadly, the most exciting part of my life."

"I'm sure that's not true."

"I assure you, it is."

Because while Sarah had been living it up in her twenties—with zero regrets—she was now in her thirties and discovering that her friends were all planning weddings or already married and looking forward to starting families or already parenting the little ones running around. And while it was true that a few were already divorced—or heading in that direction—at least they'd had the experience of falling in love and planning a life with someone special.

"So it wasn't an office romance gone bad that made you leave the company?" he pressed.

"No."

Her immediate reply made his brows lift.

"Have you never been in love?" Andrew asked.

"Sure," she said. "Probably too many times. Unfortunately, I have a tendency to be swept off my feet by handsome and charming men looking for nothing more than a good time. And while that's always fun while it lasts, it never lasts long, and then I'm alone again."

"Being with someone isn't always a buffer against loneliness," he noted. "In fact, it can highlight the distance between you."

"It sounds as if you're speaking from personal experience," she mused.

"I've had some failed relationships," he acknowledged with a shrug. "And yet, I keep trying."

"Why do you think that is?" she asked, genuinely interested in his response. "Are human beings unable to learn from their mistakes and decide they'd rather be alone than risk heartbreak again?"

"None of the mistakes were mine," he deadpanned. "The blame lies entirely with the women I've dated."

She laughed. "Even if that was true, wouldn't you bear some responsibility for choosing to get involved with them?"

"Okay, maybe I do have a weakness for blue-eyed women with great smiles."

"You're wasting your time flirting with me," she told him.

"I don't think so," he said. "But if I am, isn't it my time to waste?"

"You're getting ready to reopen the bakery—your time is at a premium," she reminded him, carrying her plate and wineglass to the sink.

Andrew followed with his own. "Thanks for dinner," he said. "I have to admit, your chicken marsala was excellent."

"Excellent?" she echoed with a frown.

"Is that inadequate praise?"

"It's several grades below legendary. The scale starts at 'good' then goes to 'really good' followed by 'excellent,' then 'exceptional' and 'amazing' and then 'legendary,'" she said, ticking each of the descriptors off on her fingers.

"So kind of like how 'cute' is lower on the scale than 'hot,'" he noted.

"That would depend on whose scale it is," she argued. "To a six-year-old cuddling a puppy, cute is probably at the very top."

"Well, you're not a six-year-old and I'm not a puppy, but the cuddling part sounds pretty good," he said.

"There will be no cuddling."

"That's not what you said at Crooked Creek Ranch."

"It was cold that night," she reminded him.

"I remember."

"Also, I'd had three glasses of wine."

"How many glasses have you had tonight?"

"Only two. I never have more than that when I'm driving. Although I do live close enough that I could walk," she admitted.

"Or you could stay."

"You said some things that night, too," she recalled. "Including that, if you ever came back to Haven, you'd find me."

"I said that *when* I came back to Haven, I'd find you," he clarified. "And I had every intention of doing so, but you found me first."

"Only because I needed a cupcake."

"I don't care about the reasons," he said. "I'm just glad you're here."

"I'm not going to sleep with you, Tex."

His lips curved. "Do you always lead with that?"

"Actually, the first time we met, I said I wasn't going to go home with you."

"And you didn't," he acknowledged.

"But since we're already at your house, I thought it important to clarify."

"That you're not going to sleep with me...*tonight*?"

"Or *ever*."

His gaze heated; his lips curved. "Challenge accepted."

"It wasn't a challenge but a statement of fact."

"Since I returned to Haven, I've been preoccupied with the renovations of the bakery," he admitted. "But not a day has gone by that I haven't thought about you and looked forward to seeing you again."

"You expect me to believe that you've been thinking about a woman you know nothing about?"

"You think I didn't know anything about you because you refused to tell me your name?" he challenged. "Your Main Street walking tour gave me plenty of character insights."

She frowned at that. "Like what?"

"The stories you shared showed interest and character. Instead of highlighting the potentially scandalous aspect of two seventy-year-olds having an affair, you focused on the fact that they'd found love together."

"I'm pretty sure they make the bedsprings creak, too. Because Frieda Zimmerman blushed like a schoolgirl when Donna Bradley asked how she injured her hip."

"And you're only telling me that now because you're obviously uncomfortable being depicted as a romantic."

She couldn't deny it.

"Then there's your enduring affection for the ex-boyfriend," he continued. "Which shows not only that you're loyal but also suggests that you might hold on to relationships that have already failed because it's less risky than taking a chance on a relationship that might work."

"Apparently I'm an open book," she said dryly.

"If you are, I've barely had a chance to skim the first chapter. There's still a lot that I don't know but that I'm very much looking forward to discovering."

"Sorry, you missed your chance, Tex."

"You're telling me that you don't think about that night under the stars?"

"My new philosophy is to look forward, not back."

"Which isn't actually an answer to my question," he noted.

"I'm not interested in picking up where we left off."

His fingertips brushed over the fluttering pulse point on her throat, making it race. "So why is your heart beating so fast?"

"Apparently there's some chemistry between us," she acknowledged.

"Some very potent chemistry that tells me our being together isn't a question of *if* but *when*."

Before she could argue the point, he dipped his head and brushed his lips over hers.

It was as much a question as a kiss, and she didn't answer by pulling back or pushing him away. She responded by rising on her toes to fit her mouth more firmly to his. Following her cue, he wrapped his arms around her middle and drew her closer, so that their bodies were aligned, their hearts beating in tandem.

Her lips parted beneath his, allowing him to deepen the kiss. A soft moan emanated from deep in her throat, destroying any illusion that she didn't want this. Didn't want him.

He continued to kiss her, long and slow and deep, until they were both breathless. When he finally eased away to draw air in his lungs and was able to speak again, he simply said, "Stay."

And for almost half a second, she considered his request.

Then, somewhere in the distance, she registered the sound of a door opening, followed by footsteps in the hall.

She pulled out of his arms and took a quick step back just as a gorgeous woman appeared in the doorway.

"Surprise!"

Chapter Seven

"Surprise!" Lilah echoed, rushing into her dad's arms.

Tilda followed her younger sister with markedly less enthusiasm, while Rachel remained in the doorway, grinning mischievously as her gaze bounced between Andrew and Sarah.

He hugged his daughters tight, sincerely happy to see them if not overjoyed by the timing of their arrival.

"I wasn't expecting you guys until tomorrow," he said, looking at Sarah and trying to gauge her reaction to this surprise.

"The girls got out of school on Wednesday and finished packing by Thursday. Since they were obviously eager to see you, we decided to start our journey yesterday," Rachel explained.

"Lilah was eager," Tilda said. "My vote was to stay in Texas."

"Well, I'm glad you're here," he said.

And he was.

He also wished someone had apprised him of their revised ETA. But, of course, that would have ruined the surprise.

He watched as Rachel's gaze shifted to the remnants of their dinner, including the two wineglasses and half-empty bottle of red.

"Apparently our early arrival was a bigger surprise than we anticipated," she remarked dryly.

His daughters, having clued into the same thing, were uncharacteristically silent, though he didn't expect that would last long.

"You always did like to make an entrance," he noted, silently cursing himself for not explaining his situation to Sarah when he had the chance. Now he could practically see the gears turning in her brain, no doubt leading her to all kinds of wrong conclusions.

"For a minute, I thought the wine was for me, even though you know that I prefer white," Rachel continued. "But apparently, while I was schlepping your kids across state lines, you were enjoying a romantic evening."

She shifted her attention to Sarah then. "And since Andrew isn't making the introductions, I guess I'll have to do it," she said, offering a hand. "I'm Rachel Morrow."

"Sarah Stafford," she responded politely. "And I was just leaving."

Sarah couldn't get out of there fast enough.

Whatever she might have anticipated when Andrew asked her to stay and have dinner with him (and her imagination had admittedly gone down several different paths), it wasn't that the evening would end with the arrival of his wife and two kids. Because she hadn't known that he had either a wife or kids—and what kind of a fool did that make her?

She breathed a sigh of relief that she'd parked on the street rather than pulling into the driveway; otherwise, she'd be boxed in. And wouldn't that have been fun—having to ask the wife of the man she'd just been kissing to move her vehicle so that Sarah could get out of the way of their happy reunion?

I'm not married.

His words echoed in the back of her mind; the obvious lie making her blood boil.

She felt betrayed by his deceit and her own willingness to

trust him. Because he'd seemed not just like a really nice guy but one who was genuinely interested in her.

How could she have been so completely wrong about him?

Maybe the problem wasn't a lack of decent single men in Haven but the fact that her own judgment was lacking when it came to interactions with the opposite sex.

The one person—the only person—she could always count on was Claire, and when she got home, before she was even out of her car, she reached for her phone to call her BFF.

Then she remembered that Claire and Devin were having dinner with Claire's parents tonight. And even if they'd returned home by now, Sarah was trying to be respectful of the fact that they were married, to remember that she shouldn't just walk into their home and intrude on their time because she was feeling out of sorts.

Before Claire and Devin exchanged vows, the bride had promised her best friend that the change in her marital status wouldn't affect their relationship. But, of course, it did. And it would be foolish—and selfish—to wish otherwise.

And just because she couldn't lament her poor choices over a glass of wine with her best friend didn't mean she couldn't have that glass of wine.

So resolved, Sarah dropped her phone back into her purse, pushed open the driver's side door and climbed out of her vehicle. She'd leave her friend alone tonight and see her tomorrow to celebrate her birthday—

Dammit.

Without the cupcakes that she only now realized she'd left behind when she made her escape from Andrew's house.

She was lamenting that oversight when an unfamiliar vehicle—with Texas plates—pulled into the driveway behind her SUV.

Rachel popped out of the driver's seat, a smile on her face and two white boxes in her hands. "You forgot your cupcakes."

"Thank you," Sarah said, a little warily, as she accepted the offering.

"Andrew asked me to bring them to you," Rachel explained. "He seemed to think that if he came, you might throw them back in his face, and apparently it was important for you to have them for tomorrow."

"My best friend's birthday," Sarah heard herself say.

Rachel smiled again, and Sarah was struck anew not just by the other woman's beauty but her grace and poise. Or maybe she was just a really good actor who was secretly thinking of various and painful ways to make her husband pay for entertaining another woman in their new home.

"You're obviously a good friend," Rachel said now.

Sarah hoped it was true. Certainly the longevity of the friendship suggested that she'd had good instincts when she'd decided, way back in fifth grade, that Claire would be her BFF. It was only later in life—or maybe only in her relationships with men—that her instincts seemed to fail her.

"I peeked in the box," Rachel admitted now, still smiling. "Chocolate caramel nut?"

Sarah nodded.

"Any chance you'd invite me in for a cup of coffee and a cupcake?" the other woman asked hopefully.

Invite her in?

The wife of the man who'd been kissing Sarah when she'd walked in the door?

No way was that going to happen, if for no reason other than that Sarah wanted to spare her neighbors the sight of crime scene tape strung up around her property in the morning.

But, of course, she couldn't say any of that to the woman standing in front of her. Instead she asked, "Aren't you eager to get back to your family?"

"The girls need some time to catch up with their dad and, after twenty-eight hours on the road with them over the past two days, I need a break. I mean, they're my nieces and I love them to bits, but twenty-eight hours is. A. Very. Long. Time."

Sarah blinked. "Your…nieces?"

Rachel laughed. "You heard the last name and assumed I was his wife, didn't you?"

"It seemed a reasonable conclusion to draw, considering that in combination with the rings on your left hand and the fact that you showed up with two girls calling him dad."

"My husband's surname is Kuczerepa, which, after three years of marriage, I still struggle to spell, so you can guess why I decided to keep mine when we married. As for the girls, Andrew wanted them to finish out the school year in Beaumont, but obviously he needed to be here to oversee the renovations. So being the wonderful sister that I am, I offered to stay with them and finish packing up his house. Now we're here and the moving truck should be arriving on Monday."

"He did mention a sister," Sarah suddenly recalled.

When Claire had questioned his knowledge of women's shoes, he'd said that he had a sister with a fondness for designer footwear.

"That would be me," Rachel confirmed.

And, sure enough, the sneakers on her feet were unmistakably Tory Burch.

So he'd been telling the truth about that, which meant that maybe he wasn't the lying rat bastard she'd accused him of being—if only inside her own head.

But he'd definitely never mentioned having kids, and while she'd be curious to hear him attempt to explain *that* oversight, Sarah decided that what she needed right now was some female companionship.

"Would you like to come in for a cup of coffee and a cupcake?" she offered.

"Twenty. Eight. Hours," Rachel said again. "Any chance of upgrading the cup of coffee to a glass of wine?"

"It so happens that I have a really nice bottle of chardonnay in my refrigerator."

The other woman grinned. "Now you're speaking my language."

The only way Andrew could have blown things more spectacularly with Sarah would have been with a brick of C-4 and a blasting cap.

But how could he have known that Rachel and the girls would show up early?

Still, he blamed himself for Sarah's obvious surprise—and the flicker of hurt—he'd seen in her eyes. Because it wasn't as if he hadn't had opportunities to tell her.

When she joked about him having a wife tied up in the attic, he could have told her that it was actually his ex-wife. Not living in his attic, obviously, but in California with her new boyfriend. Instead, he'd let the moment pass.

And when she commented about his house being big for one person, he should have told her that he wouldn't be living alone for long, that he had two kids who would be joining him as soon as they were out of school for the summer. Another opportunity missed.

He'd never outright lied to her, but he hadn't been honest, either. And he knew he couldn't blame her for walking out.

He also couldn't go after her to explain, even if she was willing to listen to him. Because how would he explain that to his kids?

Hey, it's great to see you, but I'm going to chase after Sarah—who you've never heard me mention and only met for the first time right now—in the hope that she'll let me apologize for being an idiot, and I'll catch up with you later.

Obviously that wasn't an option, because as much as he might want to make things right with Sarah, his daughters were and always would be his number one priority. The reason for everything he did—including this recent move to Nevada.

So after he sent his sister off with Sarah's cupcakes, he tried to put her out of his mind to focus on Tilda and Lilah, starting with a tour of their new home—in which they showed much less interest than Sarah had done.

"It's old and creaky," Tilda said, as the stairs seemed to groan in protest of being trod upon.

"It's older than the house in Beaumont," he agreed.

"And bigger," Lilah noted.

"Plus it has character," he told them.

"Are you referring to the ghosts in the attic?" Tilda asked, with a sly look toward her sister.

Lilah sucked in a breath. "Ghosts?"

He gave Tilda a pointed look before turning to Lilah. "There are no ghosts in this house."

"How do you know?" she asked worriedly.

"I asked the real estate agent. Their professional code of conduct requires them to disclose any evidence of paranormal activity."

Tilda snorted at his obvious fabrication.

Lilah looked at him hopefully. "Is that true?"

"I don't know," he admitted. "But I promise there are no ghosts in this house."

"But how do you know?" Lilah pressed.

"Because everyone in this town seems to know everyone else's business and if there were any rumors about it being haunted, I would have heard them."

"There's something else this house doesn't have," Tilda noted.

"What's that?"

"Beds."

"They're being shipped with the rest of our furniture."

"How come *you* got new furniture?"

Because he hadn't wanted to move the bed that he'd shared with his wife to his new home. "Because Aunt Rachel needed somewhere to sleep while she was staying with you guys, and I didn't want to sleep on the floor for two weeks."

Tilda's jaw dropped. "Are you saying we have to sleep on the floor tonight?"

"No," he said. "You can have my bed." (Conveniently made up with fresh sheets before Sarah had arrived.) "And Aunt Rachel can have the bed in the den."

"Where will you sleep?" Lilah asked worriedly.

"On the floor in the spare room," he decided.

"That doesn't sound very comfortable."

"It's only for a couple of nights."

Apparently the girls were tired out from their two days of travel, so after he made them a snack of scrambled eggs and toast—they'd always got a kick out of breakfast for dinner—they said good-night and went upstairs to crash in his bed.

Andrew had tidied up the dishes from his dinner and theirs and was settled in the living room with the baseball game on TV when his sister finally returned from delivering Sarah's cupcakes.

"Did you get lost?" Andrew asked, as she lowered herself into the second lawn chair and stretched her legs out in front of her.

"Nope," she said easily.

Of course, he'd sent a text message when he realized she'd been gone nearly an hour, simply asking "OK?" and she'd responded with a thumbs-up emoji.

"I gave you a three-minute errand and you've been gone almost two hours. Where have you been?"

"At Sarah's."

"For two hours?"

Rachel shrugged. "We had a glass of wine together. Actually, a couple of glasses."

"You had wine with Sarah?" He wasn't sure if that revelation was surprising or just unnerving.

"A really nice chardonnay from Oregon with aromas of apple and pear, subtle spice and vanilla."

"I didn't ask for your tasting notes," he said dryly. "Which I suspect you got from the label on the back of the bottle."

"What were you asking, then?" she said.

"I wasn't really asking anything. I guess I was just…surprised that Sarah invited you in."

"Truthfully, I invited myself," Rachel confided. "Because I wanted to get to know the new woman in your life."

"I'm not sure she'd agree with that title, especially after your untimely arrival."

"Well, there was a definite vibe when we came in. And she was clearly reluctant to let me over the threshold at first— probably because she suspected I was a jealous wife who would stab her in the back when she was pouring the wine."

"Why would she think you were a jealous wife? I told her I'm not married."

"Did you tell her you had kids, though? Because I got the impression that was a surprise to her."

"My parenthood status didn't exactly come up in conversation," he hedged.

"Uh-huh," she said, in a tone ripe with disapproval. "And that kind of secret is a major red flag, especially to a woman who already has trust issues."

He frowned at that. "What makes you think Sarah has trust issues?"

"I can recognize a kindred spirit," she assured him.

Of course he knew at least some of what his sister had been through. Married for five years to her high school sweetheart who worked in sales and cheated on her every time he had a business trip out of town. And there were a lot of business trips out of town. Following her divorce, she dated a few other guys, none of those relationships lasting very long, until she found herself alone at a bar one night, having been stood up by a guy she'd met online, and ran into her former divorce attorney. Six months after that, they were married.

"Do you think she'll ever forgive me?" Andrew asked his sister now.

"I'd say that depends on what you do next."

"I could use some advice here."

"Do you really need me to tell you to be honest with her?"

"No, I could figure out that part," he assured her.

"Belatedly," she muttered.

"I was hoping for something a little more concrete," he prompted.

"Start with an apology," she said. "And make it a good one."

Though it was tradition to give Claire a single cupcake on her birthday, Sarah decided to package up four of the treats for her friend to share with her husband. That left her with six out of the original dozen, after she'd offered one to Rachel the night before, and the other woman had enjoyed it so thoroughly, Sarah had been unable to resist the temptation of sampling one herself. But she had no intention of keeping the extra cupcakes, because she didn't need any more temptation—or any reminders of her ill-advised bargain with Haven's new baker.

It was a relief to know that he hadn't lied about his marital status—she couldn't bear the thought of being "the other woman" again—but he'd still been less than forthcoming about his relationship history and that made her wary. Not that she'd expected him to offer up details of all past romantic contacts, but a passing mention of an ex-wife and kids didn't seem too much to ask.

"I've had some failed relationships," he'd said. Neglecting to mention that one of those failed relationships—a nearly ten-year marriage, according to his sister—had made him a father twice over was an unforgiveable oversight.

And she'd really liked him, *dammit*.

Not to mention that his kisses were even more amazing than his delicious cupcakes.

But she determinedly pushed all thoughts of him out of her mind as she made her way to Crooked Creek Ranch, continuing past the main house to the old bunkhouse that her grandfather had renovated for his personal use when he vacated the primary residence for Spencer and Kenzie after their wedding. Because the Blake name might be synonymous with mining in northern Nevada, but Jesse Blake's heart would always belong at Crooked Creek Ranch. He'd turned over the reins of Blake Mining to his kids long ago and gone back to ranching, motivated by pleasure rather than the need for profit this time around.

He now had a small herd of cattle and a stable full of horses, and he'd taught each and every one of his grandkids to ride, instilling in them an appreciation and affection for the gorgeous animals that were essential to ranching operations. And now he was doing the same for the next generation.

In addition, he continued to help his grandson Spencer—another of Sarah's numerous cousins—at Channing Horse Trainers as well as enjoying a romance with Helen Powell. And no, it wasn't lost on Sarah that her eighty-year-old grandfather was in a committed relationship of half a dozen years when most of her romances expired more quickly than a jug of milk.

Collecting the box of cupcakes, she pushed open the car door. Before her feet even hit the ground, Luke was there, dancing around, begging for attention. As if Gramps's now five-year-old Labradoodle didn't have people fussing over him 24/7. But she crouched down to rub the soft curls on his head and scratch behind his ears, then she gave him one of the doggy treats she'd learned to always carry in her pocket, and he happily trotted off.

A glance toward the nearby paddock revealed that Gramps was working with a young paint horse. He gave her a nod, acknowledging Sarah's presence, but carried on with the lesson. So she waited and watched while her grandfather put the yearling through its paces.

"Who's this?" Sarah asked, when Gramps led the sorrel beauty over to the fence.

"Rembrandt." He rubbed a hand over the animal's flank with obvious affection.

"He's gorgeous," Sarah noted. "But what do you need with another horse?"

"What do I need with all the money I've got?"

She laughed. "So you bought him just because you could?"

He shrugged. "And because I knew Claire could use the cash—and a vacant stall at Twilight Valley."

Which hadn't remained vacant for long, hence Claire's plans for a second barn.

"I thought the name sounded familiar," Sarah said, recalling now that she'd seen it on paperwork at Twilight Valley. "But he wasn't at the rescue for long, so I don't think I ever got to meet him."

"I scooped him up before you started working with Claire," Gramps admitted. "I asked if she had a mount that might be suitable for a young barrel racer, and she invited me to come out to the ranch to meet Rembrandt."

"Dani wants to barrel race?" Sarah guessed.

Gramps nodded again.

"How do her parents feel about that?"

"Spencer rose to fame and fortune on the back of bulls, so he's hardly in a position to object," he pointed out. "Kenzie wants to be supportive, but I think she's worried about Dani following in her mom's footsteps."

Because Kenzie was Dani's stepmother, having married Spencer six years earlier, less than a year after his return to Haven with his four-year-old daughter in tow.

"So what brings you out to Crooked Creek today?" her grandfather asked.

Sarah held up the bakery box.

Gramps winced. "Oh, honey—you didn't try your hand at baking again, did you?"

She huffed out an indignant breath. "No, I didn't."

Evidently relieved by her assurance, he accepted the box and lifted the lid to peek inside. "So where'd you get the fancy treats? Because last I heard, the bakery wasn't reopening until the end of the month."

"Then there's obviously nothing wrong with your hearing."

"But I still haven't heard you say where these came from," he noted.

"I made a deal with the devil."

His bushy white eyebrows lifted.

Sarah shook her head. "Never mind. It's a long story."

"I've got time," Gramps assured her.

"I don't," she said. "I'm on my way to Twilight Valley where, by the way, that cold saltwater spa you funded is already getting lots of use."

Now those bushy eyebrows drew together in a scowl. "That donation was supposed to be anonymous."

"And it was," she confirmed. "I wasn't one hundred percent certain the money came from you until just now."

"You think you're clever, don't you?"

"I *know* I'm clever. I take after my grandfather. Grandpa Stafford, I mean."

"You're sassy, too," he said, an unmistakable note of pride in his voice.

She grinned and touched her lips to his weathered cheek. "Share those cupcakes with Dani and Owen."

He tucked the box behind his back. "What cupcakes?"

Sarah was laughing as she turned toward her car.

"Before you rush off," Gramps said, halting her in her tracks, "make sure you keep your calendar open the first weekend in November."

She accessed the app on her phone to check the date. "So far so good."

"And try to rustle up a date for yourself," he said.

"A date for what?" Sarah asked warily.

He puffed out his chest and grinned. "My wedding."

"Really?" She was grinning now, too. "You and Helen are finally getting married?"

He nodded as he accepted her hug.

"I've been trying to get Helen to move in with me for years, but she refused to do so without a ring on her finger—so I finally put a ring on her finger."

"I hope your proposal was a little more romantic than that," she said dryly.

"Don't you worry," he said. "Your old grandpa's still got some moves."

"I'll take your word for it," she decided.

"You don't have to take my word, you can take hers," he told her. "It was *yes*."

"And I'm happy for you both," she said. "But now I really have to run."

"Since you're making deals with the devil, maybe you could ask him to find you a date for the wedding," Gramps suggested, with a wiggle of his bushy brows. "Better yet, you could invite him."

Not going to happen, Sarah vowed.

But the idea lingered in her mind, tempting her, long after she'd driven away from Crooked Creek.

Chapter Eight

Kids had a way of changing a man's perspective. And the morning after his dinner with Sarah was unceremoniously interrupted, Andrew was refocused on his priorities.

He'd woken up early—partly because he was trying to get accustomed to the early morning hours of a baker and partly because he'd slept like crap on the floor of the guest room. He still had work to do at the bakery, but he was on-track for the grand opening and felt it was important to spend some time with his daughters on their first day in their new home.

Lilah had been the first one up after him, and when she made her way downstairs, her disposition was as bright as the sun. Rachel had wandered in a short while later, drawn by the scent of coffee, as he was pouring batter into the pan on the stove. And now, finally, Tilda found her way into the kitchen.

"I'm making pancakes," Andrew said.

"I'm not hungry."

"You don't have to be hungry to want pancakes," he said easily.

"I'll have another one, Daddy," Lilah said, holding up her empty plate. "Please."

Andrew flipped the cake out of the pan and onto her plate.

"Yay, breakfast theater," Tilda said dryly.

"And here I was worried that the happy mood you took to bed last night would be absent this morning," he remarked.

"Did you really expect me to be happy that we moved halfway across the country?"

"No," he admitted. "But I expected—or at least hoped—that you'd come here with an open mind."

Tilda didn't respond to that as she tugged on the door of the refrigerator.

"Juice is already out," he told her.

She retrieved a can of diet cola from the fridge.

He glanced at the clock on the stove. "It's not even nine thirty in the morning."

"I'm thirsty."

"Pour yourself a glass of juice."

She made a face. "Juice is full of sugar."

"At least it's natural sugar. That stuff is nothing but chemicals." But he'd bought it for her, anyway, stocking both of the girls' favorite treats so the place would feel more like home when they arrived.

"Chemicals that taste good," she said, defiantly popping the top and taking a long swallow.

Rachel got up to make another cup of coffee, clearly signaling her intention to stay out of this battle. Andrew bit his tongue, deciding to save his energy for the next one. Because lately, it seemed as if there was always another battle with Tilda.

Once upon a time, she'd been as easy to please as her little sister. The onset of adolescence had changed things, but she'd been even more difficult since her mom announced she was moving to California—and downright ornery since Andrew decided to move them to Nevada.

"So how did you girls sleep last night?" he asked now.

"Great," Lilah said.

"Horrible," Tilda immediately countered. "She thrashes in her sleep."

"I'd forgotten that," Andrew admitted. "Whenever she had

a bad dream when she was little, she'd crawl into bed with me and Mom—and I'd go sleep on the sofa rather than wake up black and blue."

Lilah frowned. "I don't do it on purpose."

"I know." He dropped a kiss on her forehead, to ensure she knew there were no hard feelings. "And you," he said to Tilda, "would turn yourself around so that you were sleeping sideways—so I got kicked out of the bed by you, too."

"I did?" Tilda asked, surprised.

"You did," he confirmed.

"And that's why Rob and I have already agreed that, if and when we have kids, there will be a strict no-sharing-our-bed policy," Rachel chimed in.

Andrew smirked at his sister. "A policy that will go out the window the first time your child wakes up crying in the night and can't be consoled with anything but cuddles."

He set a plate with a pancake on it in front of Tilda.

"I said I didn't want any."

"But you love pancakes."

"No," she denied. "Lilah loves pancakes."

He bit his tongue again, despite the fact that he couldn't count the number of weekend mornings that he'd made stacks of pancakes for the girls—and they'd both gobbled them up, slathered in butter and maple syrup. But Tilda clearly didn't want to remember those mornings right now.

"Do you want me to make you something else?" he offered.

"I told you I'm not hungry."

"You need to eat."

"Tilda doesn't eat breakfast anymore," Lilah remarked.

"Since when?"

"I eat if I'm hungry," Tilda said defensively. "I'm just not hungry."

"You weren't hungry at lunch yesterday, either."

Tilda glared at her sister. "My hamburger tasted like it had been sitting under a heat lamp all day."

"Mine tasted fine."

Andrew sent an apologetic look at Rachel, having a whole new appreciation for the journey his sister had endured with his bickering daughters. "I'm realizing that I can't thank you enough for everything you've done for us over the past two weeks."

"You're right," she agreed. "But you can give me a ride to the airport this afternoon."

As Sarah made her way down the long drive toward Claire and Devin's house, she caught a glimpse of her friend in the distance, racing over the rolling hills on the back of a horse that looked surprisingly familiar. She parked behind Devin's truck and, before she'd even opened her door, Ed was there.

The German shepherd/collie mix was always excited for visitors, though Sarah liked to think that she and Ed had formed a special bond as she'd been the first person to visit after Claire brought him home from the shelter. And even though he saw her almost every day now that she was working at Twilight Valley, he never failed to greet her with enthusiasm. Another reason she should consider abandoning any thoughts of romance in favor of a canine companion.

"Eduardo!" She crouched to give the dog the attention he craved—and one of his favorite treats.

When he trotted off with his biscuit, she straightened up and attempted to brush the dog hair off her pants.

"Good luck with that," Devin said dryly.

She glanced over to see him leaning against one of the support posts on the porch.

"Good afternoon to you, too," she replied to her cousin.

"There's coffee, if you want," he told her. "Claire just went out for a ride, but she'll be back soon."

"Coffee sounds good." She opened the passenger side door of her SUV to retrieve the remaining bakery box from the front seat, then followed him into the house. She set the box on the counter and washed her hands before accepting the mug of coffee he offered with a "thanks."

"You know where cream and sugar are, if you want them."

"I do—and I do," she said, adding some of each to her cup before joining him at the table. "I saw Claire as I drove in—on a horse that looked a lot like Mystic."

"Probably because it is Mystic," he admitted.

She frowned. "Did his buyer back out of the sale?"

"Not exactly," Devin hedged.

"So why don't you tell me—*exactly*—what happened?" she suggested.

"The buyer, Tom Broadbent, is a friend of mine from Stanford. I asked him to inquire through the website about Mystic because I knew Claire wouldn't admit that she wanted to keep him until someone else showed an interest. But then she insisted that it would be good for him to move on, that Twilight Valley was always meant to be a temporary home for the horses that came here. So Tom agreed to buy the horse, with the understanding that when Claire realized she missed him, I'd buy Mystic back."

"So it was all just a subterfuge?"

He frowned. "*Subterfuge* is a rather harsh word."

"What would you prefer? *Lie? Deceit?*" She folded her arms on the table. "And what is it about a man's DNA that renders him incapable of being honest with a woman?"

"Why do I get the feeling that you're mad…but not necessarily at me?"

"I *am* mad at you," she said, because she was. But he was right in that she was madder at Andrew. And since Andrew wasn't here, she refocused her attention on the topic at hand. "Because I wasted my time doing a thorough background check on your friend to ensure that Mystic would be going to a good home."

"Instead, he's staying in a good home," Devin pointed out.

"And that's great," she agreed. "I'm just saying, you could have told me what you were up to and saved me the trouble of checking the guy's references."

"I thought about it," he admitted. "But I didn't trust you not to open your big mouth and spoil the surprise."

"I can keep a secret," she told him, a little indignant that he would suggest otherwise.

"From Claire?" he challenged.

She considered that as she sipped her coffee. "Probably not," she finally conceded. "Especially not when she started crying over Mystic the other day."

Devin grimaced. "She cried?"

"Did you think she wouldn't?"

"I thought—*I hoped*—I'd have a chance to put the bow around Mystic's neck before she got to that point."

"Well, you thought wrong," she told him.

"Anyway, she's happy now that she knows Mystic is staying," Devin said, a defensive note in his voice.

"Of course she is," Sarah said. "And it's a fabulous gift because it shows that you know her heart."

"I'm learning, anyway," Devin said, flushing a little in response to her praise.

A happy bark sounded from outside—Ed's signal that Claire had returned from her ride.

"I'll go take care of Mystic, so you and Claire can visit," he said, rising to his feet.

"Thanks, Dev."

"You can thank me by telling Claire that one of those cupcakes has my name on it."

"Only one?"

"I not only know her heart, I also know not to get between my wife and chocolate," he said.

Sarah was laughing at that when her friend walked into the kitchen.

"Happy birthday!" she said, greeting her friend with a hug before presenting her with the bakery box.

Claire lifted the lid, her eyes growing wide. "Ohmygod! I don't believe it."

"You thought I'd forget your birthday?" Sarah teased, choosing to forget that she'd almost done exactly that.

"Never," her friend promised. "But I thought you'd have to stick a candle in a muffin from The Daily Grind this year."

"Well, the cupcakes aren't from Sweet Caroline's, obviously, but they are chocolate caramel nut."

"Did you make them?" Claire, unlike Gramps, only sounded a little wary.

Sarah laughed. "I love you too much to do something like that—especially on your birthday."

"So where did they come from?"

"I'll tell you," she promised. "But first, I want you to tell me how dinner was with your parents last night."

"Surprisingly pleasant," Claire said. "It helps that my parents really like Devin. And he earned bonus points this time by solving the dessert dilemma."

"How did he do that?" Sarah wondered.

"He sweet-talked Bonnie Reidel into making a lemon cheesecake."

Why hadn't it occurred to Sarah to go to Bonnie for cupcakes?

If she'd done so, the whole scene with Andrew and his sister and his kids would have been avoided.

And she would have still been in the dark about him.

So maybe the whole scene had served a purpose, after all—

if only to remind Sarah that she was better off alone rather than with a man who couldn't be honest.

"And Bonnie confirmed that she'll still be working at the bakery when it reopens as Sugar & Spice. Apparently the owner has two daughters who inspired the new name, because 'sugar and spice and everything nice.'" Claire licked caramel off her thumb. "Isn't that sweet?"

"It is," Sarah agreed. And then, "I slept with him."

The words spilled out of her mouth as if of their own volition.

Claire choked on a mouthful of coffee and had to grab a napkin to wipe the liquid dribbling down her chin.

"Who?" she asked, when she managed to speak.

"The new owner of Sweet Caroline's."

"Last night?"

Sarah shook her head as she refilled her coffee mug. "Six weeks ago."

"Six weeks ago?" Claire echoed indignantly. "And I'm only hearing about this *now*?"

"Because I didn't know he was the new owner of Sweet Caroline's at the time, and I thought he was leaving town the next day. For good, I might add."

"Six weeks…" Claire said again, her tone speculative now. Then she obviously put the pieces together, because her eyes went wide. "The hottie who thought you were a stripper is the new owner of the bakery?"

Now Sarah nodded.

"Well, well, well." Her friend lifted her mug to her lips again, sipping cautiously this time. "I guess he wasn't entirely wrong, was he? Assuming you did take your clothes off before you did the deed, of course."

"The only reason it happened is that I didn't think I'd ever see him again."

"You didn't find him the least bit attractive or charming?" her friend challenged.

"Okay, it's not the *only* reason I invited him to come home with me," she acknowledged. "But it was a significant factor."

"And now there's a chance you could cross paths with him on any given day."

"Exactly," she said.

"I still don't understand why you seem to think that's a problem," Claire admitted.

"Because I was in the process of making changes to my life," Sarah reminded her. "No more doing a job I didn't want to do. No more worrying about other people's expectations. And definitely no more falling into bed with hot guys who made me feel good in the moment."

"You planned to fall into bed with not-hot guys who made you feel good? Or hot guys who didn't make you feel good?"

"You know what I mean."

"What I know is that you're too hard on yourself," Claire said gently. "So what if you've had a few relationships that didn't work out? If you like this guy and he likes you—and it seems obvious there's an attraction on both sides—why not give it a chance?"

"Because I promised myself that I wasn't going to get involved with a man unless there was more than physical attraction."

"Physical attraction can be a solid foundation for a relationship."

"It was a one-night stand."

"So you're not interested in hooking up with him again?"

"He's got an ex-wife and two adolescent daughters."

"Everyone has a history," Claire pointed out.

"History suggests something in the past. His kids are very much in the present. And they're not little kids—they're fourteen and twelve."

"So you're not going to win them over with story times and snuggles," Claire acknowledged. "But maybe trips to the mall or mani-pedis at Serenity Spa?"

"I don't think there's much hope of winning them over. They did not look at all happy to discover that their dad had company when they showed up last night."

"I think you skipped that part of the story," Claire said. "So spill it now, Stafford."

Sarah obliged by summarizing the events of the previous evening for her friend.

"I can see how that would have been awkward," Claire admitted. "And he definitely should have given you a heads-up about the kids. But before you completely write him off, maybe you could give him a chance to explain?"

"Maybe," she allowed.

"And when he does, you can tell him that his are the best chocolate caramel nut cupcakes I've ever had."

"I don't think his ego needs the stroking."

"Well, you can stroke other parts, if you'd prefer," Claire said with a wink. "But I'm going to be at the grand opening of Sugar & Spice in two weeks to see what other magic he makes in the kitchen."

Tilda stood on the porch, watching as her dad's car pulled out of the driveway. He was taking Aunt Rachel to the airport in Elko so that she could fly back to Texas, and Lilah had decided to go with them. Tilda had been invited, too, but after the twenty-eight-hour drive from Beaumont, the last thing she wanted was to spend more time stuck in a vehicle.

Her dad had been hesitant to leave her alone but had finally relented, giving her strict instructions to stay at the house. He didn't want her wandering off in an unfamiliar town, especially when he wasn't going to be around.

As far as Tilda could tell, there wasn't anywhere to go, anyway. There wasn't even a mall in Haven—just a handful of shops on Main Street. Apparently the nearest shopping mall was in a town called Battle Mountain. But she had no idea how to get there and when she punched the address into her Uber app, she got zero available drivers.

Zero.

"I'm in hell."

"If the rumors are to be believed, hell is a lot hotter than Haven, Nevada."

She'd been certain she was alone, so when she heard the response to her muttered remark, she sucked in a breath and spun around.

"Sneaking up on someone like that is a good way to get kicked in the balls," she told the boy standing at the bottom of the steps leading up to the porch.

"You'd need a lot longer legs than what you've got," he pointed out. "Considering that I'm at least fifteen feet away from you."

He was tall—close to her dad's height, she guessed, which she knew to be six feet—but skinny. His shoulder bones were visible through his shirt and his knees were knobby beneath the hem of his cargo shorts. On the front of his T-shirt was a graphic of a d20 with the words "this is how I roll." His hair was somewhere between dark blond and light brown, his green eyes were amplified by the wire-rimmed glasses he wore, and he carried a foil-covered tray in his hands.

A stereotypical D&D geek, she decided.

The type of guy she wouldn't have been caught dead talking to at Wharncliffe Middle School.

And though she was a long way from there now, she scowled at him. "And anyway, I wasn't talking to you."

He made a show of looking around, highlighting the fact that there was no one else nearby. "So who were you talking to?"

"Myself," she snapped.

"Do you do that a lot?" he asked curiously.

"Sometimes it's the only way I can have an intelligent conversation."

His brows lifted. "Someone has a high opinion of herself."

"What are you doing here, anyway?"

"I live there," he said, nodding toward the house next door. "My mom made a chicken broccoli casserole to welcome your family to the neighborhood."

"I stand corrected," she said. "This isn't hell, it's worse. It's a fifties sitcom neighborhood."

"Are you going to take the casserole?" he asked, a little impatiently.

She stomped down the steps to accept the dish. "Thanks."

"My name's Warren."

He reminded her of Lilah—open and approachable. Willing to make friends with everyone who crossed her path.

Yin to her sister's yang.

"I don't care."

He took a step back, startled by her blunt response. "O-kay, then."

She'd been rude—inexcusably rude—and felt the prickle of embarrassed heat crawl up her throat.

"I just want to be alone right now," she said.

Not an apology but an explanation.

"I'll leave you to it," he said, and walked away.

And she was glad.

Really.

Chapter Nine

When Sarah returned home after her visit with Claire, she found Andrew sitting in one of the turquoise Adirondack chairs on her porch, holding…a branch?

As she made her way to the door, she looked at the stem covered in silvery green leaves—and then him—warily.

Or perhaps quizzically, because he said, "It's an olive branch."

And he offered it to her.

Not just a proverbial olive branch—a real one.

Though she was willing to give him credit for creativity, she refused to be charmed.

"Claire loved the cupcake," she told him, accepting the branch and extending her own. "In fact, she said it was even better than the one I gave her from Sweet Caroline's last year."

"I'm happy to hear it."

"So thank you—for making them and also for having your sister deliver them to me."

"You're welcome."

"And now that we've dispensed with those pleasantries, why don't you tell me why you're here?"

"I'm hoping you'll give me five minutes of your time to apologize and explain," he said.

"Not necessary," she said.

"My mother taught me to apologize when I did something wrong. Five minutes," he said again. "Please."

She turned her wrist to tap the face of her Apple watch, starting the timer. "The clock is ticking."

"Can we go inside? Or do you want the neighbors to see me groveling on your front porch?"

After a brief hesitation, she unlocked the door and led him inside.

"Four minutes and fifty seconds."

"I'm sorry."

"Look at that—you didn't even need half a minute."

"Any chance I could get a cup of coffee in the time I have left?"

"Apparently your mother didn't teach her kids not to invite themselves into other people's houses and offer themselves beverages," she remarked dryly.

But she selected a pod and dropped it into the single-serve coffee maker, then set a mug beneath the spout.

"Do I need to apologize for my sister as well as myself?" he asked.

"No, just yourself," she told him. "It turns out that I like your sister."

"Ouch," he said, as she handed the mug to him. "But as it turns out, she likes you, too."

"Cream or sugar?"

He shook his head. "This is fine."

"She told me that you're divorced."

"About four years now," he confirmed. "Me and Miranda both knew it was over long before we went our separate ways, but we tried to stick it out for Tilda and Lilah."

"And you have custody?"

"Officially, Miranda and I have joint custody, which worked well when we were all living in Beaumont. Eight months ago, she decided to take a new job in Calistoga, and the girls have only seen her three times since the move."

"That must be hard on them," she noted.

He sipped his coffee. "It has been," he agreed. "And I worry that I might have made things worse by moving them out of Texas and completely upending their lives."

"But that's why you moved from Texas to Nevada," she realized, setting a second mug beneath the spout of her coffee maker. "To be closer to her."

"To facilitate visitation between the girls and their mom," he clarified.

"Most people would have found a way to work some of that information into a conversation," she said.

"You're right," he acknowledged.

"We spent *hours* together. You told me that you wanted to be a rodeo clown when *you* were a kid but somehow you never got around to mentioning that you *have* kids."

"You didn't want to know anything about me," he reminded her. "You wouldn't even let me tell you my name."

"Because I didn't think I'd ever see you again after that night," she pointed out.

"You mean you didn't *want* to see me again after that night," he guessed.

Apparently the man was more intuitive than she'd given him credit for.

"Maybe you're right," she allowed, "Maybe we should both just chalk up that night as a mistake and forget it ever happened."

"I don't think I could forget that night if I wanted to—and I don't want to. But the reality is that I'm a single dad of two daughters who aren't thrilled with the move halfway across the country."

"I understand," she assured him.

"I'm not sure that you do," he said. "Because notwithstanding all of that, I don't want to pretend the connection we have doesn't mean anything, because it's been a long time since I've felt the way I feel when I'm with you."

"That feeling is chemistry," she said dismissively. "Common enough and destined to fizzle out."

"Chemistry doesn't always fizzle out," he argued. "Sometimes it makes magic—like when the heat of an oven transforms the molecular structure of batter into cake."

"That's not magic," she said dismissively. "And anyway, you have other things that require your attention right now and I'm not looking for a relationship."

"Sometimes we don't know what we're looking for until we find it," he pointed out.

"Now you're a philosopher as well as a baker?"

"Or maybe just a man who doesn't want you to shut the door on the possibility of something between us."

"You shut the door when you lied to me," she told him.

"I never lied."

"But you didn't exactly tell the truth, either."

"You're right and I'm sorry."

"And now we're back to the beginning again and your five minutes were up a long time ago."

He set his empty mug on the counter. "Thanks for the coffee."

Sarah watched him walk to the door and told herself it was better this way.

But she didn't really believe it.

When Andrew was gone, she googled "how to care for an olive branch." Then she filled a vase with water, placed some river rocks from her front garden in the bottom and carefully sliced the bottom of the branch upward to assist with the intake of water before sliding it into the vase.

The branch had an earthy fragrance, slightly bitter with just a hint of smokiness, and she smiled as she breathed in the scent—then immediately chastised herself for mooning over the stupid branch like it was a bouquet of roses.

But the truth was, she would have been less impressed with

roses. While the perennial flowering plant boasted gorgeous blooms, roses were a common sight in any florist shop. And perhaps olive branches were, too, but Sarah didn't think so, and she was touched by Andrew's thoughtfulness—even if she didn't want to be.

But she'd listened to his explanation, and she was willing to admit that she might bear some responsibility for shutting him down the first night they met. But there was no excuse for him not telling her when she was with him the night before.

And now that she thought about it, she realized it wasn't the sellers who'd painted the upstairs bedrooms pink and purple—it was Andrew who'd done that for his daughters. Which would have been the perfect opportunity to tell her about them—saying this is Tilda's room and this is Lilah's room. Instead he'd said nothing, allowing her to be completely blindsided when they walked through the door.

He'd evidently been surprised by the timing of their arrival, too—but at least he'd been aware of their existence.

But it was water under the bridge now.

He was a divorced, single dad on the verge of opening a new business and she was a never-married thirty-two-year-old woman who was only now starting to take control of her own life. She couldn't imagine that he had time for a romantic relationship, even if he wanted one, and she wasn't willing to open up her heart to yet another man whose own was otherwise engaged.

I don't want to pretend the connection we have doesn't mean anything, because it's been a long time since I've felt the way I feel when I'm with you.

It had been a long time since she'd felt that way, too.

And though she'd dismissed the feeling as chemistry destined to fizzle out, after six weeks, it showed no signs of fizzling.

But Sarah was accustomed to wanting what she couldn't

have, and so long as she remembered that the town's sexy baker fell into that category, she had nothing to worry about.

The problem was that her subconscious wasn't willing to fall in line with that plan, and when she slept, she dreamed about him. And in her dreams, she remembered how completely he'd turned her on with just a kiss, how she'd yearned to feel his hands on her and his hard body moving in tandem with her own.

"We should probably be heading back," he said, when he'd eased away after kissing her until they were both panting and breathless.

She nodded, more than a little disappointed that their limited time together was already at an end.

"You've got an early flight in the morning," she remembered.

"Not all that early."

"Then maybe, instead of dropping me off at my car, you could give me a ride home?"

It was an invitation offered—and accepted.

He ignored the speed limit on the drive back to town, following the directions she gave him to her place. The door was barely closed behind them before they were tearing at one another's clothes, leaving a trail of garments all the way to her bedroom.

They tumbled onto the mattress together, their mouths fused, their bodies straining.

His hands stroked over her skin, stoking her desire. His thumbs brushed over the already tight peaks of her nipples through the lacy fabric of her bra, sending sharp, shocking arrows of pleasure from the tips to her core. Then he replaced his hands with his mouth, suckling her through the fabric barrier, first one breast, then the other, until she was practically whimpering.

He responded by releasing the clasp at the front of her bra and peeling back the cups. Then his mouth was on her bare skin, teasing and tasting, and she did whimper.

But he wasn't finished yet. He made his way down her body, exploring every inch of her with his hands and his lips. Touching and kissing, stroking and sucking.

He brushed his lips over her belly button, then continued his downward trajectory. When he parted the soft folds of skin at the juncture of her thighs, everything inside her tightened in anticipation.

His fingertips danced over the ultrasensitive nub at her center, more of a tease than a touch. And then again and again, taunting her with the promise of something more.

She had a moment—when he was sheathing himself with the condom she'd taken out of the drawer of her nightstand—to wonder if she was making a mistake. And she acknowledged, if only to herself, that she might very well regret this in the morning. But right now, in this moment, there wasn't anything she wanted more than to be with him.

Then he was rising over her, thrusting into her. Again and again, long and deep strokes that pushed her ever closer to the edge of the abyss...and over.

He found his own release immediately after, collapsing on top of her. She welcomed his weight, her own body thoroughly sated, though her silly heart still yearned for more...

"Thanks for making dinner tonight, Tilda," Andrew said, as they sat down to a meal of chicken tacos.

"I shredded the cheese," Lilah chimed in.

"And you did an excellent job," he responded.

"Yeah, you have a special talent for sliding a block of cheddar over a grater," Tilda told her sister.

Andrew gave his eldest daughter a disapproving look.

"You've both been great about picking up the slack around

the house while I've been busy at the bakery," he continued. "And I appreciate all the help."

"Maybe you could show your appreciation by buying pizza for dinner tomorrow night?" Tilda suggested hopefully.

According to her, Jo's Pizza was the only good thing about this town.

"We had pizza on Sunday," he reminded her.

"I could eat pizza every day," Lilah chimed in.

"And if I let you, I'd no doubt get a visit from child services."

"They only take away your kids if you don't feed them, not if you feed them pizza," Tilda said.

"Well, I'm not taking any chances with my favorite girls," he said.

"We're your only girls," Lilah pointed out.

He winked at her. "Probably why you're my favorite."

Tilda snorted as she added salsa to her taco.

"Are you looking forward to camp at Adventure Village next week?" he asked Lilah.

She nodded. "I found out today that Rory's going, too."

Rory—short for Aurora—was the same age as Lilah and lived next door. They'd been introduced only a few days earlier but were already fast friends.

"I've got some plans for you, too," he said to Tilda.

"I can't wait to hear all about them," she said, sarcasm fairly dripping off her words.

"Since you insisted that you're too old to go to camp—"

"Because I am," she interjected.

"—and you're not thrilled with the idea of helping out at the bakery—"

"That's an understatement."

"—I downloaded an application so that you can volunteer at Twilight Valley this summer," he finished, choosing to ignore her interruptions.

Tilda bit into her taco. The hard shell cracked, spilling the contents onto her plate.

"Twilight Valley?" She made a face as she pushed the chicken, lettuce and cheese into a pile. "It sounds like somewhere old people go to die."

"Actually, it's where old horses go to live out their final years," he told her.

"Before they die."

He held back a weary sigh. "I've filled out most of the information. You just have to sign it."

"Thanks but no thanks," she said. "Volunteering is just another way of saying 'working without pay.'"

"It wasn't a suggestion or a request," he told her.

She scowled across the table. "You can't make me."

"You're right," he acknowledged. "But I'm not going to let you hang around the house all day doing nothing, so it's Twilight Valley or Sugar & Spice. And Twilight Valley is only two days a week—Tuesdays and Thursdays."

"How do you even know about this place?"

"When I had lunch with Kyle last week, he told me that a lot of local students do their mandatory volunteer hours at the horse rescue."

"Isn't *mandatory volunteer* an oxymoron?" she challenged.

"And there's proof that you earned that A-minus in English."

She pushed away from the table, grabbed a can of diet cola from the fridge and stomped out of the room.

"I kind of feel sorry for the horses," Lilah said. "They shouldn't have to live out their final years in the company of angsty teenage girls."

Sarah didn't hear from Andrew again until Tuesday. And that was fine. Truthfully, she had no expectations about when— or even if—he'd reach out to her again.

She was mixing supplements into the horses' feed when her phone signaled receipt of a text message and she saw his name on her screen. Her heart skipped, and then raced as if to make up for that single missed beat.

At the same time, Claire wandered into the barn and leaned over Sarah's shoulder to see what her friend was looking at.

"Is that...a ransom note?"

"Andrew thinks he's funny," Sarah said.

"Apparently you do, too, because you were smiling when you opened the message."

"Maybe I'm just easily amused."

"'Be at 27 Morningstar Road at 6 pm tonight if you want to see your paws again,'" Claire read aloud.

Sarah swiped the screen of her phone to show her friend the photo he'd sent with the message: a picture of her faux fur oven mitts tied together with rope.

Claire laughed.

"I guess you're easily amused, too," Sarah remarked.

"You have to give him points for creativity," her friend said.

"Or deduct points for playing juvenile games," she countered.

"He's making it hard for you to stay mad at him, isn't he?"

"I'm not mad at him," Sarah denied. "I'm simply not interested."

"The problem with lying to your best friend is that she knows when you're lying," Claire said.

Sarah closed the screen on her phone and set it aside without responding to Andrew's message.

"You have to show up to get your oven mitts," Claire said. "I bought those for you."

"I know you did. And I love them, but..."

"But you're so chicken you could be marsala?"

Sarah stuck out her tongue.

"Now who's juvenile?" Claire said.

"Anyway, he's not really going to harm my oven mitts."

"Of course not," her friend agreed. "This is his way of telling you that he likes you. And obviously you like him, too, or you wouldn't think twice about brushing him off."

Sarah sighed. "I do want my oven mitts back. But the whole situation is…complicated."

"Because he's got kids? Or because you already did the horizontal naked mambo?"

"We did *not* mambo."

"Cha-cha? Rumba?" Claire suggested as alternatives.

"Someone's been watching *Dancing with the Stars* again."

"My guilty pleasure," her friend admitted.

"I'm not judging," Sarah assured her.

"I'm not judging, either," Claire said. "But I do think you should give the guy another chance. Give *yourself* a chance to be happy."

It was good advice, Sarah acknowledged. But she didn't know if she was brave enough to take it.

Chapter Ten

"You're punctual," Andrew noted, when he opened the door in response to Sarah's knock at 5:59 p.m.

"I didn't want to give you any excuse to harm my paws."

"I assure you, they are completely unharmed." He frowned when she handed him an envelope. "What's this?"

"The ransom."

His brows lifted when he opened the flap and saw what was inside. "I didn't ask for any money."

"I know, but I realized that I never paid you for the cupcakes," she told him now.

He handed the envelope back to her. "Your legendary chicken marsala was payment enough."

"You're not going to stay in business long if you give cupcakes away to anyone who asks," she pointed out.

"I wouldn't give them away to just anyone," he said. "But I'm always happy to help out a friend."

"Are we friends now?"

"I hope so."

"Does that mean I can have my oven mitts back?"

"Of course," he said. "But I'm hoping that, before you go, you'll stay for a meal you didn't have to cook this time."

"Pizza from Jo's?" she guessed.

"No, lasagna from the freezer section of the grocery store."

Sarah hesitated.

"With salad and garlic bread," he added, aware that the offer of a prepackaged entrée probably wasn't overly appealing.

She looked at him warily. "Why are you doing this?"

"I want you to have a chance to get to know my daughters."

"Did you ever consider just asking instead of holding my oven mitts hostage?"

"I considered it," he admitted. "And I didn't like my chances of getting a positive response."

"Next time, just ask," she advised.

"I will," he promised, pleased that she seemed willing to consider the possibility of a next time.

"Okay."

"You'll stay for dinner?" he prompted.

She nodded.

He grinned and gestured for her to make her way to the kitchen.

"You've got furniture," she noted, glancing into the living room.

"You like the leather sofa better than the folding chairs?"

"It works better for the overall aesthetic of the room," she said.

"I've got a dining room set now, too," he pointed out.

"And now this place actually looks lived in."

"You want to see lived in? You should see the girls' bedrooms," he told her.

"Or you could respect our privacy and not let strangers into our personal space," Tilda said, appearing in the doorway of the kitchen.

Andrew managed a smile, but Sarah could tell that it was forced.

"My eldest daughter, Tilda," he said, then turned to the teen. "Tilda, this is Sarah."

"It's nice to see you again," Sarah said.

"Yeah," Tilda agreed.

"I'm Lilah," his younger daughter said, her greeting bright and friendly as she exited the kitchen with a big bowl of salad in her hands.

"Hi, Lilah."

"Lilah, why don't you take Sarah into the dining room while Tilda helps me serve up dinner?"

"Okay," she agreed easily.

"Dad sits there, Tilda sits there and I sit there," Lilah said, pointing at the chairs around the table. "That leaves that one for you."

"Thank you," Sarah said, settling into her assigned seat.

Lilah took the seat adjacent to their guest and started chatting away while Andrew dished up the pasta and Tilda carried the plates to the table.

He hadn't dated much since his split from Miranda, and he'd never before brought a woman home for a meal with his family. And while this wasn't a date, because Sarah had made it clear that she wasn't interested in dating him, he could see that Tilda wasn't happy that there was a woman who wasn't her mom at the table with them.

And while he wished she'd at least make an effort to be polite, he knew that calling out her behavior would only exacerbate it.

"So what do you girls have planned for the summer?" Sarah asked, as she tore off a piece of garlic bread.

"I'm going to camp at Adventure Village next week," Lilah said. "And Rory, my new best friend who lives next door, is going to the same camp."

"That sounds like fun," Sarah said, then shifted her attention to Tilda. "Are you going to camp, too?"

"No. But in July we're going to spend two weeks in California with our mom."

"I told you it might not be two weeks this summer," Andrew cautioned. "Your mom just started a new job and she's not sure how much time she'll be able to take off."

"She doesn't need to take time off," Tilda said, pushing her pasta around on her plate. "It's not like we need a babysitter."

"Where in California does your mom live?" Sarah asked.

"Napa Valley."

"One of my favorite places in California."

"You've been there?" Lilah asked.

Sarah nodded. "A few times."

"We haven't been yet," Lilah confessed. "Mom's new house is under renovation."

"Well, I'm sure you'll love it when you get to visit."

"Our mom's a sommelier," Tilda said. "She knows a lot about wine."

"I'll bet she does," Sarah agreed.

"What do you do?" Lilah asked.

"I work at a local ranch."

Tilda made a face as she poked at a tomato wedge with her fork. "So you're like...a cowboy?"

"Actually, I mostly handle the business side of things, but I'm happy to help muck out stalls and groom horses when help is needed."

"Do you get to ride the horses sometimes?"

"Every day," Sarah said.

"Lucky," Lilah said.

"Can I be excused?" Tilda asked.

Andrew frowned at the food left on her plate but nodded.

"You may both be excused," he told his daughters. "We'll clean up later."

"Or I can help you clean up now," Sarah said.

"That's not necessary," he protested.

She shrugged. "If you don't want my help, then I'll take my oven mitts and go."

"Do you want to rinse or load?" he asked.

Sarah chuckled at his abrupt change of tune.

A short while later, she decided that she should have taken her oven mitts and made a quick escape when she had the chance, because helping Andrew tidy up after dinner turned out to be an exercise in sexual frustration. Somehow while they ate, the huge kitchen had shrunk to a fraction of its previous size, so that every time they crossed paths, there was some kind of physical contact between them. And no matter how unintentional or fleeting that contact, it had the effect of sending currents of electricity sparking through her veins.

She scraped the remnants of food off Tilda's plate—had the girl eaten any of her lasagna?—then rinsed it under the faucet. As she was doing so, Andrew sidled by to return the container of Parmesan to the refrigerator.

His hip grazed her bottom, and the plate slipped out of her grasp. Thankfully it didn't break, but it clattered loudly enough to catch his attention.

"Sorry," she said.

"No worries." He retrieved the plate from the sink and placed it in the dishwasher.

She wondered if the heightened attraction was a result of her determination that the single dad of two was off-limits, similar to how someone on a diet might obsess over the foods they wanted to avoid.

Thankfully, Sarah had some experience in turning away from the things she wanted, and she took a step back now.

"I think that's everything," she said.

He slid the rack into place, then closed the door.

As Sarah dried her hands on a tea towel, she spotted a glass dish on the counter. "Is that my baking pan?"

"It is," he confirmed.

She stepped closer to look at the sugar-dusted squares of fried dough in the pan, tightly covered in plastic wrap. "What are those?"

"Those are what all the kerfuffle is about," he told her.

"Beignets," she realized.

And he was right that they had been the subject of much kerfuffle when Haven's residents learned that the new baker was replacing doughnuts with its French cousin.

"More specifically, those are my chai latte beignets."

"Why are your chai latte beignets in my pan?"

"Because one of the other things my mother taught me was never return a food dish empty."

"They're for me?"

He nodded.

"Thank you," she said, surprised and pleased by the gesture.

"You can have one now, if you want. I just realized that I didn't offer you anything for dessert."

"I don't usually eat dessert, anyway," she confided. Or doughnuts, though she couldn't deny that the beignets were tempting. "Or maybe, since there are two in the pan, you were hoping that I'd offer one to you?"

"Nope, they're both yours."

"That's right—you don't eat what you bake. You only sample."

"As we discussed when I caught you checking me out."

"That was before," she told him.

"Before?"

"Before I found out that you were a single dad of two kids."

"And my parental status somehow changes the appearance of my butt?"

"No, but it changes everything else."

"You're no longer attracted to me?"

"It's not about attraction. It's about the fact that we're at different stages of our lives, with very different priorities."

"So you *are* still attracted to me."

She blew out a breath. "Did you hear the part about different stages of our lives and different priorities?"

"I heard it," he said. "I just don't happen to think that matters as much as the chemistry between us."

"And on that note, I'm going to take my baking pan and my oven mitts and go," she decided. "Please tell your daughters it was a pleasure to meet them and goodbye."

He followed her to the front door. "How about a little wager?"

She eyed him warily as she slipped her feet into her shoes. "What kind of wager?"

"You try one of those beignets, and I bet you come into the bakery on the day of the grand opening for more."

"And if I do?"

"If you do, then you agree to give us a chance to see where the attraction between us leads."

She didn't need a map to see where the attraction would lead—straight to the bedroom.

"And if I don't show up at the bakery?"

He smiled. "You will," he assured her. "But if you don't, then I will defer to your wish to ignore the attraction between us."

"You specified the grand opening," she noted. "So if I were to come in the day after for more beignets—or two days after that—I'd still win the bet?"

He nodded. "Is that a wager you're willing to make?"

She shifted the baking pan to one hand and offered him the other.

After a perfunctory shake to seal their deal, he tugged on her hand, drawing her closer.

"I look forward to seeing you soon—and definitely on the twenty-eighth."

"The twenty-eighth?" she echoed, feigning surprise. "Is that the grand opening?"

His gaze narrowed. "You know it is."

"I think I'm going to be out of town that weekend."

His gaze narrowed, then he shook his head. "I don't think you are."

"Did you take a peek at my calendar when I wasn't looking?"

"Of all the things I'd like to take a peek at, your calendar isn't one of them," he assured her.

"Then how do you know I'm not going to be out of town?" she challenged.

"Because you're not the type to cheat to win."

"There you go again, thinking you know me."

"Maybe I'm wrong," he allowed. "And maybe I'm wrong, too, in thinking that you're drawing out this conversation, hoping I'll clue in to the fact that you want me to kiss you goodbye."

"I haven't been—"

The rest of her indignant protest was muffled by his kiss.

When Dad told her and Lilah that he'd invited a friend for dinner, Tilda had assumed it was a guy friend because he'd never before invited a female friend to eat with them. (She specified "female" rather than "girl" in her mind because she didn't even want to think "girlfriend" for fear that might make it true.)

She knew it was silly to feel hurt that he might be involved in a romantic relationship. After all, her parents had been divorced for more than four years and Mom had dated several different guys in that time.

But Dad hadn't had much of a social life since the divorce. In fact, she didn't know for certain that he'd even been on a single date. Tilda had always suspected that was because he was still in love with her mom, and she'd always believed that they'd eventually get back together again.

But that was before Mom moved to California with Perry.

Before she claimed that he was her only chance for real happiness.

Was that why Dad was suddenly interested in dating? Had he given up on reuniting his family?

The thought made her uneasy, because if Mom and Dad weren't together, she didn't know where she was supposed to be.

But the thought of them getting back together made her uneasy, too, as she remembered the tension and the arguments and feeling as if she needed to tiptoe around the house so her mom didn't find a reason to yell at her, too.

They tried not to fight in front of the kids, but sometimes Tilda heard them, anyway. And when you heard things you weren't supposed to hear, you learned things you didn't want to know.

She was scowling at the ground when her phone pinged with a text message. She yanked it out of her pocket to peer at the screen.

Hey

The message was from London.

When she first told her BFF that she was moving, London promised that they'd text all the time. And for the first few days after school finished, she'd kept that promise. Then she'd been hanging out at the beach with Damien or shopping at the mall with Kellie or sipping Frappuccinos at Starbucks with Tanya. There was always a reason she was too busy to reach out—as she'd explained when she finally responded to Tilda's overtures. As if sending a text message to say "hey" took more than three seconds.

But this was the first time any of her friends had initiated contact in four days, and Tilda had started to feel as if she was already forgotten.

Maybe she should wait to reply, so that London didn't think she'd just been sitting around waiting to hear from her. But she was afraid that if she delayed, London might get bored and move on to something else.

So she replied:

Hey

How's haven?

I HATE it

She didn't usually bother with capitalization or punctuation in her text messages, which drove her dad nuts, but the depth of her emotion warranted the effort this time.

Not surprised

I looked on a map—it's the middle of nowhere!

U don't have to tell me

When r u coming back?

I wish!

U should come for the 4th

Party at D's

D was Damien, London's sometimes boyfriend.
I'm 1800 miles away

Actually, the specific number was 1,892 miles, according

to Google Maps. Because yes, she'd looked it up, needing to know exactly how far away from civilization she was.

U could hitch

No way.

Tilda wasn't so desperate to get out of Nevada that she'd risk her life getting into a stranger's vehicle. She'd heard too many horror stories about girls being abducted and trafficked, and she wanted to live to see her fifteenth birthday—and not locked up in a garden shed in some trucker's backyard.

My dad would KILL me

He should've asked if u wanted to go to NV before he dragged u there

That was the truth.

And it wasn't only that he hadn't asked but that, when she protested his plans, he'd responded that he was sorry she wasn't looking forward to the move but she was a kid and therefore didn't get a say.

It wasn't fair.

Mom had moved to California, which sucked, but at least Tilda and Lilah and Dad had stayed where everything was familiar.

Then, just when she was getting used to the new normal, Dad decided to move to Nevada to open his own bakery, claiming it had been a longtime dream or something like that. But he didn't pick Las Vegas, the interesting part of Nevada, where she might meet lots of cool people and maybe have something resembling a social life. Instead, he dragged them to the middle-of-freakin'-nowhere.

And apparently she'd taken too long to respond to her friend, because London messaged again.

Gotta run
Mtg D at Starbcks

Have fun

Hope to see you the 4th

Yeah, like that was ever going to happen.

She tucked her phone back into her pocket.

"That was a heavy sigh."

She glared at Warren, who'd apparently decided it was okay to invade her peace—and her backyard.

"Why don't you leave me alone?" she asked, not so much because she wanted to be alone but because she couldn't understand why he'd make a second effort when she'd shot down his first.

He shrugged. "Apparently I have a soft spot for sad girls."

She folded her arms over her chest. "I'm not sad."

"You don't look happy," he noted.

She glared at him.

"That's better," he said, lowering himself to sit beside her on the wrought iron bench.

"Seriously—why are you here?"

"Because I think you need someone to talk to."

"You think I'd talk to you?" Her tone dripped with derision.

He shrugged, unfazed by her attitude. "I might not be your first choice, but it looks like your options are limited."

He was being nice to her—for no reason. And she didn't want him to be nice to her, because suddenly her throat felt tight. As if she was going to cry. And no way was she going to cry in front of him.

"Why don't you go play D&D with your geeky friends?"

"At least I have friends," he retorted.

Ouch.

"I hate you," she told him.

"Do you?" he wondered. "Or do you hate yourself?"

She felt her heart pinch. "You don't know anything about me."

"And you know even less about me," he pointed out reasonably. "So why are you so sure that you hate me?"

"I know your type."

"What is my type?" he asked curiously.

"A straight-A student who does his homework during his lunch period so he can help Mom and Dad around the house after school and who never misses curfew because his only social activities are D&D with his geeky friends and playing trumpet in the high school band."

"How do you manage to make those things sound like character flaws?" he asked, sounding more amused than insulted by her assessment.

"It's a gift."

He surprised her by laughing at that.

"FYI, I play alto sax, not trumpet." He rose to his feet. "If you change your mind about wanting to talk, you know where to find me."

Then he was gone.

But Tilda stayed outside, watching YouTube videos on her phone until Sarah got into her SUV and drove away.

Chapter Eleven

Andrew glanced up from the list on his iPad when Tilda stomped into the house, letting the screen door slam at her back.

"Sarah said to tell you goodbye," he said.

Tilda pulled a can of diet cola out of the fridge and popped the top. "How do you know her, anyway?"

"I met her on my first visit to Haven."

"Is she the reason we're here?"

"Her name is Sarah," he said again. "And no. Of course not."

Tilda didn't look convinced. "Mom followed Perry to California."

"I promise you, I didn't follow anyone here. We came to Haven because it was the best choice for our family."

"According to you."

"According to me," he confirmed. "Because I'm the dad, I get to make those tough choices."

Tilda swallowed another mouthful of soda. "Is she—*Sarah*—your girlfriend?"

He shook his head. "No."

Not yet.

His daughter didn't look convinced. "So what was with the wine at dinner?"

"Sometimes it's nice to have wine with a meal."

"Since when?"

"Actually, there's evidence to suggest that wine has been drunk since humans created the first permanent settlements."

She rolled her eyes. "I meant, since when do *you* have wine with a meal?"

"Not often," he acknowledged. "Not anymore."

"You and mom used to drink wine with dinner all the time," she remembered.

"We did," he confirmed.

"Back in the days when we all used to have dinner together. When we were a family."

"We're still a family, Tilda. We might not live under the same roof anymore, but your mom's still your mom and I'm still your dad."

Her gaze skittered away. "We don't even live in the same state anymore."

"That's just geography."

"Yeah, well, geography is wreaking havoc on my social life."

"I know this move hasn't been easy for you."

"You know nothing," she said. "You've been here three weeks and you're already dating."

"I'm not dating," he said. "Sarah is a friend who happens to be a girl but she's not my girlfriend and we haven't been on a single date."

"But do you want to date her?"

He put down the iPad and looked his daughter in the eye. "What's with all the questions, Tilda?"

She shrugged. "I just think I have a right to know if you plan on adding a stepmom to our family."

"Not anytime in the near future," he assured her.

"But you like Sarah?"

"Yes, I like Sarah," he confirmed. "And I think, if you gave her a chance, you'd like her, too."

She tipped the can to her lips again before asking, "What happened with you and Mom?"

"You want to know why we got divorced?"

She nodded.

He pushed back the stool next to him—a silent invitation for her to sit. After an almost imperceptible hesitation, she did so.

"Sometimes people grow apart, no matter how much they love one another, and realize they're better off alone than together."

"Mom's not alone. She's with Perry."

"Well, I'm not alone, either," he pointed out. "Because I've got you and your sister."

She traced the logo on her can with a fingernail. "Did you want us...or did you get stuck with us?"

He was sincerely shocked that she would ask such a question. "I wanted you. *Always*," he assured her. "And your mom wanted you, too."

Tilda rolled her eyes at that.

"It's true," he said. "But we agreed that, because of your mom's late hours at the restaurant, I could provide a more stable home for you and Lilah."

"And did you agree that she should quit her job at the restaurant and move to California?"

"Your mom wasn't happy with her job in Beaumont."

"She seemed happy enough until she met Perry."

"And now she's even happier," he pointed out, because there was no doubt it was true. By all accounts, Perry adored Miranda, and there was nothing Miranda liked more than being adored. But there were some things about their marriage his children didn't need to know, and he wasn't going to say anything that might negatively alter their perception of their mother.

"And now she doesn't have any time for us," Tilda noted.

"She's been busy with the new house and the new restaurant," he acknowledged.

At least that was the excuse she'd given every time he tried to pin down a date for their daughters to visit. But finally the renovations were complete on the house she shared with Perry so they could visit, whenever her schedule might allow.

"You're busy with the bakery," Tilda pointed out.

"Yeah, but you live with me, so you get all my free minutes," he said, hoping to earn a rare smile.

"Until you get a girlfriend," she guessed.

"Tilda," he began, not quite sure what else to say.

But she didn't stick around to listen to anything more.

The new sign was installed at the bakery the next day, and several passersby stopped to watch the unveiling. Kyle's wife, Erin, had designed the logo for him—*sugar & spice* in lowercase script flanked by inward-facing silhouettes of two little girls created from pictures of his daughters in their younger years.

When he showed them the design, Lilah had been thrilled and Tilda mortified. Apparently being immortalized as a five-year-old was cool when you were twelve but not when you were fourteen.

But he got several compliments from the passersby—followed by even more inquiries about the menu offerings. He responded to all the latter with the suggestion that the potential customer should be there for the grand opening to find out.

But today, he was taking a break from the last-minute preparations to meet Kyle for lunch again, and he was perusing the menu when his friend settled on the barstool beside him at Diggers'.

"This time I'm late," his friend acknowledged. "I took the kids to the park so Erin could have some peace and quiet to get some work done and then had trouble dragging them away."

"Enjoy every one of those moments while they last," Andrew advised his friend. "Because before you know it, your kids will be tweens and teens and they won't want to spend any time with you and you won't be able to do anything right."

"Is it really that bad?"

"Not always." He shrugged. "Some days it's worse."

"Something to look forward to, then," Kyle said dryly.

They paused their conversation to order.

"It's been a rough year for the girls, and I get that," Andrew said, after the bartender had set their drinks in front of them.

"Having second thoughts about the move?" his friend asked.

"About everything," he confided.

"You can't expect the pieces to fall into place overnight. You all need some time to adjust. In the meantime, me and Erin are here, if we can help in any way."

"You've both already done so much," Andrew said. "You put me in touch with Caroline when you knew she wanted to sell, and Erin designed a kick-ass website for Sugar & Spice."

"My wife has real talent—and the website is kick-ass," Kyle agreed, nodding his thanks to the bartender when he set their plates in front of them. "And although you haven't shared the details of your opening-day menu, I thought I would mention that Erin loves your sticky buns."

"All the women do."

"Hey—that's my wife you're talking about," Kyle protested.

"You're the one who said she loved my buns," he felt compelled to point out. "And they are on my list for the grand opening, so I'll put some aside for her."

"That won't be necessary. She plans to be there when the doors open."

"I appreciate the support," Andrew said sincerely. "It will be nice to see a familiar face."

"I would think they're all familiar faces now, since everyone's been making the rounds of The Daily Grind when you go for your afternoon coffee run."

"It's not just my imagination, then?"

Kyle chuckled. "Definitely not."

"That doesn't mean any of them will show up next Saturday," Andrew noted.

"Are you kidding? There's going to be a line out the door."

"Because the residents of Haven have been deprived of peanut butter banana croissants for so long?"

"Chocolate peanut butter banana," his friend corrected him. "And that might be part of it, but the biggest part is that they're all curious about the new owner of Sweet Caroline's."

"Sugar & Spice," he corrected.

"You can put whatever name you want on the sign," Kyle cautioned. "It's going to take the locals a while to get used to calling it anything but Sweet Caroline's."

"I knew what I wanted when I came to Haven—a business of my own and a new start for the girls. Maybe for me, too." Andrew nibbled on a fry. "Now I find myself wanting things I have no business wanting."

"Sounds to me like you've got a woman on your mind," Kyle said, lifting his burger from his plate.

"Yeah," he admitted.

"What's the problem? Your interest isn't reciprocated?"

"I think it might be," he said cautiously. "But with everything else going on, it's probably not the right time to pursue a relationship."

"There's gotta be more to life than work."

"I've got more," Andrew reminded him. "I've got Tilda and Lilah, and they need to know that they come first with me." He sipped his beer again. "Although Lilah seems to be doing just fine. It's Tilda that I'm most worried about."

"How old is she now?" Kyle asked. "Thirteen? Fourteen?"

"Fourteen," he confirmed. "She'll be starting high school in September."

"Tough time," his friend said sympathetically.

"For the move?"

"For life in general," Kyle clarified. "In some ways, high school was the best time of my life. In others, it was a nightmare—especially freshman year. Starting a new school at any age can be hard. Walking into high school without knowing anyone is going to be even harder."

"That's why I wanted to make the move at the beginning of the summer. So she'd have time to make friends before school starts."

"It's only been a few days," his friend pointed out.

"You're right. But she's so mad that she had to leave her friends in Beaumont, she's stubbornly refusing to put any effort into making new friends here."

"Maybe she could invite one of her old friends to come here for a visit," Kyle suggested.

Andrew shook his head. "Aside from the fact that there's no direct transportation from there to here, her friends were one of the reasons that I jumped at the opportunity to move both girls out of Texas." London, in particular, had been testing her parents' boundaries and encouraging Tilda to do the same, leading to ignored text messages, missed curfews and the smell of cigarette smoke—and sometimes weed—on her clothes when she finally did come home.

"Erin suspected that you made the move to be closer to Miranda, possibly in the hope of a reconciliation."

"She's half-right," he said. "I did want to be closer to Miranda, but only to facilitate visitation between Tilda and Lilah and their mom.

"They've seen her all of three times since she left Texas—and each time, she made the trip to Beaumont because she was temporarily living in a one-bedroom apartment with the boyfriend while their house was being renovated, which meant that they didn't have a spare room for guests."

"Do Tilda and Lilah get along with the boyfriend?"

"They haven't really spent much time with him. And when Miranda came back to Beaumont for those visits, he didn't come with her."

"Have they spent much time with your new girlfriend?" Kyle asked.

"I don't have a girlfriend, and that wasn't a very subtle fishing expedition," Andrew chided his friend.

"At least tell me who she is—this woman you're thinking about who isn't your girlfriend."

"No way," he said.

"Because I know her," Kyle immediately guessed.

"Odds are good, considering that you know almost everyone in this town," Andrew pointed out.

And then she walked into the bar—and right into the arms of another man.

He frowned. "Who's that?"

"Sarah Stafford," Kyle said, having followed the direction of his friend's gaze.

"I mean the guy she's with."

"Zack Kruger."

The high school boyfriend.

He didn't realize he'd spoken aloud until Kyle responded, "Yeah, they were an item back then. But how do you know about Sarah and Zack?"

"She mentioned him in passing," he said, silently cursing himself for the giveaway.

"I didn't know you knew Sarah."

"We actually met here, at Diggers', the first time I visited Haven."

His friend didn't have any trouble connecting the dots. "I

have to say, you're setting the bar pretty high if that's where your interest lies."

He dragged his gaze away from Sarah and Zack. "What do you mean?"

"You've heard of Blake Mining?"

"Of course." When Kyle first told him about Sweet Caroline's being offered for sale, he'd done some cursory research on the northern Nevada town.

"Well, Sarah's last name might be Stafford, but her mom was a Blake."

Apparently the woman who claimed to be a stickler for honesty had some secrets of her own, Andrew mused.

Zack rose to his feet when Sarah approached the table he'd snagged and greeted her with a fierce hug. "Damn, you're a sight for sore eyes."

"You, too," she said, aware of the curious glances other diners cast in their direction as she slid into the booth across from him. Some of them were no doubt wondering about the identity of the man she was with—because at thirty-two, he didn't bear much resemblance to the skinny kid he'd been at sixteen. Others would remember, and they'd talk, because people always had something to say about Sarah's unlikely friendship with Zack.

A lot of them said that Zack Kruger was all wrong for Sarah Stafford. The truth was, she'd been all wrong for him.

Though they'd grown up in very different worlds, the attraction had been real. And maybe part of the attraction was the knowledge that being together was a great big middle finger to the rest of the world. Sarah had used Zack to get a reaction from her parents; he'd used her for the veneer of respectability their relationship gave him in the community.

And they'd both gotten what they wanted, at least for a while.

They ordered lunch when their server came to the table, then picked up their conversation again.

"So how's life in Seattle?" Sarah asked.

"Good," he said. "Business is *really* good, which means I'm working longer hours, including evenings and weekends sometimes."

"How does Imani feel about that?" she asked, naming the girlfriend he'd mentioned on his last visit.

"She puts up with it. Not just the long hours but my distraction when I'm prepping for trial and my frustration when I lose—" he grinned "—which thankfully isn't very often. And through it all, she still loves me."

"Sounds like you've got a keeper there," Sarah said lightly.

"You're right about that," he said with another grin. "Which is why we're getting married in October."

"Wow."

Zack was getting married?

Sarah was…surprised.

And perhaps more surprising, genuinely pleased for him.

"Congratulations."

"Thanks. In light of our…history, I wanted to tell you in person, before you heard it from anyone else."

"I'm happy for you, Zack."

"I'm happy, too," he said. His gaze moved around the bar, no doubt as aware as she was that they were the subject of much scrutiny. "I'll bet no one around here would have guessed that I'd actually make something of myself someday."

"I would have," she said.

He laughed.

"I would have," she insisted. "I always knew you were capable of so much more than anyone gave you credit for."

"Plenty of folks gave me lots of credit for causing trouble."

But she knew he didn't cause trouble so much as he'd been unwilling to walk away from it. Yeah, he'd been suspended from school a few times for fighting, but it was usually in defense of a smaller kid being picked on by bullies.

And maybe it was true that he'd been quick to use his fists, but it was also true that he looked out for his mom and his little brothers, giving his mom more than half the pay from his part-time job toward household bills. And every week, he took Mrs. Sanchez's list to the grocery store to do the shopping for his elderly neighbor, always ensuring she got back the correct amount of change to the very last penny.

And when Sarah finally decided that they should go all the way (and it had been *her* decision—Zack might have made it clear that he wanted her, but he'd never put undue pressure on her), he didn't brag about it after the fact. Another guy might have told his friends that he'd nailed Sarah Stafford, but Zack hadn't said a word to anyone, ensuring that her first intimate experience remained intimate.

"You were one of the good ones," she said now. "Even if I didn't realize it at the time."

"I was crazy for you," he admitted.

"We were both more than a little crazy back then," she noted. "But we had some good times together."

He smiled. "We had some *really* good times—and not only back then."

She smiled, too. A little sadly because she knew those good times had already come to an end. And even if she'd realized, a long time ago, that there was no going back, the letting go was still bittersweet.

"Do you want your jacket back?" she asked him now.

"What jacket?"

"Your vintage Levi's jean jacket. The one you gave me the night we went up to Lookout Point, because—in a ridiculous effort to look sexy—I was wearing only a skimpy little top and miniskirt."

He smiled at the memory. "The top was pale blue, with a

ribbon that laced up the front. The skirt was a slightly darker shade, with a little ruffle at the bottom. And you were sexy as hell," he assured her. Then he winked. "Still are."

She rolled her eyes at that. "Do you want the jacket or not?"

"It was vintage sixteen years ago," he noted. "You really still have that old thing?"

"Not only do I still have it, I still wear it," she told him.

He shook his head. "You always did have a sentimental streak."

"You're not the only one who's accused me of that in recent months."

"Sounds like there's a story there," he mused.

Now she shook her head. "Not even a first chapter."

"Don't close the book before it gets interesting."

"Too late."

"I hope that's not true," Zack said. "Because if this guy is worth it, he won't let you go that easily."

And that was the story of her life: every man she'd ever been with—even the ones who'd claimed to love her—had let her go. And maybe she bore some responsibility for pushing them away, as she'd admittedly done with Andrew, but the result was the same.

She always ended up alone.

Chapter Twelve

"This *sucks*," Tilda said, delivering the line with all the considerable disdain a fourteen-year-old could muster.

"You've been here less than two weeks and that refrain is already sounding tired," Andrew told his daughter. "Could you at least mix it up a little? Use different words? Expand your vocabulary?"

"Child labor is illegal in this country," she protested, as she pushed the mop over the pink-and-white checkerboard flooring.

It wasn't what Andrew would have chosen, if he'd picked out the flooring, but he couldn't justify the expense of replacing perfectly good tiles. And, as it turned out, the soft sage color he'd selected for the walls worked well with the tile flooring and the off-white bistro tables and chairs for the seating area.

"A parent is allowed to employ a child in a family business," he responded to his daughter now.

She dunked the mop in the bucket, sloshing water over the sides. "An employee gets paid to work."

"You're being paid room and board."

He could practically hear her eyes roll as she responded, "That. Is. So. Lame."

"That's reality, kiddo."

"I *hate* reality." She lifted the mop again and pushed it around the floor. "I wanna go back to Beaumont."

"Well, that's not happening," he told her.

"Then let me go to California, to live with Mom."

He ignored the pain that slashed through his heart like a jagged knife, because he knew she hadn't intended her words to hurt him. It wasn't that she didn't want to live *with him*, it was that she didn't want to live *here*: a town in northern Nevada without a Starbucks or a McDonald's or—horror of horrors—a shopping mall.

So he didn't point out that his ex-wife hadn't shown any interest in having either Tilda or Lilah make the move to Napa Valley with her and her winemaker boyfriend. The girls were hurting enough without being reminded that their mom had prioritized her new romance over maintaining proximity to—and her relationship with—her children. In fact, Miranda had been scheduled to visit the previous weekend and canceled at the last minute, which he suspected was a contributing factor to his daughter's current mood.

"That's not happening, either," he said, keeping his tone deliberately casual. "Also, you missed the far corner by the front window."

"It's too dark to see what I'm doing."

"There's plenty of light."

"But no natural light," she pointed out. "Why'd you paper over the windows, anyway?"

"Because I didn't want anyone passing by to see what we're doing here until we're ready to open."

"You mean, you don't want the local authorities to see you exploiting child labor," she grumbled.

"Our grand opening is Saturday—the local authorities can see you working behind the counter then," he responded mildly.

She huffed out a breath as she pushed the mop into the corner. "It's not fair that I'm stuck working here while Lilah's at a birthday party."

"It's not," he agreed. "But your sister still has a couple of years before she turns into a sullen teenager, which is probably why she's already managed to make friends."

"She made friends with the kid next door," Tilda noted dryly. "That didn't require much effort aside from moving in."

"And yet you've put considerable effort into ignoring Rory's brother."

"Because he's totally lame."

"How can you possibly know that when you've never had a conversation with him?" he challenged.

"I've had a couple of conversations with him," she said. "And the first time I talked to him, he was wearing a D&D T-shirt."

"So?"

"So...totally lame," she said again, dropping the mop back into the bucket. "Can I be done now?"

He wasn't sure the floor was clean, but it was definitely wet. His gaze shifted to the clock on the wall showing that it was almost six o'clock.

"Sure." He pulled a couple of twenties out of his wallet and handed them to his daughter. "Why don't you go to Jo's to grab a pizza for dinner?"

She pocketed the money. "Okay."

The bell over the door jangled as she let herself out.

He felt confident that she knew her way around town, and if he worried about the fact that she'd yet to make any friends, that fact was less worrying than the friends she'd said goodbye to when they left Texas.

Miranda's decision to move to Calistoga might have been the unwelcome catalyst that precipitated his recent move and career change, but once he'd had some time to think about it, he'd decided that a fresh start could very well be the best thing for all of them. And if he'd chosen Nevada because it was close to California and he was (perhaps foolishly) optimistic that his ex-wife would soon realize how much she missed her daughters, well, that wasn't anyone's business but his own.

In the meantime, he was going to do everything in his power to let Tilda and Lilah know that they were still—and always would be—his number one priority.

"I'm so glad you were able to meet," Jenna said, giving her sister a hug before sliding onto the barstool beside her.

"I'm glad you called," Sarah said. "It's been a long time since we've done this."

"We used to do it all the time, when you worked in the office beside mine."

"You mean when we'd leave at the same time and equally desperate for a drink?"

Jenna laughed as Duke came over to take their order. "Yeah. Good times."

"If you invited me to meet to try to convince me to go back to Blake Mining, I'm leaving," Sarah warned, when their wine had been poured.

"I didn't," Jenna hastened to assure her. "I wouldn't. I'm not sure I'd ever be brave enough to venture out on my own, but I'm proud of you for doing it. For following your dreams."

"Thank you," Sarah said.

When Jenna reached for her glass, Sarah finally spotted the diamond on her third finger.

"Ohmygod." She snatched Jenna's hand for a closer inspection of the ring. "You're engaged?"

Jenna smiled and nodded.

"When? How?"

"Today. At lunch. Harrison packed a picnic basket and took me to the park for our four-month anniversary."

"You had a picnic in the dog park?"

Her sister laughed. "Not in the off-leash part, obviously,

but the other side of the park that's actually set up with picnic tables for people."

"That makes more sense," Sarah noted.

"We had sandwiches with lettuce and tomatoes from his greenhouses and homemade potato chips and fresh lemonade."

Harrison was an organic farmer who offered his produce for sale through The Trading Post and also supplied fresh fruits and vegetables to The Home Station. He wasn't likely to get rich doing what he did and didn't seem to have any ambitions in that direction, but he was passionate about his farm, his dog and Jenna.

Sarah was thrilled for her sister, who was obviously as head over heels in love with Harrison as he was with her. But as she listened to Jenna recount every detail of the oh-so-romantic proposal, she realized that she was a little envious, too.

And she hated that, because Jenna deserved every happiness.

But didn't she deserve happiness, too?

"You'll be my maid of honor, won't you, Sarah?" Jenna asked now.

"Absolutely," she immediately replied.

"We don't have a date yet," the bride-to-be said. "But I know that I don't want a long engagement—I want to be Mrs. Harrison Raczynski as soon as possible."

"First you have to learn to spell it," she said, recalling Andrew's sister's explanation for her continued use of her maiden name.

"R-A-C-Z-Y-N-S-K-I." Jenna rattled the letters off easily.

"Someone's been doodling her future husband's name in her notebook," Sarah couldn't resist teasing.

"It did take some practice," her sister admitted. "But taking his name ensures our future children will be one more step removed from everything implied by the Blake name in this town."

"Speaking of… Have you told Mom and Dad?"

"Not yet." Jenna glanced at her watch as she finished her wine. "But Harrison's picking me up so we can go to Miners' Pass to do just that, so I have to run."

"Don't you want to savor your engagement status for a while longer before they trample all over your joy?"

"I do," Jenna agreed. "But I won't hear the end of it if they happen to hear about our engagement from anyone else."

"That's true," Sarah acknowledged, standing when Jenna did to give her sister a hug. "Just remember, whatever happens with them, I'm here for you—whatever you need."

"I know. And thank you."

Sarah settled back on her stool as Jenna hurried out the door to meet her fiancé.

"Is everything okay?" Duke asked Sarah, as he tipped a glass under a tap to pour a draft beer for Jerry Tate, a regular seated at the other end of the bar.

Sarah managed a smile for the bartender. "Everything's great."

"Are you sure? Because you've hardly touched your wine."

"Too busy chatting with my sister, I guess," she said, picking up her glass now.

"You want anything to eat?" Duke asked, when he returned after delivering Jerry's beer.

"No, thanks. I'll get something at home." She pulled some money out of her wallet and set it on the bar to pay for her drink.

As she exited the restaurant, she realized she couldn't remember what she had in her fridge and decided she didn't feel like prepping and cooking, anyway. Instead, she pulled out her phone and ordered pizza.

Jo's Pizzeria had a front entrance with a sign over the door that said "Restaurant" and a side door designated for "Takeout." Sarah walked in the side entrance, her stomach growling as she breathed in the heady scents of tomato sauce and oregano.

Laurel Walsh, working behind the counter, found the order with Sarah's name on it and set the box on the counter.

"Large pizza," she noted, a speculative gleam in her eyes. "Are you planning to share that with someone?"

Sarah shook her head. "The large with three toppings was the special tonight, and leftover pizza freezes well."

"That's disappointing," Laurel said. "Especially following reports that you were cozied up with the hunky new baker at The Daily Grind a couple weeks back."

"I had a three-minute conversation with him while we both drank coffee," Sarah said, determined to nip any rumors in the bud.

"A three-minute conversation about...?"

She pulled out her wallet to pay for her pizza. "Cupcakes."

Laurel wiggled her eyebrows as she rang up the order. "Is that a euphemism?"

"It is not."

"Then you're not calling dibs on the hunky new baker?" Laurel asked, passing Sarah's change across the counter.

"Definitely not."

"If I wasn't still reeling from my divorce, I might be tempted," Laurel said. "Because the number of desirable, eligible men in this town seems to be dwindling with each day that passes. And apparently Harrison Raczynski was recently spotted looking at engagement rings in The Gold Mine, so if your sister says yes, he'll be off the market, too."

"She did say yes," Sarah said, smiling to ensure the other woman could see how happy she was for Jenna and Harrison. "They got engaged today."

"She's only been dating the guy—what? Four months?"

Sarah nodded. "Apparently when it's right, you know."

"Or when you want it to be right, you convince yourself

it is. I don't mean your sister," Laurel hastened to clarify. "I was just thinking about my personal history. Of course, I was barely out of high school—and pregnant—when I walked down the aisle."

"Funny how you think you know everything as a teenager and only realize how much you don't know until you've grown up," Sarah mused.

"Isn't that the truth?" Laurel agreed, as Sarah's cell phone vibrated inside her purse. "Anyway, tell Jenna 'congrats' for me."

"I will," Sarah promised, reaching for her phone to check the display.

"Excuse me a sec," she said, stepping away from the counter to connect the call.

Laurel nodded as she collected another order from the pass-through window.

After a brief conversation with Twilight Valley's insurance agent regarding additional coverage for the incoming group of summer students, Sarah turned around again—just in time to see her pizza walking out the door.

"That was quick," Andrew said, when his daughter returned to the bakery with a large flat box a short while later.

Tilda shrugged. "They weren't too busy."

"I'm not complaining," he said, his mouth watering in anticipation as he lifted the lid. He'd worked through lunch—*again*—and had even skipped his usual afternoon coffee break at The Daily Grind because the hours that remained before the grand opening were rapidly dwindling.

"Sausage, peppers and olives?" he said, inventorying the toppings on the pie from which a single slice was missing. Apparently his daughter had been so hungry, she'd dug into their dinner on her way back to the bakery.

"What's wrong with sausage, peppers and olives?" Tilda asked.

"It's not our usual order."

She shrugged. "You didn't ask for the usual order. And besides, you're always telling me to try new things."

"Yeah, but since when do you listen to me?"

She rolled her eyes. "Take the win, Dad."

He decided to take the win.

"It would have been a bigger win if you'd waited to eat with me," he said.

"I was hungry," she said. "You made me work through lunch."

"I didn't make you work through lunch," he denied, feeling guilty nonetheless that he'd lost track of time and hadn't realized that she was working through lunch right along with him.

"Is that what you're planning to tell the Labor Board?"

She was obviously joking, and he was grateful for the rare glimpse of humor, so he responded in kind.

"That's my story and I'm sticking to it," he confirmed.

He took a big bite of the pizza while Tilda began to unpack a box of take-out containers, transferring them to the cupboard beneath a display case.

"You don't even like olives," he noted, after he'd chewed and swallowed.

"I don't like *green* olives," she clarified.

The bell over the door jingled, startling Andrew.

He didn't lock it during the day, because he figured the paper covering the windows and doors would keep people out.

"We're not open," he said automatically.

"I know."

"Sarah." He dropped the half-eaten slice of pizza into the box and stepped away from the counter.

"I'd apologize for interrupting your dinner," she said, "except that it's *my* pizza you're eating."

He frowned. "Your pizza?"

"Hot sausage, roasted red peppers and black olives."

"I'm sorry," he said, immediately apologetic. "There must have been some kind of mix-up at Jo's."

But when he glanced at Tilda for confirmation, he realized that his daughter was paying far more attention to aligning stacks of napkins than the task warranted, and the sinking feeling in the pit of his stomach warned him that maybe he was wrong.

"There wasn't a mix-up," Sarah said, and he was struck again by the fact that her voice managed to sound sexy even when she was obviously annoyed. "I ordered the pizza, I paid for the pizza, and when I turned away from the counter to take a phone call, your daughter walked out of the restaurant with my pizza."

"I'm sure you're mistaken."

Sarah shifted her attention to his daughter. "Am I mistaken, Tilda?"

His daughter finally abandoned the cupboard and straightened up.

"It was a harmless prank," she said, in the defensive tone he knew only too well.

Andrew was mortified. "You stole Sarah's pizza?"

"I didn't *steal* it," she denied.

"Did you pay for it?" he challenged.

She didn't meet his gaze. "I didn't have to. It was already paid for."

"Because *I* paid for it," Sarah said. "Because it was *my* pizza."

"I gave you money," Andrew reminded his daughter.

"And told me to grab a pizza, so I grabbed a pizza."

"I'm so sorry," he said to Sarah.

"It's just a pizza," Tilda said. "What's the big deal?"

"I think it's probably a good idea for you to go home now, Tilda," he told her. "We'll talk about the big deal later."

"What more is there to say?" she challenged.

"I'm sure I'll think of something," he promised. "Likely starting with the word *you're* and ending with *grounded*."

"Grounded from what?" she grumbled, turning toward the kitchen to exit through the back door. "There's nothing to do in this town, anyway."

"You're letting her off the hook pretty easily," Sarah noted, when Tilda was gone.

"She's not off the hook yet," Andrew assured her.

"You didn't even make her apologize."

"I apologized."

"You didn't steal my pizza," she pointed out. "And now that you've given her a free pass on this, what do you think she's going to do next?"

"I didn't give her a free pass," he said, pulling his wallet out of his pocket. "And I'm not having this conversation with you."

"It's not about the money," she said, when he thrust a handful of bills at her. "It's about the fact that your daughter is pushing against your boundaries and she's going to keep pushing until you push back."

"Here's an idea," Andrew said. "When you have kids of your own, you can tell me how to raise mine."

With a huff of frustration, Sarah turned on her heel and walked out the same door she'd entered, leaving him alone with her pizza and no appetite for it.

Warren was outside, washing his mom's car in the driveway, when Tilda walked past on her way home. He glanced up, but she pretended she didn't see him.

So what if he was the only person close to her age in the neighborhood?

She wasn't that desperate for a friend.

She stomped up the steps and flung open the screen door, letting it slam shut behind her.

If Dad was home, he'd give her hell for that for sure.

But he wasn't home and she was already in trouble, so what did it matter?

She stomped up the stairs to her room and slammed that door, too.

She hated her new room.

So what if it was bigger than the room she'd had in Beaumont?

She didn't want a new room—she wanted her old room in their old house in Texas.

But that house was gone now. Sold to a young couple with a three-year-old son and a second baby on the way. A couple looking to make happy memories, blissfully unaware that they could apparently fall out of love as easily as they'd fallen into it, go their separate ways, tear their family apart.

"This isn't working, Andrew."

"So let's figure out what we need to do to make it work."

"Maybe I don't want to make it work."

"What are you saying?"

"I want a divorce."

"We've got two daughters, Miranda. Maybe you should think about what they want instead of what you want."

"I'm not going to let my children hold me hostage in a marriage that isn't working."

"Hold you hostage? Isn't that a little melodramatic?"

"It's how I feel. I'm not happy, and I haven't been for a long time."

"Then let's try counseling."

"I don't want to go to counseling. I want a divorce."

Tilda felt tears burn behind her eyes, blinked them away.

A tentative knock sounded. "Tilda?"

"Go away."

Instead of doing as she requested, Lilah turned the knob and pushed open the door. "What's wrong?"

"Nothing."

Her sister held out a bag of sour cherry blasters. "Want some? I got them in my goody bag from Rory's birthday party."

"No." Tilda knocked the bag out of her sister's hand, spilling sugary gummies all over the floor.

"Hey!" Lilah's lower lip trembled, as if she was going to cry. "Why'd you do that?"

"Because I don't want any of your stupid cherry blasters."

Lilah dropped to her knees and began picking the candy off the floor. "You could have just said 'no, thanks.'"

"I don't want any candy and I don't want any company."

"Why are you mad?"

"I'm not mad!" Which she realized might have been more believable if she hadn't yelled the words at her sister.

Lilah opened her mouth, as if there was something else she wanted to say.

"Go away," Tilda said again.

This time, Lilah went away.

Leaving Tilda alone with all kinds of uncomfortable feelings churning inside her.

Chapter Thirteen

She could have handled that better, Sarah acknowledged, as she walked home from the bakery.

Andrew said he'd talk to Tilda later, and she should have left it at that. But there was something about his daughter that set off her internal radar. Something that warned her the girl was either trouble or in trouble. Maybe both.

Because she knew it wasn't a mix-up, as Andrew tried to explain it away. The girl had blatantly stolen her pizza.

Okay, maybe theft under twenty dollars wasn't a felony, but it was definitely an annoyance and one she didn't need at the end of a long day.

Her heavy mood lifted when she turned onto Fieldstone and saw Claire's vehicle in her driveway.

"This is a nice surprise," she said, managing a smile for her friend.

"Devin had plans with Trevor tonight, so I decided to come into town with him to hang out with you."

"Come on in," she said, sliding her key into the lock. "I'll open a bottle of wine."

"Dev will probably have a couple of beers with his brother, so I'll stick with tea in case I need to drive back."

Sarah filled the kettle with water and set it on the stove before selecting a bottle of cabernet franc from her built-in wine rack. As she uncorked the bottle, she remembered that she hadn't eaten since breakfast.

"Do you want a grilled cheese?" she asked Claire.

Her friend shook her head. "No, thanks. We had dinner before we came into town."

She started to collect the ingredients for her sandwich, then pivoted to the stove when the kettle started to whistle.

"I've got it," Claire said, turning off the burner and pouring the hot water into her mug. "You make your sandwich and tell me why you haven't stopped scowling since I got here."

"I think I'm hangry," she admitted, dropping her sandwich into the pan.

"You didn't have lunch today, did you?"

"No. I wanted to finish up the grant proposal before I had to leave to meet Jenna at Diggers'."

"They have food at Diggers', you know."

"I did hear something about that," she said, flipping her sandwich.

"Is everything okay with Jenna?" her friend asked cautiously.

"Yeah, she's doing great," Sarah said. "In fact, she's getting married."

Claire sipped her tea. "When?"

"They haven't set a date yet, but soon, she hopes."

"Something else is on your mind," Claire noted.

"Yeah," she said again, turning her sandwich onto a plate.

"Want to share?" Claire asked, when Sarah sat down across from her.

Sara nibbled on her sandwich. "Do you remember when I stole that bottle of wine cooler from The Trading Post in high school?"

"I was your lookout," her friend reminded her.

"I knew it was wrong, but I did it, anyway. Even though I had the money to pay for it."

"You were underage. There was no way Mr. Hawkins would have sold it to you."

"That's not an excuse."

"Of course not," Claire agreed. "But it was fifteen years ago—I'm sure the statute of limitations has run out so that even if you went to Mr. Hawkins today and confessed to the crime, you wouldn't be thrown in jail for it."

"I was a troublemaker."

"You sometimes acted out in an effort to get your parents' attention," her friend acknowledged.

"I stole a car."

Claire rolled her eyes. "*You* didn't steal a car. *Zack* stole a car."

"I was in the car with him when he got pulled over." And fifteen years later, she still remembered the terror that had gripped her heart when she spotted the red and blue lights flashing in the mirrors—followed by a combination of dread and anticipation twisting in her belly when the arresting officer told her that her parents were on their way to get her.

"Not that I don't appreciate this trip down memory lane, but where's this coming from?" Claire asked.

Sarah summarized her interaction with Andrew and Tilda for her friend.

"I think this is about more than his daughter stealing your pizza," Claire guessed. "I think you're still upset that he never told you he had a daughter—never mind two of them."

"Maybe," she allowed.

"And you have a right to be upset," her friend assured her. "Especially because I'm sure you told him all your secrets."

Sarah popped the last bite of sandwich into her mouth and took her time chewing before she responded, "I don't have any kids that he doesn't know about."

Claire swallowed another mouthful of tea. "Have you told him about your parents?"

"I'm sure he could guess that I have parents," Sarah said dryly.

"But would he guess that your parents are filthy rich?"

"They are. I'm not."

"So he doesn't know that you're a Blake?"

"My mother's a Blake," she clarified.

"That's a fine line you're balancing on," her friend cautioned.

"I would have got around to telling him eventually, but I'm not sure it matters now. He seemed pretty mad at me for being mad at his daughter for stealing my pizza." She sighed. "I know I overreacted... I think I was feeling a little sorry for myself after Jenna shared her news, because it seems like everyone I know is married or getting married or having babies."

Her friend fell silent.

Uncharacteristically silent.

And somehow, Sarah knew.

"You're pregnant," she realized.

Claire nodded.

"Ohmygod." She pushed away from the table to hug her friend tightly. "This is so...*wow.* You're going to have a baby. You're going to be a mom." She grinned. "And I'm going to be an auntie."

Claire laughed at that. "You're already an auntie to your brother's kids."

"And I love them to bits, but my BFF is going to make me an auntie again and—" she had to swallow around the lump that rose in her throat "—I really couldn't be happier for you and Devin."

"It's early days yet. The baby's not due until February," her friend said. "But you're the first person I wanted to tell—after Devin, obviously, and I'm sorry for the timing—"

"No," Sarah interjected. "Don't you dare apologize for sharing the best news ever."

"Yeah?" Claire said hesitantly.

"Yeah," she confirmed, and hugged her friend again. "And I'm going to be your baby's favorite auntie."

"As if there was ever any doubt."

Andrew was rolling out the dough for sticky buns Friday night when there was a knock on the open kitchen door. He glanced over his shoulder, surprised to see Sarah standing there.

It wasn't fair that any woman should be so effortlessly beautiful. And she was even more so today, as instead of her usual jeans and T-shirt, she was wearing a sleeveless summery dress with a skirt that flirted with her knees and Louboutin sandals with a skinny ankle strap that added several inches to her height and gave him a second jolt.

He must have been staring, because she explained, "There was a reception at The Home Station tonight—a thank-you to some of Twilight Valley's big donors."

"You have to spend money to make money," he agreed.

"Anyway, since I was in the neighborhood, I stopped by your place. Lilah told me you were here—and to come to the back door."

"She should have also told you that I was busy," he said.

"I knew you would be." She stepped over the threshold to peruse the trays on the counters. "You've got a big day tomorrow—and it smells amazing in here."

He appreciated the compliment, but he remained wary—and at a distance, because he really wanted to haul her into his arms and kiss her until they were both breathless.

"Why are you here, Sarah?" he asked instead.

"You might recognize this," she said, holding up the olive branch he'd given to her the day after his sister and daughters crashed their dinner.

"It does look vaguely familiar," he acknowledged.

"I owe you an apology. I overstepped the other day and

some of the things I said obviously rubbed you the wrong way."

Finally, he turned to give her his full attention, a slow smile curving his lips. "And you want to make it up by…rubbing me the right way?"

A flush of pink color spread across her cheeks.

"I want to *explain*," she clarified.

"That doesn't sound nearly as much fun," he lamented, "but I'm listening."

"It's kind of a long story," she warned.

"I've got lots of baking to do."

"Okay." She nodded. "It starts a few years back, when a pregnant Labradoodle took shelter in the barn at Silver Star Ranch. Five weeks later, my brother, Patrick, had a dog and six puppies.

"Brooke Langley, one of our local vets—and now Patrick's wife—helped with the birth, and her son, Brendan, named all the puppies after *Star Wars* characters. And like everyone else who saw them, I fell head over heels and laid claim to the one named Han.

"But when it came time to actually take him home, I started to have second thoughts about the amount of time that I spent away from home and whether that would be fair to the puppy, and I balked. So my sister, Jenna, snapped him up."

Andrew was a little confused as to how her story related to the pizza incident with his daughter, but he figured she'd get to the point eventually and only said, "It's nice that Han stayed in the family."

"That's what I thought, too," she agreed. "Until, four months ago, when Jenna met Harrison at the off-leash dog park, courtesy of Han getting up close and a little too personal."

He chuckled. "As dogs have a tendency to do."

"It is kind of funny," she acknowledged, with just the hint

of a smile. "A real meet-cute, according to Claire. And I'm happy for my sister, of course. Because she's dated her share of duds, too, and absolutely deserves a happy ending. It's just that there's a part of me that wonders…"

"If the man of her dreams might have been the man of your dreams if you'd been the one at the dog park?" he guessed.

"It sounds silly when you say it out loud, but yeah."

"It's human nature to wonder about the path not taken," he said.

"And now, instead of shopping for a wedding dress, I'm going to be a bridesmaid. Again."

"They're getting married?"

She nodded. "Jenna told me when I met her for a drink on Wednesday. And all the time I'm asking about her wedding plans, the back of my mind is echoing the warning—three times a bridesmaid, never a bride.

"And while I've never put much stock in old sayings like that, considering this will be my sixth time standing next to a bride, I have to wonder if that means I'm twice as unlikely to ever marry."

"I'm sure that's not true," he said.

"It's not even the wedding, though," she told him. "It was the sudden and depressing realization that I might never find someone to share my life.

"Of course, I know that isn't the worst-case scenario. Being alone is certainly preferable to being in a toxic relationship like my parents' first marriage."

"I didn't know your parents were divorced."

"Divorced and remarried," she told him.

"They both remarried?"

"They remarried each other," she clarified. "But only after hooking up with various other partners and ensuring their kids had an intimate understanding of relationship dysfunction.

"Sorry—that was an unnecessary tangent and probably

more information than you ever wanted to know about my family. But that's the convoluted story about why I was in a mood when I went to Jo's to pick up my pizza."

"And my daughter walking out with the pizza you'd paid for did nothing to improve your mood," he acknowledged.

"I was hangry," she admitted. "And feeling much more like my usual self after I had a grilled cheese."

"You didn't go back to Jo's for another pizza?" he asked, surprised.

"And have to explain to Laurel what happened to the first one?" She shook her head. "None of us needed to deal with the potential fallout from that."

He hadn't considered how that might have affected Tilda. It was bad enough to be the new girl without being the new girl who stole a pizza from Jo's.

"Thank you," he said, sincerely grateful for her discretion.

"Anyway, I shouldn't have presumed to give you parenting advice just because your daughter reminds me of myself at her age."

He finished arranging the cinnamon rolls on top of the base of brown sugar and butter and pecans. "It seems to me that you turned out okay."

"You wouldn't have given me favorable odds if you'd known me when I was a teenager," she told him. "The truth is, it took a long time and a lot of work to break some self-destructive habits. And some I'm still working on."

"Such as?" he wondered.

"Falling into bed with men I barely know."

"You don't have to worry about that with me," he told her, wiping his hands on a towel. "Because you know me a lot better now than you did eight weeks ago."

"That's true," she acknowledged. "But still not very well."

He drew her into his arms. "So let's spend some time together."

"I think, between your daughters and your bakery, most of your time is already accounted for."

"I seem to have a few minutes right now."

"Be still, my heart," she said dryly.

He smiled at that and lifted a hand to cup the back of her head, his thumb brushing over the pulse point at the base of her jaw. "Your heart *is* racing."

She swallowed. "You're invading my space."

"Actually, you invaded mine."

"I brought an olive branch," she reminded him. "A symbol of peace and friendship."

His gaze dropped to her mouth, and he knew it would taste sweeter than anything on his menu. "And I'm suddenly feeling very friendly toward you."

She laughed, a little breathlessly. "I can't believe I ever accused you of not having game."

"The first time I saw you, I couldn't help but trip over my tongue," he said. "You completely took my breath away."

"You had enough air to imply that I was a stripper," she remarked dryly.

"I was definitely intrigued by the possibility that you might take more clothes off." Thinking back to that night, he couldn't help but smile. "And then you did."

"That was much later," she pointed out.

"And later still after that before I realized that I never got to see your tattoo."

"It's not exactly hidden," she said. "You'd already guessed that it was on my shoulder blade, but that's on my back and…"

He quirked a brow. "I was on your front?"

She swallowed. "Yeah."

"Next time we won't be so rushed," he promised, lowering his head to brush his lips over hers. "And I'll be sure to appreciate every inch of your body."

"There's not going to be a next time," she said, even as her body swayed into his. "I don't do one-night stands anymore."

His mouth skimmed over her jaw, down her throat. "But we've already spent one night together, so when we get naked together again, it won't be a one-night stand."

"That's a rather self-serving argument," she noted.

"But also persuasive, don't you think?"

When she opened her mouth to respond, he covered it with his own. A hum sounded low in her throat as she lifted her hands to his shoulders, holding on to him as he deepened the kiss. Their tongues danced together in an erotic and arousing rhythm that had all his blood migrating south…and an annoying buzzing sound echoing in his head.

With obvious reluctance, Sarah eased her mouth from his.

"Oven timer," she said.

"What?"

Then reality returned and he swore under his breath as he stepped away from her to pull the trays out of the oven.

He examined the mini cakes, tested a random sample and breathed out sigh of relief.

"What are they?" Sarah asked, peering over his shoulder.

"Right now, they're just white cakes. Tomorrow they'll be Chantilly cakes."

"With whipped cream and berries?"

He nodded as he removed two more trays from the oven. "And these chocolate cakes will be layered with milk and dark chocolate mousse and frosted with chocolate Italian buttercream."

"Obviously you've got a lot of work to do before you open."

"Bonnie will be here to help in the morning."

"And the beignets?" she asked, her tone deliberately casual. "When do you make those?"

He grinned. "Not until tomorrow."

She sighed with obvious regret, and he knew he'd be seeing her the next day.

"I should get out of your way so that you're not stuck here all night," she said now.

"I wouldn't mind being stuck here all night if you were with me," he told her.

She rolled her eyes, but she was smiling. "Good night, Andrew."

"Good night, Sarah." He followed her to the door. "I'll let you know when the girls make their plans to go to California so we can schedule our date."

"You seem pretty confident that I'll be here for a beignet tomorrow," she mused.

"My fingers are crossed."

"If I do show up, you should know that it's because I'm tempted by more than your fancy doughnuts."

And then, after one last, all-too-brief kiss, she walked out the door.

Chapter Fourteen

Andrew didn't stay at the bakery very long after Sarah had gone, because he knew he'd be back there at 4:00 a.m. the following morning to ensure all the display cases were full before the doors opened at eight o'clock. But he had too much on his mind to be able to sleep right away, so he turned on the TV and decided to unwind with the baseball game before bed.

Kyle was right—running his own business was a lot different from simply making desserts for someone else's menu. Of course, he would still be making desserts for The Home Station, and he was grateful to his friend for offering an arrangement that guaranteed at least a minimal income for Sugar & Spice even if no customers walked through the door.

But worries about the opening weren't even the biggest part of what preoccupied his mind. Tonight, like almost every night since he'd met her, he was thinking about Sarah.

"Dad?"

The softly spoken query jolted him back to the present, and he turned to see his youngest daughter at the foot of the stairs.

"Why are you still awake?" he asked Lilah.

"I couldn't sleep."

He patted the empty cushion beside him, inviting her to sit. "Something on your mind?"

She shrugged as she dropped onto the sofa to snuggle against him.

"You don't know if there's something on your mind? Or you don't know if you want to tell me what's on your mind?"

"The second part," she admitted.

"Well, I'm here," he said. "If and when you decide you want to talk about it."

She was quiet for a minute—perhaps watching the ball game playing on TV or perhaps preoccupied with her own thoughts.

When the Rangers jogged off the field at the middle of the fifth inning, she finally said, "Tilda doesn't like it here."

"If you're worried that you're talking behind her back, don't be. She's made her feelings on the matter perfectly clear."

"Okay," Lilah said, seemingly relieved by this bit of information.

"What about you?" he asked now. "Do you like it here?"

She nodded.

"You don't miss your friends in Beaumont?"

"Sure, but we message and chat online, and I've already made some new friends here. Rory and Kylie and Teagan."

"I'm looking forward to meeting them."

It had always been his rule for both his daughters: if they wanted to spend time at a friend's house, he had to meet that friend—and the friend's parents—beforehand.

"You've met Rory. And her mom and dad," Lilah reminded him.

The day after Rachel arrived with Tilda and Lilah, Rory's mom had sent over a chicken-broccoli casserole so that they wouldn't have to worry about putting together a meal while they were unpacking. She'd even included a list of ingredients—in case anyone had allergies to worry about—and instructions for reheating in both the microwave and the oven. It had been hearty and delicious, feeding all three of them for dinner that night and leftovers for Andrew for lunch the next day.

"That reminds me, we've still got Mrs. Aldridge's casserole dish," Andrew said now.

"I can take it over tomorrow," she offered.

"You can't take it back empty."

"We could put some of your sticky buns in it," Lilah suggested.

"Or you and Tilda could make your famous peanut butter cookies," he suggested as an alternative.

"They're not famous," she said. "And Tilda doesn't want to do anything with me these days."

He'd noticed that his eldest daughter had been uncharacteristically snappy with her sister, but he'd hoped that Lilah might remain oblivious.

He brushed a hand over her hair. "I'm sorry, Lilah."

She shrugged as she nibbled on her thumbnail.

He gently pulled her hand away from her mouth. "I thought you stopped biting your nails a couple years ago."

"Mostly."

"I know there's been a lot of upheaval in your life these past few months."

"It would be more upheaval to go back again," she said.

"We're not going back," he told her.

"That's what you say now, but Tilda always gets what she wants."

He was stunned, not just by the words but by the resigned tone that warned she believed them. "I'm sorry if it seems that way to you, but I assure you, it's not true. And I promise that we're not going back to Texas. This is where we live now."

"Okay."

She'd always been an easygoing child, sweet-natured and quick to smile. Of course, puberty hadn't hit her with its full force yet, and he had no doubt it would all change soon enough, but for now he was happy to appreciate her sunny disposition.

She snuggled in again. "Can we get a dog?"

"Is this a test? To see if I'll give you what you want?"

"If you said yes, I'd have to admit that I sometimes get what I want, too."

"What if I said *someday*?"

"*Someday* works," she said. "If you really mean it."

"Why not?" he decided. "I'm not saying someday soon, but once the bakery is up and running and we've settled in, we could take a trip to the local shelter and see what dogs they've got available."

"They might have cats, too."

"I'm sure they do."

"Just something to think about," she told him.

He chuckled softly and hugged her close.

People showed up.

The grand opening of Sugar & Spice was scheduled for 8:00 a.m., but there was a line of customers waiting outside the door an hour before that. On Bonnie's recommendation, he'd hired another former employee of Caroline's to work the counter. And from the time Andrew unlocked the doors at seven thirty, he and Bonnie and Mabel had been running nonstop. Tilda and Lilah had been enlisted to help, too, and they spent several hours bussing tables and doing dishes.

For the grand opening, he'd decided to offer three kinds of beignets—plain sugared, lemon filled and chai latte with cinnamon sugar—all of which proved popular. He'd also made sure there were chocolate peanut butter banana croissants (thank you, Bonnie), and nobody was more surprised than him that his sticky buns sold out before the croissants. In fact, by three o'clock that afternoon, his display cases were almost empty and Andrew was giddy with happiness and relief and exhaustion.

He knew that business wouldn't always be this brisk. That half the people who came through the door were motivated by curiosity. But he had faith that whatever they'd chosen to sample on their first visit would entice them to come back again.

Sarah had stopped by for a couple of chai latte beignets—and left with a box filled with various other treats, too. But while she was there, she offered to cook dinner for him and the girls—an offer he was quick to accept. Not just because it saved him having to come up with a dinner plan, but because it meant that he would get to see her again later that day.

Unfortunately, he forgot to tell the girls that Sarah would be bringing dinner over, and when he made his way down the stairs after stealing a quick shower, she was already at the door.

"Dad didn't tell us that we were having company tonight," Tilda—always the gracious hostess—said.

"Well, I assure you that he was aware of my plan to bring dinner so that he'd have one less thing to worry about on the day of the grand opening."

"Aware and grateful," Andrew interjected, nudging his daughter aside so that he could take the slow cooker from Sarah's hands and she could cross the threshold.

"Mrs. Aldridge sent over a casserole the day we moved in," Tilda remarked, following them to the kitchen. "But she didn't expect to sit at the table and eat it with us."

"Tilda," Andrew admonished, mortified by his daughter's rudeness.

"I'm just saying."

"Sending food is a neighborly thing to do," Sarah responded to his daughter. "Bringing food is a friendly thing to do."

"So how long have you and Dad been...friends?" Tilda asked.

"I promise, she has manners," Andrew interjected again. "But I think they might be in one of the moving boxes yet to be unpacked."

"All my stuff is unpacked," Tilda said. "Lilah's the one who still has boxes in her room."

"So maybe your manners ended up in one of her boxes," he said. "Why don't you go see if you can find them? And while you're up there, tell your sister to come down for dinner."

Tilda stomped up the stairs, clearly aware—and unhappy—that she'd been dismissed.

"I'm sorry," Andrew said.

"I already told you that you don't have to apologize for your daughter."

"Well, now that we're alone." He leaned in and touched his mouth to hers. "Hi."

She smiled. "Hi."

But when he went to kiss her again, she took a deliberate step back.

"Your daughters are upstairs," she reminded him.

"Believe me, we'll hear them when they come down the stairs."

Sure enough, almost before the last word was out of his mouth, heavy footsteps sounded.

"What did I say?"

She responded with a smile. "Why don't you get out the plates so I can dish up dinner?"

Per their dad's instructions, Lilah set out napkins and Tilda got the cutlery, and in short order, they were seated around the dining room table.

"What is this?" Tilda asked, poking at the meat on her plate.

"Apple butter and sage pork roast with sweet potatoes," Sarah said. "There's also spinach salad with a red wine vinaigrette."

Tilda began to separate the apple slices from the potatoes. "I don't like sweet potatoes."

"They're just like regular potatoes," Andrew told her. "Only...sweeter."

"And orange," Tilda noted.

"Do you suddenly have a bias against orange food?" her dad asked.

"I don't like sweet potatoes," she said again.

"I like sweet potatoes," Lilah chimed in, not wanting Sarah's feelings to be hurt by her sister's rejection of the meal she'd prepared. "Especially sweet potato fries."

"Those are my favorite, too," Sarah said.

"Have you decided what movie you're going to see tonight?" Andrew asked his daughters.

"There are only two screens and since one of them is showing a horror flick, which Lilah won't watch, we don't exactly have a choice," Tilda told him.

"We're not officially on the payroll at Sugar & Spice," Lilah explained to Sarah. "But because we worked hard today, Dad gave us each twenty dollars so we can go see a movie."

"Twenty dollars will buy you a movie ticket and a popcorn-drink-candy combo at Mann's Theater," Sarah told her.

"Do they have cherry blasters?" Lilah said.

"I don't know," Sarah admitted. "I'm more of an M&M's girl myself."

"Plain or peanut?"

"Peanut all the way."

"Those are my favorite, too," Lilah said. "If I'm going for chocolate. But my first choice is always cherry blasters."

While they chatted, Tilda scraped the sauce off her meat, ate three tiny bites of pork, complained the apple was mushy and pushed the sweet potatoes around on her plate.

"I hope you're at least going to eat some salad," Andrew said, when he saw the remnants of the meal on her plate.

She acquiesced by taking one small scoop of salad, claiming that she wanted to leave room for popcorn.

"What time is the movie?" Sarah asked.

"Seven thirty," Lilah said. Then, as the idea suddenly struck, "Do you wanna come with us?"

Tilda sent her sister a dark look across the table.

"Thanks, but I think I'll help your dad tidy up here and then head home. I imagine he's got another early day tomorrow."

"Another very early day," he confirmed. "And now I'm suddenly wondering what was so bad about starting my day at noon and making desserts for somebody else's restaurant."

"Nothing was bad about it," Tilda immediately jumped in. "That's why you should think about going back to your old job in Beaumont."

"We're not going back to Beaumont," Andrew said firmly.

"We're staying here and getting a puppy," Lilah told her sister.

"A puppy?" Tilda echoed skeptically.

"And maybe a kitten, too."

"We can't have a cat," Tilda reminded her. "Mom's allergic."

"Mom doesn't live here," Lilah pointed out.

"But she might decide she wants to come back."

Sarah quietly pushed her chair away from the table and carried her plate to the kitchen, giving Andrew and his daughters some privacy.

"Your mom isn't coming back," he said, his tone gentle but firm.

"How do you know?" Tilda challenged.

"Because she lives with Perry in California now."

"She lived with Alvin in Westbury, too, but that didn't last long."

"You're right," he acknowledged. "But even if things don't work out between your mom and Perry, she and I are not going to get back together."

"Why not?"

"Because as much as we love both of you, we don't love each other anymore."

"But if you fell in love once, why can't you fall in love again?"

"I think that's a question for another day," Andrew said. "Because if you guys don't leave for the movie soon, you're not going to make it on time."

Chairs scraped against the floor as the girls pushed away from the table.

"Money and phones?" Andrew asked, as they were getting their shoes on.

"Check," Tilda said.

"Check," Lilah echoed.

"Text me when you get there," he said.

"Yes, Dad," they intoned dutifully.

Sarah heard the door shut. Then, a few minutes later, Andrew carried the rest of the plates into the kitchen from the dining room.

"Was that as much fun for you as it was for me?" he asked her.

"Real life is messy—and there's nothing more real than life with kids," she said. "Also, it's perfectly normal for kids to fantasize about their divorced parents reconciling."

"Is it?"

"And sometimes it actually happens—which isn't necessarily a good thing."

"You're talking about your parents," he realized.

She nodded.

"Parents divorcing really does a number on their kids, doesn't it?"

"It doesn't have to," Sarah said. "And for what it's worth, I thought you handled that really well."

"And now I have a two-hour reprieve that I'd like to spend with you—if my daughters haven't made you want to run for the hills."

"They're not going to run me off that easily," she promised.

"I'm very glad to hear that," he said, drawing her into his arms.

Tilda had been trying to work up the nerve to ask her dad about the Fourth of July for more than a week. She'd already told London that she would be there, so she needed to figure out a way to get Dad to say yes to her plans—and soon— because the holiday was coming up fast.

The grand opening had been a huge success and the Day Two crowd equally impressive—with a surge of customers through the door following each of the local church services, people wanting sweet treats with their coffee or tea or cakes or pies or assorted pastries to take home for dessert after their Sunday dinner.

She crossed her fingers, hoping that his happy mood would work in her favor. And when Dad said that he needed to go back to the bakery after dinner, to prep doughs and batters for the next day, she'd volunteered to go with him.

He'd always been willing to let his daughters help in the kitchen, and by the time Tilda started kindergarten, she knew how to beat, blend, combine, fold, stir and whisk, and her vocabulary included words like *fondant* and *ganache*. By third grade, she could make a birthday cake from scratch—without a recipe card. And by the fifth, she could frost that cake with homemade Italian meringue buttercream.

She had so many happy memories of time spent in the kitchen with Dad and Mom.

Before everything had fallen apart.

It hadn't happened all at once, like the collapse of a soufflé out of the oven, but a more gradual deterioration, like an ice cream cake melting in the sun.

Tilda pushed that unhappy thought to the back of her mind as she filled the pastry bag with pink buttercream.

Tonight Dad had put her to work frosting a batch of cup-cakes, always one of her favorite tasks. She liked how she could create totally different effects depending on whether she used an open or closed tip and whether she started on the outer edge or in the center. For this batch, she was using a closed star tip to create a pretty ruffled effect, then adding a sprinkle of sanding sugar.

"Those look great," he said approvingly.

"Thanks." For the next batch, she switched to an open star tip and pale blue frosting, then blurted out the question be-fore she lost her nerve. "Can I go to London's next weekend?"

Dad glanced up as he continued to knead the dough he was working with. "London?"

She rolled her eyes. "You know, my best friend for the last ten years?"

It was admittedly something of an exaggeration. Because while she'd known London for more than ten years, they hadn't really started hanging out much until middle school.

"I know who London is," he said. "I'm just a little surprised you think I'd say yes to taking you back to Texas when you moved to Nevada only two weeks ago. Not to mention right after we opened the new bakery."

"I didn't ask you to take me anywhere," she said. "I asked if I could go."

He returned the dough to the bowl and the bowl to the proofing drawer. "You're suggesting that I should buy you a ticket and put you on a plane?"

"A plane would be faster than a train," she agreed.

"No."

"No, it's not faster?" she said dubiously. Because she'd looked at the train schedule and found that there was no di-rect route from Haven to Beaumont. As a result, it would take several transfers and almost three days to make the trip by train. Bus options had been similarly limited.

"No, you're not going to Texas," he responded bluntly.

She folded her arms over her chest. "Why not?"

"Because you live here now."

"My friends live in Texas."

"You'll make new friends here," he said confidently.

"You have no idea how hard it is to be a teenager plunked into a new town where everybody's known everybody else practically since kindergarten."

"You have to make an effort," he acknowledged. "And it wouldn't hurt you to smile."

She scowled at him.

"Just like that," he said.

Her scowl deepened. "I bet Mom would let me go to Beaumont." Using the other parent as leverage was something she'd learned from her friend Kellie, whose parents had been divorced a lot longer than they were married.

Except that Dad didn't take the bait.

"Well, you don't live with your mom, so it's not her decision," he said.

"Maybe I should go live with Mom."

But they both knew it was an idle threat, considering that Mom hadn't even invited Tilda and Lilah to visit since moving to California.

"What's going on in Beaumont next weekend?" Dad asked now.

"London's having a Fourth of July party."

"Is it July next weekend already?"

"It follows June every year," she told him.

"Well, it turns out they celebrate the Fourth of July here, too," he said. "Sarah was telling me about the activities at Prospect Park, and I thought it would be fun if we all went together."

"*All* meaning you and me and Lilah…and Sarah?"

He nodded.

"Doesn't sound like fun to me."

"It's that or stay home," Dad said, in a tone that told her the subject was firmly closed. "Because you're not going to Beaumont."

When Tilda dropped the subject of a potential trip to Beaumont, Andrew wasn't reassured. And though she stuck around to decorate a third batch of cupcakes, he knew that she wasn't happy with him. When she finished and said she was going home, he promised to follow soon after.

And though he still had filling to make for his beignets and choux pastry to bake for his cream puffs, he took a break to call Miranda first, knowing that she'd likely be at work when he finished.

"I've got ten minutes before I have to be out the door," she said, apparently having no time to waste on pleasantries.

"We need to talk about Tilda."

"You wanted custody," she pointed out. "If there's a problem, I have no doubt that you're capable of handling it."

"We have shared custody with the girls' primary residence being with me," he reminded her. "If either of us has a concern, we try to figure out solutions together and present a united front."

"So what's the concern?"

He knew Miranda loved their daughters, but she'd been an only child doted on by parents who always put her needs first, and even now she expected everyone else to do the same.

"Tilda's not happy about our move to Nevada," he confided.

"Well, of course she's not," Miranda said. "She's a fifteen-year-old girl who's been taken away from her friends and everything familiar."

He had to bite his tongue to hold back from reminding his ex-wife that their eldest daughter was still only fourteen, choosing to focus instead on the bigger issue.

"You were as worried as I was about Tilda's so-called friends," he reminded her now. "Friends with whom she'd skipped classes and stayed out past curfew and snuck out of the house to hang with when we grounded her."

"You're right," Miranda acknowledged. "But they're her friends, not ours. Maybe what we think doesn't matter."

"We're her parents."

"Exactly."

He frowned at that unexpected response.

"Did your parents like all of your friends?" she challenged.

"Yeah." He didn't have to pause to think about it. He and Calvin and Stuart had walked to school together, played on the same soccer team and camped out together in one another's backyards.

"Well, mine didn't," Miranda confided.

Which didn't really surprise him. It had taken nearly half a decade of marriage before her parents started to warm up to him—but they cooled off quickly again when Miranda decided that she didn't want to be married anymore.

He pushed those memories aside to refocus on the point of this conversation.

"Tilda wants to go to Beaumont for a party at London's on the Fourth of July."

"So let her go," Miranda said easily.

"I'm not letting her go."

His ex-wife sighed. "If you didn't want my opinion, why did you call?"

"Because I think she could benefit from some one-on-one time with her mom."

"In other words, she's giving you a hard time, and your solution is to dump her on me," Miranda guessed.

"I don't want to dump her anywhere," he immediately denied. "I'm only trying to think about what our daughter needs and how we can meet those needs."

"I'm almost five hundred miles away," she reminded him, "so I'm not sure how much *we* can do."

"Make some time for her, Miranda. Please. If she had plans to spend the Fourth of July weekend with you, I know she'd forget all about Beaumont."

She sighed. "I'll let you know when I've got time, but it's not going to be the Fourth of July. The winery hosts special festivities that weekend and I'll be working Friday, Saturday and Sunday."

Andrew said goodbye and ended the call, frustrated that she wouldn't make their kids a priority. And even more annoyed to realize that while he'd initiated the call to specifically discuss his concerns about Tilda, she hadn't once asked about Lilah.

Chapter Fifteen

Maybe this wasn't the best idea, Tilda acknowledged, as she cast another glance at the oversize clock on the wall.

The guy at the counter hadn't blinked when she said she needed a ticket to Reno. He didn't even ask for ID to prove that she wasn't a minor. Probably the makeup that she'd applied did the trick of making her look older. Just some mascara to darken her lashes and lipstick to color her mouth, both of which she'd "borrowed" from Mom's stash the last time she visited, since Dad wouldn't let her wear makeup until high school. (Though he'd reluctantly let her put some gloss on her lips for her middle school graduation.)

But high school wasn't too far away now, and the prospect of reaching that milestone—and being in a different school from her little sister—made her stomach feel funny. Somehow excited and scared at the same time.

But it was the journey in front of her that was making her stomach hurt now. And with every minute that ticked past, the pain grew sharper.

Because Haven wasn't on any of the major rail routes, her trip was going to take a lot longer than the twenty-eight hours she'd spent in Dad's car with Lilah and Aunt Rachel. From Reno she'd have to get on a different train to Sacramento—because apparently going west was the only way to travel east—then transfer to Los Angeles and again for the final leg of the journey to Beaumont. She'd made careful notes on the station names and departure times to ensure she arrived in time for the party, but it was going to take more than three days!

Once she got to Reno, her transportation options expanded. She could even fly to Texas, which would get her there in a matter of hours rather than days. But she didn't have high hopes that she'd be able to get through airport security without a parent and only her middle school ID card, so she was stuck traveling by train. Or bus, which was even less appealing.

London had promised that the weekend would be fun like she'd never experienced, but if Tilda was being honest, she was more apprehensive than excited. Maybe it was the circuitous train route that made her uneasy. Or maybe it was that she'd snuck out of the house without telling Dad where she was going. Most likely it was that London's idea of fun had started to diverge from her own.

Yeah, she wanted to see her friends again. To feel as if she fit in somewhere, because she definitely didn't belong in Haven. She wasn't even sure she belonged in her family, anymore.

And London had been so excited to hear that Tilda was going to be at the party that she had to believe whatever trouble she might get into for disobeying her dad would be worth it.

But now that she was actually at the station, about to embark on a three-day journey, she was a lot less certain.

She double-checked the app on her phone, to confirm that the train was on schedule, and breathed a sigh of relief that she only had another eight minutes to wait. Because once she was on the train, there would be no chickening out. No turning back.

She dipped her hand into her front pocket, where she'd put all her money. Every single dollar she had—and what she'd borrowed from her sister—because it was ridiculously expensive to travel by train. At least she wouldn't have to spend any money on food, because she'd tossed a few granola bars and her refillable water bottle in her duffel bag.

She glanced at the clock again—and caught a glimpse of a sheriff's vehicle. Suddenly her armpits were damp and her heart was pounding really hard against her ribs.

But the vehicle only cruised slowly through the parking lot, then pulled out onto the main road and drove away.

A whistle sounded in the distance, and other passengers on the platform began to move around in anticipation of the train's arrival. Tilda exhaled a shaky sigh of relief as she slung the strap of her duffel bag over her shoulder.

Then she turned around and found herself face-to-face with Sarah.

"What are you doing here?" Tilda demanded.

Beneath the panic, Sarah thought she detected a hint of relief in the girl's voice.

Relief that she'd been found before she could board a train that her dad probably didn't know she had a ticket for?

Or maybe Sarah had imagined the relief, because the expression on Andrew's daughter's face was one hundred percent defiant.

"Funny, that's what I was going to ask you," she responded lightly.

"I asked first."

She nodded, an acknowledgement of the fact. "I'm here to pick up my grandfather's fiancée's great niece who's coming to celebrate the Fourth of July with the family."

Tilda's gaze narrowed. "That sounds totally made up."

"Truth," Sarah promised, raising her right hand as if taking an oath.

"Why didn't your grandfather—or his fiancée—come to pick her up?"

"Because Crooked Creek Ranch is a long way out of town

and I don't like my grandfather driving any further than he has to, so I volunteered to play chauffeur."

"How old's your grandfather?"

"Eighty."

"That's kinda old to be driving," Tilda agreed.

"Your turn now," Sarah said to the teen.

"I'm going to visit a friend," Tilda hedged.

"In Beaumont?" she guessed.

"That's where all my friends are."

"And your dad approved of this plan?"

The teen's gaze flitted away. "Yeah."

"I'm surprised he didn't say anything to me," Sarah mused.

"He doesn't have to tell you everything," Tilda shot back at her.

"No," she agreed. "But considering that we were talking about the four of us spending the holiday together at Prospect Park, it seems like something he would have mentioned."

"It was a recent change of plans."

"That's your story and you're sticking to it, huh?"

The girl's cheeks flushed, but she folded her arms over her chest.

She was a study in contradictions: guilty and defiant. Uncertain yet determined. Scared and brave.

Sarah could see everything Tilda was feeling, and her heart ached for her. Because despite having grown up in Haven, she'd been that girl—out-of-sorts and overwhelmed and desperately wanting to feel as if she belonged...somewhere.

She'd had no shortage of friends—because she was a Blake and, even at a young age, she'd understood that the Blakes were akin to royalty in Haven. At the same time, she was aware that most of her friendships were superficial. That the same girls who invited her to hang out at Jo's or asked to be part of her study group always expected her to pay for the pizza and questioned whether her parents had bought her a spot on the honor roll.

She didn't think she would have survived those years without Claire—her one true friend. Even with Claire, she'd struggled with anxiety and insecurity. And those struggles had taken her to a dark and dangerous place.

The same dark and dangerous place she suspected was beckoning the girl in front of her.

"Question," Sarah said now.

Tilda eyed her warily.

"Do you really want to go back to Texas to see your friends or to punish your dad?"

"I want to see my friends," Tilda responded.

"Did you think at all about the fact that your dad would freak out when he realized you were gone?"

"I'm not sure he'd even notice…"

Busted.

"I mean, if he didn't know I was going, because he said I could go," Tilda hastened to add.

A quick recovery, Sarah mused, if not exactly a credible one.

"Change can be tough, especially when you're a teenager," she noted. "If you ever want someone to talk to—"

"If I want someone to talk to, it won't be you," Tilda interjected.

"I'm not your enemy, Tilda."

"You're not my friend, either."

"I could be."

"Thanks, but no thanks." The teen pulled her phone out of her pocket, clearly indicating that she was finished with their conversation.

But Sarah wasn't giving up just yet.

"I can't imagine that there's a direct train from Haven to Beaumont," she remarked, her tone deliberately casual. "So you're probably going to… Reno first?"

Tilda nodded.

"And then…" she prompted.

"Los Angeles," the girl admitted.

Jesus. Just the thought of this pretty, young—and obviously naïve—girl on her own in a big city made Sarah's blood run cold.

Before she could decide on an appropriate response (because forcibly wrestling Tilda into the backseat of her car to prevent her from getting on the train now visible in the distance was probably a little over the top), Andrew stepped through the station doors and onto the platform.

Tilda obviously spotted her dad at the same moment, because she sucked in a breath and whirled on Sarah.

"You called him," she said accusingly.

"When would I have done that?" Sarah challenged.

The teen frowned.

"Then you texted him," Tilda decided.

"I didn't. But I was planning to," she admitted, in the interest of full disclosure.

Tilda scowled. "Then how did he know where to find me?"

"You told me that he knew you were here—and where you were going," she reminded the girl.

Color flooded the teen's cheeks again.

Andrew stopped in front of them, glancing from Tilda to Sarah and back again.

"Popular place today," he remarked idly.

"Apparently," Sarah agreed.

Tilda remained silent, her gaze fixed on her sneakers.

"Let's go," her dad said.

The girl sighed wearily as she lifted her backpack from the ground and slung it over her shoulder.

"Give me your ticket, Tilda," Sarah said.

"Why?" she asked suspiciously.

"Just give her your ticket," Andrew advised. "You don't have any use for it."

Tilda thrust the ticket at Sarah and walked away with her dad.

Sarah's original plans for the Fourth of July had included Andrew and both his daughters. She'd been looking forward to spending the day at Prospect Park and showing them that, despite being a tiny dot on the map, her hometown knew how to throw a party that brought the whole community together.

But as a result of Tilda's secret excursion to the train station and attempted defection to Texas, she was grounded until her dad said otherwise. Of course, she blamed Sarah, even though Andrew admitted that he'd tracked his daughter's location via an app on her phone—and even after Sarah gave her the money she'd made the ticket agent refund (despite it being a non-refundable ticket) because he'd failed to ask for ID before letting a minor purchase it.

Anyway, it didn't seem fair to Sarah that Lilah should be punished along with her sister, so after she finished her usual morning workouts with the horses at Twilight Valley—and showered and changed—she picked up Andrew's youngest daughter to attend the celebrations with her.

"I kind of feel bad that Tilda's missing all this," Lilah said, dipping her hand into her bag of kettle corn as they wandered around the park.

"You shouldn't," Sarah told her. "If you want to feel bad for someone, it should be your dad. He actually wanted to be here. Your sister would rather be in Texas."

"You're right," Lilah agreed, munching on her snack. "And the truth is, part of me feels sorry for her but a bigger part is glad she's not here."

"Emotions are rarely simple and straightforward," Sarah noted.

"We used to have a lot of fun together, but now she just complains about everything and makes everyone else unhappy."

"Unfortunately we can't control how other people think and feel, we can only control how we respond."

"You're saying she can't make me unhappy if I don't let her?" Lilah guessed. "Like choosing to come here today to have fun with you instead of staying home and then feeling sad that I missed out?"

"Like that," Sarah confirmed, as they finished their tour of the food booths—offering everything from foot-long hot dogs and pizza slices to candied nuts and snow cones—and turned toward the activity stations. There was a dunk tank and pie throwing booth and half a dozen carnival-type games with all the proceeds going to local charities. There was also a clown making balloon animals for the kids, a bouncy castle and an enormous inflatable slide.

Of course, there were permanent play structures in the park, too. Swings and climbers and a splash pad where dozens of little ones were dancing in the fountains and shrieking with laughter when an unexpected spray erupted.

At the face painting booth, they crossed paths with Macy and Liam Gilmore, whose kids were waiting their turn in line.

"At my school in Beaumont, there was a sister and a brother in the grade below me who were twins, but I've never met any triplets before," Lilah said to Sarah, as they continued on their way.

"Ava, Max and Sam are the only triplets I know, too," Sarah said. "But there are several sets of twins in my family."

"Several?" Lilah said skeptically.

She nodded. "In fact, one of my cousins—the woman supervising the little boys in the sandbox—has two sets."

Sarah introduced Lilah to Regan and Sawyer and Sutton.

"Where are Piper and Poppy?" Sarah asked, naming the boys' older sisters.

"At the bouncy castle with their dad," Regan said.

"He didn't have to work today?"

"Tonight—which is why we brought reinforcement baby-sitters," she said, as Deacon Parrish and Sierra Hart, recently engaged, wandered over to join them—the latter in the third trimester of her second surrogate pregnancy.

"Are you having twins, too?" Lilah asked the expectant mom.

Sierra laughed. "Nope. One at a time works for me."

"We can't all be overachievers," Regan said with a shrug.

"And I'm okay with that," her sister-in-law said.

"Have you seen either of my brothers?" Regan asked Sarah now.

"Jason and Alyssa were at the splash pad with their kids and Spencer and Kenzie were heading over to the dunk tank."

"Caleb Gilmore volunteered to sit the first shift at the dunk tank," Sierra noted, her eyes dancing with amusement. "Sky Kelly paid for five balls and dunked her brother five times."

Sarah had to laugh at that. "Well, she was the star third baseman of Diggers' softball team for a number of years."

"The best, though, was when Brielle took a ten-dollar bill out of her pocket and offered it to her sister-in-law so she could throw five more.

"Poor Caleb must have been waterlogged by the time she walked away."

"She didn't walk away. Jake had to drag her."

Sarah laughed again.

"So what do you think of Haven?" Regan asked, turning her attention to Lilah.

"I've only been here a few weeks, but I like it so far," she said.

"What grade are you going into?"

"Seventh."

"Same as Brendan," Regan noted.

"My nephew," Sarah explained. "We haven't met him yet, but we're headed toward Patrick's usual site—where he hopefully has burgers grilling—right now."

"Then we'll no doubt see you again in a while," Regan said. "But if not, it was nice meeting you, Lilah."

"And all of you," she responded politely.

But of course they crossed paths with several other people en route who wanted to say a few words to Sarah or be introduced to the girl by her side. Including Olivia and Adam Morgan, whose three sons—Easton, Hudson and Colton—were kicking a soccer ball around a field. Easton was also going into seventh grade and so was his buddy Elliott, who jumped into the game with his sister Avenlea, while their parents—Lindsay and Mitchell Gilmore—joined the adults' conversation.

"Do you know *everyone* in town?" Lilah asked, when Sarah dragged her away from the game.

She laughed. "Not everyone, but Haven's a pretty small town and my family's lived here a long time, so I know a fair number of them."

"I only ever lived in Beaumont before we came here," Lilah said. "But Dad and Aunt Rachel grew up in Louisiana before Grandma and Grandpa moved them to Texas."

"Louisiana, huh? I guess that would explain the beignets."

Lilah nodded. "He said they were his favorite treat when he was a kid."

"Do your grandparents still live in Texas?"

Now the girl shook her head. "Grandma got cancer a few years back and Grandpa died a few weeks after she did. Aunt Rachel said it was 'cuz his heart was broken and that we shouldn't be too sad, because now they're together again."

"That's a nice way of looking at it," Sarah decided.

By the time they got to where Patrick had spread his blankets on the lawn—claiming viewing spots for the fireworks later—Jenna and Harrison were there, along with Trevor and Haylee and Aidan and Ellie (Lilah's mind was boggled by yet another set of twins!), Devin and Claire and Gramps and Helen and Francesca, Helen's great-niece of the train station errand.

"I haven't seen you since the engagement was official," Sarah noted, greeting her future step-grandmother with a warm hug. "Congratulations."

"Thank you," Helen said. "When I lost my Harold, I was sure I'd never fall in love again—and then I met your grandfather."

"He's one of a kind," Sarah agreed.

"The very best kind," Helen said. "And though it seems a little silly to me, to be planning a big wedding at our ages, Jesse insisted that we celebrate."

"Well, if you need any help with anything, let me know."

"I appreciate the offer, but Jesse's decided to put all the details of our big day in the hands of a professional."

"The best of the best," Gramps chimed in.

"That would be Gilmore Galas," Haylee said.

"I thought your sister's company was based in California."

"It is, but Finley couldn't resist Gramps's charm."

"Very few ladies can," he said immodestly.

"Of course, it also gives her an excuse to visit her niece and nephew in Haven—and Lachlan's going to come with her to make a holiday of it," Haylee said, mentioning her sister's husband.

"Speaking of the wedding," Gramps said, turning his gaze on Sarah again. "You got a date yet?"

"I've still got lots of time," she pointed out.

"Are you working on it?"

"Thinking about it," she said.

"Try less thinking and more doing," he suggested.

"You should ask my dad," Lilah chimed in.

Gramps considered this for a minute. "Her dad's the baker who made the cupcakes for Claire's birthday?"

"He is," Sarah confirmed.

He nodded. "Ask him. And ask if he'll give your grandpa and his bride any kind of discount on a really big cake."

"Always working the angles, aren't you, Gramps?"

He winked at her. "You know it."

"I bet Dad would give you a discount on the cake," Lilah said, when Gramps's attention had shifted elsewhere.

"My grandfather can afford to pay full price—and then some," Sarah assured her.

"You could ask him anyway," Lilah said. "I mean, to be your date to the wedding."

"I don't know if that's a good idea," Sarah hedged.

"Why not? You like him, don't you?"

"Sure," she agreed, keeping her tone deliberately casual.

"And I know he likes you."

She bit her tongue, because no way was she going to pump Andrew's twelve-year-old daughter for information. But there was one question she needed to ask. "You wouldn't mind if I asked your dad to be my date?"

"I hope you do," Lilah said. "He needs someone in his life."

"He's got you and your sister," Sarah pointed out.

"That's what he says," the girl acknowledged. "But eventually we're going to grow up and go away to school and I don't want him to be alone."

"I'll keep that in mind."

"How were the fireworks?" Andrew asked Lilah, when Sarah finally brought his daughter home later that night.

"Awesome!" Lilah enthused.

"You had a good time?"

"The. Best. Time." Then she wrapped her arms around Sarah and hugged her tight. "Thank you for taking me."

"You're very welcome," Sarah said, hugging her back.

"And it's very late," Andrew said to his daughter. "Go on up and get ready for bed."

"Okay." But Lilah hugged her dad first, too. "G'night, Dad."

"Night, sweetie. I'll be up to check on you soon."

"No need to rush," she told him. "I'm sure you and Sarah have lots to talk about."

"Do we?" he asked, when his daughter had disappeared up the stairs.

"Lilah's trying to play matchmaker," she warned.

"Well, I can't fault her choice," he said. "But I'm curious to know how this came about."

"You can blame my grandfather. He asked if I had a date for his wedding and when I said no, Lilah suggested that I should ask you."

"And what did you say?"

"I promised to think about it."

"Are there any other candidates in the running for your potential date?"

"Not at the moment," she said.

"Let's keep it that way," he said, and lowered his head to kiss her.

"Mmm…fireworks twice tonight."

He grinned.

Tilda was sitting on the wrought iron bench near the stand of trees in the backyard when Warren came over. She kept her gaze focused on the book in her hand, pretending she didn't know he was there. Pretending she wasn't desperate for someone to talk to.

Without waiting for an invitation, he sat down on the opposite end of the bench. She turned the page and kept reading.

He broke the silence first, saying, "I didn't see you at the park yesterday."

She lifted her gaze from the page to him. "Why were you looking for me?"

"I wasn't looking for you," he denied. "But I saw your sister with Sarah and noticed that you weren't there."

"You're right. I wasn't."

"Why not?"

"Why do you care?"

He shrugged. "I wouldn't say that I care so much as that I'm curious."

"Well, it's none of your business."

"Your dad ground you for trying to run away?"

She slammed her book shut with a frustrated sigh. "I *hate* this town."

"Obviously."

"I wasn't running away," she denied. "I just wanted to go to Texas to spend some time with my friends."

"How'd that work out for you?"

She glared at him.

"Maybe instead of trying to go back, you should look to the future and think about the opportunities you have right here."

"I wish I could say that I appreciate your fortune cookie advice, but I don't. And someone with a perfect family and a perfect life has no right to pass judgment on anyone else."

He seemed surprised by that. "You think I have a perfect life?"

"Are you saying you don't?" she challenged.

"Every family has secrets," he told her.

"Yeah? What's yours?"

"If I told you, they wouldn't be secrets anymore, would they?"

She rolled her eyes. "You're weird."

"You're judgy."

She scowled.

Warren's phone chirped and he glanced at the screen. "And there's another snag in my perfect life."

"What snag?"

"My mom's running late and I need her car to go to the drive-in tonight."

"Haven has a drive-in?"

He shook his head. "It's in Cooper's Corners."

She didn't know where that was and she wasn't going to ask.

"Don't tell me you've got a date tonight," she sneered instead.

"Okay, I won't tell you," he said.

"With an actual girl?"

He ignored the question. "I wonder what happened to make you so mean."

"I'm not mean," she denied.

He laughed, though the sound was without humor. "The mean girls never think they're mean."

"I'm *not* a mean girl." But the heat that burned her cheeks denounced the lie. Because even if she didn't believe she was a mean girl, she had been mean to him.

"Your sister was at my place hanging out with Rory earlier today and we all ended up playing *Mario Kart* together."

"Are you trying to make a point? Or do you just like to hear yourself talk?"

"My point is that it's hard to believe the two of you are sisters," he said.

"Would it be easier to believe that we're only half sisters?" she challenged.

He nodded slowly. "Actually, yes."

"Well, there you go," she told him.

"Same dad, different moms?" he guessed.

"No, same mom, different dads."

His brows lifted. "But you live with your dad."

"Lilah's dad," she clarified.

"You call him Dad," he noted.

"Because I didn't know any different until a few months ago." And she hadn't told a single soul—so why had she opened her big mouth and blabbed to him? "Lilah still doesn't know, though—and he doesn't, either—so you better not say anything to anyone."

Warren was quiet for a long time before he asked, "So why did you tell me your big secret?"

"I don't know," she admitted. Maybe because it was a big secret—the biggest one she'd ever held on to—and the truth was eating away at her. "Maybe because, like you said, I don't have anyone else to talk to."

He took off his glasses, used the hem of his T-shirt to rub a spot of one of the lenses. "Henry's not my dad, either."

She blinked, surprised. "He's not?"

He shook his head. "My dad was a mean drunk who used to knock my mom around. She put up with it, determined to keep her family together, until I was five years old and he started hitting me, too."

"Did he—" She swallowed. "Did he hurt you?"

"Not that I can remember. Truthfully, I don't have many memories of him at all—and that's probably a good thing," he said. "We lived in Branson, Missouri then, and when my mom decided to leave him, we moved to Lakewood, Colorado, where her sister lived with her family. That's where she met Henry, a widower with a three-year-old daughter."

"So Rory's not really your sister," Tilda realized.

"Rory *is* my sister," he insisted, an unexpected edge to his tone.

"But...you don't have the same mother *or* father."

"We have the same mother *and* father," he countered. "Just because we don't share DNA doesn't mean we're not family."

"You're right," she said, feeling chastened. "I'm sorry."

After another minute, she asked, "Do you have any idea where your dad—your biological dad—is now?"

He nodded. "In prison in Missouri."

Prison? *Yikes.*

And she'd been upset when her mom moved to Napa Valley.

"Because he knocked your mom around?" she guessed.

Now he shook his head. "Because he killed a guy in a bar fight."

"My mom lives in California now—with her new boyfriend. Not that that compares to having a dad in prison," she realized.

"It's not a contest," Warren said. "And I didn't tell you so that you'd feel sorry for me or be nice to me. I told you so that you'd know that everyone has stuff going on behind the scenes, and you should think about that before you pass judgment on anyone else."

Chapter Sixteen

"You and Devin left the park early on Saturday," Sarah commented to Claire Tuesday morning, as they were untacking their mounts after their morning ride.

"Ed's not a fan of fireworks," Claire explained.

"You didn't have him with you," she pointed out.

"I know. But the neighbors behind us sometimes set off their own, and I didn't want him to be alone if rockets started exploding in his backyard."

"Well, you missed a good show."

"Did Lilah enjoy it?" Claire asked.

"She did," Sarah confirmed, as she examined and picked Bella's hooves. "Not just the fireworks but the whole day."

"She seems like a nice kid."

"She is. And she likes me, which helps balance out the fact that her sister hates me."

"I'm sure Tilda doesn't hate you," her friend said.

"She definitely blames me for ruining her Fourth of July plans," Sarah noted. "Even though Andrew tracked her through an app on her phone."

"Another reason to be glad we didn't have smartphones when we were her age," Claire remarked. "On the other hand, I shudder to think of a fourteen-year-old girl trying to navigate her way across state lines without the ability to call 9-1-1 at her fingertips. Actually, I shudder to think of a teenager making that trip even with a phone."

"Andrew yelled at her. I think it was probably the first time in his life that he ever did."

"Sometimes yelling is warranted," Claire noted.

"Exactly what I said," Sarah told her friend. Finished with the mare's hooves, she picked up a curry comb. "Anyway, Tilda is going to be here today."

Claire nodded. "I know. I signed off on her application."

"And I know you thought I should do the orientation—"

"And you will," her friend interjected.

Sarah continued to brush the horse's coat. "Did you hear me say she hates me?"

"If she does, it's only because she doesn't know you. Working here will give you both a chance to change that."

"I really think it would be better if I stayed in the background, at least for the next couple of weeks."

"You can think whatever you want, but you're not the boss here," Claire said.

"Really?" She looked over the horse's back at her friend, who was busy grooming her own mount. "You're going to play the boss card?"

"It is fun to pull it out every now and then," Claire said, a smile in her voice.

"I thought we were friends."

"Best friends," Claire confirmed. "Which is why I know you're not intimidated by a fourteen-year-old girl."

"Maybe not a normal fourteen-year-old girl with a normal amount of teenage attitude," Sarah allowed.

"I have complete faith in you."

Which is why Sarah was in the yard with her clipboard at nine thirty, the recommended first-day arrival time for student volunteers so that they could be checked in and their necessary paperwork collected before orientation began at ten.

Warren Aldridge was one of the first to arrive, along with Dylan Spears and Heidi Garwood, whom he'd apparently picked up en route. Though this was Sarah's first summer at Twilight Valley, she knew it would be Warren's third and that Claire considered him trustworthy and dependable. The other volunteers on the list were Bryce Holland, Whitney Kirk and Tilda Morrow.

When everyone was accounted for, Sarah introduced herself, then led the students on a tour of the facility so they could meet the animals in residence—the horses and goats and Ed, who'd already greeted each of them upon their arrival.

She gave a brief summary of the tasks that they might be required to perform on a rotating basis, to ensure that those who got first crack at grooming or hand-walking also had to take a turn cleaning tack and mucking out stalls.

"Proper attire is required," Sarah reminded them, with a pointed look at Whitney's sandals. "If you don't have proper attire, you won't be able to work, and if you can't work, we can't sign off on your hours.

"There are lockers available in the lunchroom for your personal belongings and a refrigerator for your snacks and drinks. Your four-hour shift includes a half-hour break for lunch and you are expected to bring your own, except on the last Thursday of the month, when hamburgers and veggie burgers will be provided. Whatever you're eating, please don't share it with the dog. I assure you, Ed doesn't go hungry, and as much as he might like people food, his digestive system does not."

"That's the truth," Warren chimed in, proving that his time on the ranch had given him some experience in the matter.

"Tasks are pinned to the board." She gestured to the magnetic board on the wall. "Grab one and get to work."

Five teens rushed to the board, angling for their preferred assignments. Tilda lagged a few steps behind.

"Looks like you're mucking out stalls," Sarah said, when she saw Andrew's daughter staring at the last remaining pin.

The girl shrugged. "I figured that's what you'd make me do, anyway."

"It's not my job to make you do anything," Sarah told her. "And no one's forcing you to be here."

"Actually, that's not true," she said. "My dad's forcing me to be here. This was his idea, not mine."

"Should I call and ask him to come and get you?"

The teen hesitated for half a second, then shook her head. "No."

"Then put on a pair of gloves, pick up a pitchfork and get to work."

Tilda didn't say much after her first day at Twilight Valley. When Andrew asked her how it went, she only said, "It was okay." But when it was time to go back on Thursday, she didn't grumble half as much as she'd done on the first day, and when the next Tuesday came around, she was ready and waiting when he returned from the bakery to take her to the ranch.

And so it seemed that they were finally settling into their respective routines. Sugar & Spice was doing steady business; in addition to volunteering at Twilight Valley, Tilda helped out at the bakery on weekends; and Lilah entertained them with her camp adventures over dinner every day.

If he had any cause for complaint, it was only one—that he didn't see enough of Sarah. Because exchanging a few words of greeting when he dropped off or picked up Tilda didn't count. He wanted to be able to spend some real time with her without wondering who might be watching.

And maybe Sarah wanted more, too, because when he dropped his daughter off Tuesday morning, she held up a hand—asking him to hold on a minute while she finished issuing instructions to one of the volunteers—then hurried over to his vehicle.

"Hey," she said.

"Everything okay?" he asked.

"If you're asking about Tilda, yeah, everything's fine," she said. "I was just wondering about you."

"What about me?"

"From what I hear, you've been working day and night since you opened Sugar & Spice."

"It's taking some time to optimize the prep and baking schedules, but we're getting there," he said.

"Is there any chance you might be able to steal away for a few hours tomorrow afternoon?" she wondered aloud.

"I think the chances are pretty good," he said. "What did you have in mind?"

"We could head out to Crooked Creek again, saddle up a couple of horses and go for a ride."

"What time should I pick you up?" he asked, willing to adjust his schedule as required to be with her.

"One o'clock at my place?"

"I'll see you then."

He'd been in such a hurry to get to Sarah's on time that he didn't think about food, so he was pleased to discover that she'd packed a picnic lunch. And an hour after they'd arrived at Crooked Creek—where her grandfather had two mounts tacked and ready, they were stretched out on a blanket on the grass by the creek, munching on sandwiches and sipping soda while their horses grazed nearby.

"The first night you brought me out here, you didn't mention that this was your grandfather's ranch," he noted.

"Didn't I?" she said, with feigned innocence.

"I think you know very well that you didn't. In fact, you've never mentioned that you're a Blake."

"Obviously someone did," she noted.

"Kyle," he told her.

"And how did that come up in conversation?" she wondered.

"We were at Diggers' the day you had lunch there with your ex."

"Zack?"

His brows lifted. "Have you had lunch with any other exes recently?"

"No."

"So why didn't you tell me?" he asked her now.

"About having lunch with Zack?"

"That you're a Blake," he clarified.

She shrugged. "Truthfully, I don't think about it most of the time. But I know that other people do, and as soon as they find out that I'm a Blake, they treat me differently. Which is how I ended up dating several guys who were more interested in my family and my connections than they were in me."

"Obviously they were fools," he said.

"Maybe. But it became an instinctive defense, to keep that part hidden, so I wouldn't have to wonder if someone wanted me or just my name."

"I guess I can understand that," he said. "And since we slept together long before I knew your name, you can rest assured that I have no interest in your family fortune—just your body."

"I think you might have to prove it one more time."

"I'll give it my best shot," he promised, and lowered his head to cover her mouth with his own.

Her lips were as sweet as he remembered, her response as passionate as he recalled, and in no time at all, they were both panting and naked and—

He rolled away from her abruptly and swore under his breath.

Then Sarah held up a little square packet between two fingers.

"I do appreciate a woman who comes prepared."

"Well, I'm still waiting for that part," she said, surprising a laugh out of him as he took care to protect them both.

Then, finally, he was inside her, filling and fulfilling her. She held on to him, her fingernails biting into his shoulders, as the world tilted and spun. The tautness of his muscles and the shallowness of his breathing told her that he was close to his release, too. But he held himself back, determined to ensure her pleasure first.

And while the creek trickled over the rocks and the horses grazed, he swallowed the cries that announced her climax. Only then did he surrender to his own.

A long minute later, he rolled off her and wrapped his arm around her, spooning her from behind. Sarah was still trying to catch her breath when she felt him press a kiss to the ink on her shoulder blade.

"You're smiling," she said.

"How can you tell?" he asked.

"I felt your lips curve against my skin."

"Okay, I'm smiling," he admitted. "Because I really like your tattoo."

She'd told him it was a lion, but it was really a lion cub. More specifically, a young Simba from the Disney movie.

He shifted so that he could kiss her lips now. "And it proves that you're not as predictable as you feared."

"And not as strong and courageous as I pretend to be," she confided. "More baby lion than king of the jungle."

"I think you're a lot stronger and braver than you realize. You're also smart and sexy and amazing and kind, and when I'm with you, I'm always right where I want to be."

And when she was with him, he made her feel as if she was all those things. And she didn't want to be anywhere else.

She'd dated a lot of men in her thirty-two years, and she'd enjoyed some pretty intense chemistry with a few of them. But only Andrew had ever turned her on so completely with just a look. Only Andrew made her insides quiver with just a smile and her knees grow weak with a casual touch.

In the beginning, the attraction had been purely physical. She hadn't known him well enough for it to be anything more. But over the past several weeks, as she'd spent more time with him, she'd discovered that she really liked him.

And if it occurred to her that her heart might be in danger, well, that was a worry for another day.

The following Sunday, Tilda and Lilah left for California to spend some time with their mom. Not the two weeks they'd hoped for, but five days.

Sarah suspected she was as excited about the trip as they were, because it meant five days—and five nights—that she could spend with Andrew.

He suggested making reservations for dinner at The Chophouse in Battle Mountain. She countered with an offer to pick up steaks and potatoes to grill at his place. He promised to provide a bottle of wine and dessert—and extra chocolate sauce for later. When she returned from Twilight Valley, after a strenuous workout with an ornery stallion who didn't seem to appreciate his change in circumstances, she took a long shower to soothe her weary muscles then rubbed scented lotion over her body. When she dressed, it was in anticipation of being undressed, in some of her sexiest underwear and a sleeveless floral print sundress.

"My mouth has been watering for steak all day," he confided, when he met her at the door. "Now I'm only hungry for you."

"We can put the groceries in the fridge for later," she suggested.

So that's what they did, then Andrew lifted her effortlessly into his arms and carried her up the stairs to his bedroom.

"I don't need to be seduced," she said, feeling foolish because her heart had actually fluttered when he scooped her off her feet.

"Seduction isn't about necessity but pleasure," he said.

She didn't realize he'd found the zipper at the back of her dress until she felt the air against her skin. The first night they'd spent together, they'd shared a desperate passion born of the knowledge that he would be gone in the morning. Tonight was different. Tonight they had time for a more leisurely and thorough exploration.

He tugged the straps over her shoulders and down her arms, then let the dress fall to the floor to pool at her feet, before shedding his own T-shirt and jeans.

"I don't think I've ever taken enough time to appreciate your lingerie before," he said, his fingertips skimming reverently over the delicate lace.

"I like the feel of soft fabrics against my skin," she confided. "Soft fabrics and strong hands."

He eased her onto the bed. "I like the feel of you."

He straddled her mostly naked body, his knees bracketing her hips, holding her in place while his hands and mouth moved over her.

She let her hands explore him, too, tracing the hard angles and ridges of muscle. She dipped her hand into his boxer briefs and wrapped her fingers around him, stroking him slowly, making him groan with pleasure.

She'd always enjoyed physical intimacy and wasn't afraid to let a man know what she liked—and what she didn't. But Andrew didn't need any guidance. He instinctively seemed to know just where and how to touch her to maximize her pleasure, stoking the fire that burned inside her. He had a way of making her feel so much, and making her yearn for even more. From the first brush of his lips, the first pass of his hands, she was his.

His mouth moved down her throat, over her collarbone.

Tasting, teasing. He suckled her breasts through the lacy fabric. His mouth hot and wet, making her the same.

He rained kisses over her belly, then nuzzled the scrap of lace between her thighs, making her gasp and yearn. He hooked his thumbs in the sides of her panties and tugged them over her hips, then nudged her knees farther apart and settled between them.

Her breath caught in her throat when he lowered his head to put his mouth on her, using his lips and his tongue to kiss and lick and drive her to the edge of reason…and over.

She flew apart, shattering like a supernova.

And when she finally came back to earth, he was there, holding her and kissing her.

"Andrew." His name was a whisper—a plea.

"Tell me what you want."

"You," she said simply.

And he gave her what she wanted. What they both wanted.

It was much later before he fired up the barbecue, and after dinner they had dessert—and then dessert again.

She didn't know what time he left for the bakery the following morning, she only knew that when she rolled over and reached for him, he was gone.

She squinted at the clock on the bedside table.

5:35.

Then rolled over again and fell back to sleep.

The next time she woke up, he was kissing her.

"Good morning, sleeping beauty."

Her eyes flickered open slowly.

"I brought you coffee and fresh beignets," he said.

"A very thoughtful gesture," she said, wriggling into a seated position so that she could take the mug and plate.

Then she set both aside and reached for what she really wanted—him.

Chapter Seventeen

Napa Valley was beautiful. As they neared the end of their almost two-hour drive from the San Francisco airport to Calistoga, Tilda had to admit that Sarah had been right about that. Outside her window, everything was lush and green, with rows and rows of vines as far as the eye could see, heavy with glossy leaves and bunches of fruit just starting to ripen.

The day had started with a ridiculously early morning flight out of Elko, and though it was only midafternoon now, she was feeling the effects of the travel. Nine hours of total travel time—including the drive to the airport and the stopover in Salt Lake City—and she was beat, which made her wonder how she would have endured three days of train travel from Haven to Beaumont. And now she'd never know.

Perry had kept up a running monologue about grape growing and wine making throughout the drive. And while Tilda was sure it was a testament to his passion for his work, she really just wanted him to shut up so that she could enjoy peace and quiet for five minutes—and maybe even exchange a few words with her mom, who seemed happy enough to let her boyfriend rattle on.

"Not too far now," Perry had said, turning off the main highway.

Twenty minutes later, he turned again, this time into a long drive leading toward what looked like a freaking castle.

"Home sweet home," Mom said.

Tilda gawked. She couldn't help it.

This was where her mother lived?

But of course it wasn't.

Perry continued to drive, past the castle, past half a dozen other buildings with the same architectural style and stunning display of stone and glass until he arrived at a house that was maybe half the size of the one in Haven.

And though it was small, it was fancy—the exterior matching that of all the other buildings on the property. Glossy wood door, gleaming windows that reflected the afternoon sun.

"This is one of the original guesthouses on the estate," Mom explained, as she ushered them inside. "Originally a one-bedroom bungalow that was renovated to add two bedrooms and another bath on the second floor." She led them up the stairs and opened one of the doors with a flourish. "This will be your room while you're here."

"Mine or Lilah's?" Tilda asked.

"Both," she said. "That's why there's two beds."

"But you said there were two rooms."

"The other one's Bella's."

Isabella was Perry's seven-year-old daughter with his former girlfriend, but she went by "Bella," which Tilda knew meant *beautiful*. (It was also, she thought unkindly, the name of one of the horses at Twilight Valley.)

"Is Bella here?" Tilda asked.

"Not right now," Mom admitted. "But she's here two weeks out of every month, so her room is full of her stuff."

"I guess that's what shared custody really looks like," Tilda mused.

Mom frowned. "You know we'd love to see you more often, it's just hard with so much distance between us."

Distance she'd put between them when she decided to move

to California, but Tilda knew there was no point in reminding her mother of that.

"Well, I'll let you girls unpack," Mom said. "We planned an early dinner tonight, figuring you'd be tired out from travel, so that you can get a good night's sleep before the fun starts tomorrow."

The early dinner was a salad of mixed greens with grilled fish and roasted vegetables. Tilda pushed her food around on her plate, more tired than hungry, and when she and Lilah were finally excused from the table, they went upstairs to get ready for bed.

Lilah fell asleep as soon as her head hit the pillow, but Tilda tossed and turned for what seemed like forever, unable to shut off her mind and go to sleep.

She'd been looking forward to this visit for weeks— *months*—thinking about all the things that she'd be able to do with Mom in California. But now that she was finally here, she wished she was back home in Haven.

She felt bad that Dad was alone—and then she considered that maybe he wasn't alone and felt even worse.

But she must have fallen asleep eventually, because when she woke up, it was morning. She reached for her phone, to check for messages, and found one from Dad, sent the night before to both her and Lilah.

Good night. Love you both. Sweet dreams.

The words were followed by a heart and a sleeping emoji.

One message in the past twenty-four hours, and that from her dad. It was a sad but true reflection of the state of her social life.

But she replied:

Good morning.

And added sunshine and kiss-blowing emojis.

Then she got dressed and made her way to the kitchen.

She took a seat across from Lilah at the table and Mom set a plate in front of her with a thick Belgian waffle topped with whipped cream and berries.

"I'm not hungry," Tilda said.

"Try the waffle," Mom urged. "You'll love it."

Before she could respond to that, Perry walked into the room. He smiled and wished them good-morning.

"You look like you're on your way out," Mom noted.

"I just need to check the veraison," he told her, picking up a mug of coffee he'd obviously left on the counter and swallowing a mouthful.

She pouted. "You said you were taking the day off."

"I won't be long," he promised.

"Make sure you're not," she said, tipping her head back.

While he was kissing her, he skimmed a hand down her back, then over her butt and gave it a squeeze.

Tilda dragged her gaze away—and didn't look at her mom again until she heard his footsteps move away and the front door open and close.

"We're only here for a few days," she said. "Do you think you could ask Perry to keep the PDAs to a minimum during that time?"

"Maybe I'm the one who can't keep my hands off him," Mom countered with a smile.

Tilda rolled her eyes. "I don't need to hear things like that."

Mom laughed. "You're fifteen years old—stop acting like a child."

"I'm fourteen," Tilda noted. "And I *am* a child. *Your* child."

"You'll be fifteen in February."

Which was more than half a year away.

"And definitely living up to the stereotype of a moody teenager," Mom noted. "I thought you were happy to be here."

"I was. I am." She attempted to spear a blueberry with her fork, but it rolled away. "But I thought we were coming here to spend time with *you*."

"We've got so many things planned. Hiking and swimming. Perry wants to give you a tour of the vineyards and the winery. And shopping—we definitely need to go shopping," she said. "Honestly, Tilda, don't you have any clothes that fit?"

"I meant, *just* you." She looked at Lilah. Not that she actually expected her sister to chime in with any kind of support. Lilah didn't like conflict and tended to go along with whatever anyone else wanted to do.

"Perry took time off so that he could get to know you and your sister better, and so that you can get to know your stepfather."

Tilda's fork slipped out of her grasp and clattered against her plate. "Stepfather?"

Mom nodded. "That's right. Perry asked me to marry him—and I said yes."

Her empty stomach churned. "When's the wedding?"

For the first time since Tilda sat down at the table, Mom looked uneasy. "Three weeks ago."

"You're already married?"

"Perry wanted us to tell you together. Tonight," she admitted. "But how could I wait to share such exciting news?"

"Apparently you waited three weeks," Tilda noted. Then she counted back and scowled. "And three weeks ago was the weekend you were supposed to come to Haven to see us."

"You said something came up and you had to go to Las Vegas," Lilah chimed in, surprising her sister.

"Well, the something was that Perry proposed," Mom told them. "And we went to Las Vegas to get married."

Tilda felt hot tears burn her eyes.

Apparently Lilah wasn't too happy, either, because she pushed away from the table and stormed off to their shared room.

"I can play hooky this afternoon if you can," Sarah said, snuggling into Andrew's embrace.

"Aren't we playing hooky right now?"

"We are," she agreed. "But I wasn't sure if you had to go back to the bakery."

"Nope." His hand skimmed lazily down her side, tracing the outside of her breast, the dip of her waist, the curve of her hip. "I told Mabel that I was playing hooky this afternoon."

"She didn't ask any questions?"

"I'm the boss," he reminded her.

"We could pack a picnic again and head back to Crooked Creek," she said.

He smiled, obviously remembering the first time they'd gone out to Crooked Creek. Or maybe the last time.

"I like that plan," he said. "But I don't know that I have the makings for a picnic."

"I'll stop at The Trading Post on my way home to get what we need."

"Why are you going home?"

"Because the dress I wore over here last night isn't really appropriate for riding."

"I'm not sure it's appropriate for grocery shopping, either," he noted.

A valid point. And while it wouldn't be the first time she'd been spotted in town wearing clothes rumpled from the night before, she knew that he was wary of any gossip making its way back to his daughters.

"So I'll go home first and then go to the grocery store."

"Or we could skip the picnic and stay here—and naked—all day."

"Hmm…another intriguing option."

"Let's see if I can influence your decision," he said, rolling on top of her.

As he kissed her, long and slow and deep, he slid a knee between her legs, parting her thighs so that he could settle between them. Her hips instinctively lifted, rubbing her pelvis against his.

He groaned, a low sound of approval that turned into a muttered curse when his phone chimed with a text message.

"Do you need to check that?" Sarah asked.

"Check what?" he asked, nibbling on her lips.

"Your phone."

"I don't have a phone. There is nothing here but you and me."

She appreciated his effort, but she could tell that he was distracted, wondering.

"Check your phone," she said. "I promise, I'll be right here when you're done."

He reached toward the nightstand to retrieve his phone.

"Just my sister," he said, setting it aside again.

"You don't want to respond to her?"

"Not right now," he promised.

Less than a minute later, his phone chimed again.

This time he sighed when he glanced at the screen.

"The bakery?" she guessed.

He shook his head. "Tilda."

Of course he couldn't ignore a message from his daughter, and she didn't expect him to.

He swiped to open the message, skimmed the content and then swore under his breath.

"Something's wrong," Sarah guessed.

Now he nodded. "Miranda just told the girls that Perry is their new stepdad."

"They didn't know that she was getting married?"

"No," he said. "And it's news to me, too."

"Are you okay?" she asked cautiously.

"To be honest, I'm not happy."

"Because your ex-wife got remarried?"

"Because of the way she handled it," he clarified. "We agreed, when we split up, that the girls would always be our number one priority. And for the first four years after, we mostly managed to present a united front, despite the divorce.

"Then she met Perry and, six months later, decided to move with him to California. There was no discussion with me or our daughters, no concern about how they might feel and no consideration of how it would impact her relationship with them.

"I was the one who had to try to explain her decision to them. And now I'm going to be the one dealing with the fall-out of the surprise nuptials."

"Tilda and Lilah don't like their new stepfather?"

"They don't really know him," Andrew admitted.

"Hopefully that will change over the next few days," Sarah said, trying to put a positive spin on the situation.

His phone chimed again.

"Unlikely," he said. "Because now they want to come home." He sent her an apologetic glance. "It looks like we're going to have to take a rain check on that picnic—and our alternate plans."

She managed to bite her tongue for a whole three seconds before she said, "That's your decision? No discussion or consideration of how it affects our weekend?"

He glanced up from the screen, already open to the airline website. "I'm sorry—what did you say?"

"Nothing important." She slid out of his bed and began gathering up her clothes.

He'd already made abundantly clear that Tilda and Lilah were *his* daughters and that her opinions weren't welcome or relevant in matters concerning them. And while she knew that his primary concern was always their best interests—and, in fact, his commitment to his daughters was one of the things she liked most about him—she was a little disappointed that he wasn't willing to make any effort to salvage their plans for the weekend.

If there had been any kind of real emergency with either of his girls, she would have been right there to help him push everything else aside. But neither of them was sick or hurt—except maybe their feelings.

"If there's something you want to say, say it," Andrew told her now.

"It's just that, from everything you've told me, this is the first time they've seen their mom in weeks," she ventured cautiously. "And they've been there less than twenty-four hours. Don't you think you should give them some time to try to work things out?"

"Work things out?" he echoed incredulously. "She just dropped the bombshell of her marriage on them."

"Which blows up their hopes of a reconciliation," she acknowledged. "That aside, I don't know your ex-wife and I'm not going to pretend to understand her reasons for not sharing her plans with Tilda and Lilah in advance, but maybe you should give her some credit for telling them that she got married. And for not hiding Perry from them when they were dating."

"Is that what this is really about? You're upset that I don't want them to know we've been dating?"

"Except that we haven't been dating," she pointed out. "We've been sneaking around and hooking up. Because your daughters aren't ready to see you with a woman who isn't their mom, even though their mom was living with—and is now married to—another man."

"I'm sorry if you're disappointed that our plans for the weekend have been upended," he said coolly.

"I *am* disappointed," she said. "Not because our plans have been upended so much as the fact that you're willing to upend them simply to placate your daughters who maybe need to learn that their dad is entitled to a life of his own."

But maybe she needed to remember that she had a life of her own, too, and get back to it.

So resolved, she headed to Twilight Valley, where the horses, at least, didn't give her mixed signals.

"That thing's getting a lot of mileage," Sarah remarked, when she returned—three hours later—from wherever she'd been and found Andrew sitting on her porch with the olive branch in his hand.

"I should probably come up with something new," he acknowledged. "But it got me in the door once before and I'm hoping it will do so again."

"I thought you'd be on your way to the airport by now."

"Not until Friday," he said.

"No flights available?"

"Could we maybe continue this conversation inside?" he asked. "I've been sitting on your porch long enough that your across-the-street neighbor has peeked through the curtains half a dozen times to ensure I know I'm being watched."

"Frank or Maria?"

"It was a man, so I'm guessing Frank," he said.

"Then I guess I'd better invite you to come in before he tells Maria, who will tell Emelia, who will tell everyone."

She unlocked the door; he followed her inside.

"After you left, I called Tilda and told her that I wasn't letting them come home early. Because you were right, they've been looking forward to this trip for weeks, and it wouldn't be fair to anyone to cut it short."

"How did she respond to that?"

"She hung up on me."

"You don't seem particularly bothered by the fact," she noted.

He shrugged. "Mad has pretty much been her mood since February, when I first told the girls that we were moving. Not that Miranda would know, because she moved to California in November, so I figure it's her turn to deal with adolescent hormones and angst."

"So where do we go from here?" she asked him.

"How about dinner?" he suggested. "I managed to finagle a reservation at The Home Station for eight o'clock."

"I appreciate what you're trying to do," she said. "But it's really not necessary. I understand why you're protective of your daughters—and why now might not be the best time for them to learn that you're dating someone."

"Except that we're not really dating until we actually go on a date," he pointed out, recycling her earlier argument.

"So then there's nothing to tell," she said.

"I feel like the luckiest man in the world when I'm with you. I *know* I'm the luckiest man in the world," he amended. "But I'm also a dad, and I need to be sensitive to my daughters' needs."

"I understand that," she promised. "I really do."

"But I also need you to know how much you mean to me," he told her. "And if I'm struggling to reconcile my identity as their father with my identity as your lover, and I know I am, it's because this is all new territory to me."

"It's possible I overreacted a little," she acknowledged. "Because this is all new territory to me, too."

"Maybe we can figure things out together?" he suggested.

She nodded. "I like the sound of that."

"So…dinner?"

"Let's see what we can rustle up in the kitchen." She

glanced down at herself and wrinkled her nose. "After I shower—I smell like hay and horses."

He drew her into his arms. "I like the way you smell."

"I'm sweaty."

"You're sexy." He touched his lips to her. "My sexy cowgirl."

"Hold that thought," she said, stepping back. "Shower first, then dinner then...well, we can play it by ear after that."

And that's what they did, taking advantage of every minute of the all-too-limited time that was already ticking away.

Chapter Eighteen

Tilda was bored.

She'd been volunteering at Twilight Valley on Tuesdays and Thursdays and helping her dad at Sugar & Spice on Fridays and Saturdays—which seemed to satisfy him enough that he left her to her own devices the rest of the time. But it was Wednesday—the middle of the week—and she had nothing to do.

Nothing except check off some of the tasks on Dad's communal chore list, and she was bored enough that she was watering the flower boxes on the railing around the porch when she saw Warren come out of his house next door with a backpack slung over one shoulder.

Because she was usually home on Wednesdays, she'd started to notice a pattern in which he left the house before 11:00 a.m. and didn't come back until after 3:00 p.m.

She set down the watering can and skipped down the steps.

"Hey," she called out to him. "Where are you going?"

He paused in midstep and glanced over his shoulder. He looked surprised, and perhaps a little wary, that she'd taken the initiative to start a conversation.

She couldn't blame him. Every time he'd made a friendly overture, she'd responded with attitude and snark.

"Why do you want to know?" he said, answering her question with one of his own.

She shrugged. "I don't really."

"Then this conversation is pointless," he noted, and continued on his way.

She should have let him go, but instead, she found herself hurrying to catch up and then falling into step beside him.

He walked for thirty minutes—a whole half an hour!—without saying a word to her. She didn't say anything, either, because she'd already asked where he was going and he'd declined to answer.

But she thought she'd figured it out when the community center came into view. As if she needed any more proof that he was a geek, he spent his Wednesdays during summer break at the local library?

He paused on the steps leading into the building and opened his backpack. He took out a water bottle and drank from it.

Tilda realized then that she was thirsty, too, but she was empty-handed, not having planned to take a thirty-minute walk. Which, of course, meant she was going to have to walk another thirty minutes back home again.

Warren glanced at his watch then took another drink from his bottle, pretending he didn't know she was there.

Or maybe he really didn't.

Maybe she was as invisible to him as she felt to everyone else in her life.

She wished he'd offer her a drink.

Of course, if he did, she'd have to refuse. Because no way was she putting her mouth where his had been.

He recapped the bottle and dropped it into his backpack again before finally speaking to her. "Are you going to follow me inside, too?"

"I'm not following you," she immediately denied.

He snorted and she flushed, because obviously she had been following him.

"So why are you here?" he asked.

"I need something to read."

"Do you know how to read?"

"Now who's the mean girl?" she challenged.

He just smirked.

Then he spotted someone else walking up the steps toward the entrance—a girl with bluntly cut reddish hair and big eyes—and his attention shifted.

"Hey," the girl said, and smiled at him.

"Hey," he responded, and smiled back.

And they turned away from Tilda and walked into the library together.

She was probably a cheerleader who needed tutoring in chemistry. That was the only reason Tilda could imagine that a girl who looked like that would be hanging out with Warren.

Still, curiosity had her following them into the building.

They walked up an open staircase to the second floor. Tilda reached the top just in time to see them head into a study room together. There were narrow panels of glass flanking the door—sidelights, she thought they were called—through which she could see a long table with three chairs on each of the sides and one at each end.

Two other people were in the room already.

A guy several inches shorter than Warren with black hair that flopped over his eyes. He was set up at the far end, with a trifold cardboard screen on the table in front of him. She'd never played D&D (as if!) but she'd seen it depicted in television shows and movies and guessed the guy behind the screen was in charge. What was he called? The game ruler? Dragon tamer? Dungeon master?

Something like that, anyway.

The other guy in the room was—another girl, Tilda realized.

Blond and perky, with a ponytail and a toothpaste-commercial smile that reminded Tilda of London. Her former best friend had always been the prettiest and most popular girl in school, and Tilda had felt lucky to be part of her chosen group—one of the "in" crowd.

But she wasn't part of London's group, anymore. She wasn't part of any group now. She was on her own.

In fact, she'd exchanged only a handful of text messages with London since she'd been a no-show to Damian's big party. (Though she'd heard from Kellie that the cops had shown up and everyone had been busted for underage drinking. Some had been caught with drugs, too—and not just pot. Another reason Tilda was glad she'd never made it to Texas that weekend—Dad would have grounded her for life!)

The red-haired girl in the study room threw her head back, laughing at something Warren said, then she reached across the table and laid a hand on his arm, almost as if she was flirting with him.

But why would a girl who could probably get any guy she wanted waste her time flirting with Warren?

Maybe he wasn't bad-looking, Tilda allowed. He did have nice eyes behind the glasses. And a nice smile. And he seemed to be a decent human being—or at least a lot nicer than she was.

Two more guys wandered in to join the group, and then they settled down to business of their game.

She didn't know why she hung around.

She certainly didn't want Warren to think that she was waiting for him. Because she wasn't. And she had no intention of spending four hours at the library.

But she also had nothing else to do, and since she'd told him that she was there to get something to read, she decided to browse the stacks.

At the public library in Beaumont, you had to show photo ID and prove residency to be able to sign out materials, so she wasn't optimistic about her chances of getting a card here with only last year's student ID from Wharncliffe Middle School. But the librarian—"Mrs. Gilmore" as she was addressed by another patron and "Lindsay" according to her name tag—looked at the name under the photo and asked Tilda if her dad was the owner of Sugar & Spice. When Tilda admitted that he was, Lindsay spent the next five minutes raving about his new lavender vanilla beignets as she input the requisite information and issued Tilda a card.

"So you go to the library on Wednesdays to play D&D?" Tilda said, falling into step with Warren again after he'd said goodbye to his fellow gamers.

"It's what I do with my geeky friends," he reminded her.

"Which is at least a little less lame than going to the library to study on your summer break."

"Happy to hear it," he said. "Because your opinion means so much to me."

She shifted the stack of books in her arms. "What if I wanted to play?"

"You'd have to find another group—ours is full."

"Oh."

He eyed her curiously. "You almost sound disappointed."

She shrugged. "I guess I'm more bored than I realized."

"And you haven't made any friends so you want to horn in on mine."

"Forget I said anything," she said, annoyed that she'd let herself show even a hint of vulnerability.

They walked in silence for several minutes before he said, "Stasia goes to Cape Cod with her family for the first two weeks of August every summer, and Dylan goes to Colorado for the whole month, to spend some time with his dad. Usually we suspend whatever campaign we're in the midst of until they get back, but if you really want to learn, add the player's handbook to your reading list and sit in on the next session to see what it's all about, and maybe the others will let you participate in a starter campaign while they're gone."

"The next session being next Wednesday?" she guessed.

"Yeah."

"Okay."

"Don't you want to check your calendar first? Make sure you don't have any other plans?"

She flushed. "I think we both know that I don't."

"Then I guess I'll see you next Wednesday," he said.

"Or tomorrow, at Twilight Valley."

"Or tomorrow, on the way to Twilight Valley."

In response to her questioning look, he said, "I could give you a ride, save your dad having to make the trip."

"Okay," she agreed. "Thanks."

Life settled into something of a routine over the next few weeks. Though Andrew hadn't officially announced to his daughters that he and Sarah were dating, they'd been spending a fair amount of time together and if Tilda wasn't overly thrilled by Sarah's presence, she at least seemed to have accepted it.

The closer it got to September, the more excited Lilah was about starting school. Unfortunately, Tilda was obviously dreading the same. She'd made a couple of friends through her volunteering at Twilight Valley and had even been hanging out with Warren sometimes. But he was a junior and she was only a freshman, so Tilda didn't expect him to acknowledge her presence at school. For now, though, she had someone to talk to, and Andrew was glad. And when he'd checked on his daughters before he turned in the night before, Tilda had been studying the *Dungeons & Dragons Player's Handbook* as if she expected to be tested on its contents.

"I think the girls had a good time tonight," Andrew said, settling on the sofa beside Sarah after they'd returned from a potluck barbecue at Claire and Devin's.

"It seemed like," Sarah agreed.

"Lilah's already counting the days until she can volunteer at Twilight Valley."

"Until then, I'm sure Claire would be happy to have her visit whenever she wants."

"Don't tell Lilah that—she'll be wanting to go every day."

"Mmm," Sarah agreed.

"Everything okay?" Andrew asked. "You seem a little distracted."

"Sorry."

"Don't apologize," he said. "Tell me what's on your mind."

"I'm afraid of overstepping," she admitted. "But I'm more afraid of saying nothing."

"About?" he prompted.

"Tilda."

He sighed. "What has she done now?"

"Nothing," Sarah was quick to assure him. "I was just wondering…has it ever occurred to you that she might have…an eating disorder?"

"What?" He scowled at the thought. "No. And what would make you ask such a question?"

"A lot of little things," Sarah said.

"Like what?" he demanded.

"Like the dress she was wearing tonight—she told me that you bought it for her eighth-grade graduation."

"That's right," he confirmed.

"Did it fit her better in June?" she wondered. "Because it looks two sizes too big for her now."

"She has lost some weight," he acknowledged hesitantly. "But she's been doing a lot more walking here than she ever did in Beaumont, plus whatever physical labor she's doing at Twilight Valley."

"Maybe she's been getting more exercise," Sarah allowed. "And maybe it's that she hardly ever eats."

"Isn't it normal for teenage girls to pick at their food?"

"*Normal* doesn't mean *healthy*," she pointed out. "And it's certainly not healthy for a teen who barely weighs a hundred pounds to count every calorie that she puts in her mouth."

"I don't think she's counting every calorie that she puts in her mouth."

"Just because she's not counting out loud doesn't mean she's not counting."

"Then why is she always going out for burgers and fries?"

"Is she?" Sarah asked dubiously. "When was the last time you actually saw her eat a burger? Or even a handful of French fries?"

"She had a burger tonight," he pointed out. "And macaroni salad and corn on the cob."

"No, she put a burger and macaroni salad and corn on her plate and, after she ate about three bites of the burger, she 'accidentally' dumped her plate on the ground. And she said she was going to get another one, but she never did."

He couldn't dispute what she was saying, because he didn't know that it wasn't true. Because he hadn't been paying close enough attention. And it troubled him, more than a little, to think that Sarah had noticed these things about his daughter that he'd somehow missed.

Being busy at the bakery was no excuse. Being preoccupied with Sarah was even less so. Because his daughters were supposed to be his number one priority, and if what Sarah was saying about Tilda was true, he'd somehow let her fall through the cracks.

"I'll keep a closer eye on her at mealtimes," he vowed. "But it's a pretty big leap from dumping one plate of food to assuming she has an eating disorder, don't you think?"

"Except that it's not about one plate of food," she pointed out. "Have you noticed how often she has an excuse for not wanting dinner? She had a late snack or a big lunch. And whenever you make her sit at the table, she spends most of her time pushing her food around her plate."

"She can be a picky eater," he acknowledged.

"Trust me," Sarah urged. "I know all the tricks."

I've used all the same tricks.

"What tricks?" he wanted to know.

"Cutting food into smaller and smaller pieces and then moving them around the plate so that it looks like you're eating when you're not."

Andrew frowned. "I know you took it personally that she wasn't a fan of your pork roast a few weeks ago."

"It wasn't just the pork roast," she told him. "She's done the same thing at every meal I've seen her eat."

"Which hasn't been that many."

"You're right," she acknowledged. "But you asked me what was on my mind and I couldn't continue to pretend that the things she's doing don't worry me."

"You don't have to worry about my daughter," he said, a touch of resentment in his tone. "That's my job."

"You're right." Sarah nodded as she pushed herself off the sofa, her heart aching. "For a minute I let myself forget that I wasn't actually part of your family—that I'm just the woman you screw on the side."

"That's not fair," he protested. "You know I care about you. I'm just having a little trouble balancing the different parts of my life."

"And maybe that's the problem. Maybe instead of trying to balance the different parts you should consider bringing them together."

"I don't know if my daughters are ready for that."

"I think the bigger problem is that *you're* not ready for that," she said.

"Maybe I'm not," he admitted. "In the past few months, I've moved my family halfway across the country and started a new business in a town where I knew exactly two people, so it might be that I need a little bit of time to catch my breath before I decide to jump into a new relationship without a parachute."

"That's a fair point," she said. "And probably something I should have considered before I went into freefall. Because I already love you and Tilda and Lilah."

And it hurt more than she'd anticipated to realize that he didn't feel the same way.

The ball was in his court.

That was what Sarah told herself—her justification for staying away from the bakery and the grocery store and the pizzeria and anywhere else that she might cross paths with Andrew. She spent extra hours at the ranch, but while the physical labor kept her hands busy, it didn't stop her mind from wandering or her heart from aching. Of course, she knew she couldn't avoid him forever, she just needed a little time for her bruised heart to heal before she found herself face-to-face with him again.

It turned out that the "little time" was less than forty-eight hours, which was when Claire oh-so-sweetly asked her to please stop at Sugar & Spice because the baby wanted chocolate cupcakes. When Sarah had suggested that Devin should be the one to deal with his wife's pregnancy cravings—after all, he was the one who'd knocked her up—Claire reminded her that Devin was at a conference out of town. She then offered to make the trip into town herself, but that didn't really make a lot of sense when Sarah lived so close.

She didn't bother to call out her friend's obvious manipulations, because Claire would then accuse her of being afraid to face Andrew and Sarah would end up going to the bakery anyway to prove she wasn't. Such was the joy of having a BFF who knew everything about you.

And that was how Sarah happened to be at Sugar & Spice Friday morning when Tilda, carrying a bin of dirty dishes from the seating area to the kitchen, fainted.

Chapter Nineteen

Of course, Andrew freaked out. Any parent seeing their supposedly healthy fourteen-year-old daughter collapse would—and then their mind would start to go down all kinds of dark paths.

Thankfully Tilda came around quickly, and she seemed more embarrassed to realize she'd fainted than she was injured as a result of the fall. Seeing the crowd that had gathered only added to her discomfort, so Sarah ushered the patrons out of the bakery to make way for the paramedics coming in.

Despite Tilda's insistence that she was fine, Andrew wasn't willing to take her word for it. He rode in the ambulance with her to the hospital and Sarah promised to pick Lilah up from camp and meet him there.

Forty-five minutes later, they found him pacing in the ER waiting room.

"Any news?" Sarah asked.

He shook his head. "They're doing tests. Checking her blood pressure and her heart rate and running a full blood panel."

Lilah, her eyes swimming with tears, slipped her small hand into her dad's much larger one. "She's going to be okay," she said, her tone a lot less certain than her words.

He managed a smile for his youngest daughter. "I'm sure you're right," he said. "But I'll feel a lot better when I hear it from a doctor."

"The last time—" Lilah's lower lip quivered, as it did when she was trying not to cry "—the doctor told Tilda to keep a journal of what she eats each day, to help her remember not to skip meals."

Andrew immediately stilled. "The last time?"

Lilah's lip quivered again and her teary gaze dropped to the tile floor.

Her dad tipped her chin up, forcing her to look at him. "Are you telling me this has happened before?"

"Mom said she was going to tell you…" Lilah's voice was quivering now, too. "She didn't tell you?"

"No." A muscle in his jaw flexed. "She didn't. So maybe you can fill me in?"

"When did this happen?" Sarah asked gently.

Lilah's gaze shifted. "When Mom took us shopping at the outlet mall in Napa."

"So…two weeks ago," Andrew realized.

His daughter shrugged. "I guess."

"Can you tell us what led up to Tilda fainting?" Sarah prompted.

"She was trying on clothes and she did a twirl to show off a new outfit and…she just crumpled to the ground."

"Jesus." Andrew scrubbed his hands over his face.

Lilah started to cry. "I'm sorry, Daddy."

He put his arm around her and hugged her close. "It's not your fault, Lilah."

"Mom said she was going to tell you."

Sarah could imagine that Andrew was having some thoughts about his ex-wife's silence on the matter, but thankfully he kept them to himself for the moment.

"I need to know, Lilah—was that the only time something like this happened?"

"The only time that I know," she said, wiping her eyes on her sleeve.

He nodded, then hugged her again. "Okay."

A nurse came into the waiting room then.

"We've finished poking and prodding your daughter for the moment," she said to Andrew. "You can go in now to see her." He nodded again. "Lilah, why don't you go ahead? We'll be there in just a couple of minutes."

"Okay," she said, and followed the nurse to the exam room.

"There's something you didn't want to say in front of her," Sarah realized.

He swallowed. "All those tests I mentioned... They're also doing a pregnancy test," he confided. "They asked Tilda when she had her last period and she said... April. So they're doing a pregnancy test."

"I think it's standard procedure to rule out pregnancy when treating a female of childbearing age," she told him.

"She's not of childbearing age," he protested. "She's a *child*."

"I hate to break it to you, but if she's menstruating, then she's of childbearing age."

"She's fourteen," he said again. "And she freaked out, too, when they asked if she could be pregnant—told me there's no way she could be because she's never had sex."

"So take a breath," Sarah advised. "And trust the doctors to do what they need to do to figure out what's going on."

"She hasn't had a period since April," he said again.

"She's only fourteen. It's possible that her cycle isn't regular yet."

"I do the shopping," he reminded her. "I buy the tampons when she puts them on the list. I didn't realize she hadn't put them on the list."

"This isn't your fault, Andrew."

"Then why do I feel like it is?"

"Because you're scared, and blaming yourself is easier than admitting that you have absolutely no control over the situation."

"I need to call Miranda."

"Why don't you wait until you have more information first?" she suggested.

"If you mean wait until I've gotten over the urge to yell at her, I'm not sure I'm going to live that long."

"Then at least wait until you've talked to the doctor."

"Okay." He let out a deep, shuddering breath, then reached for Sarah's hand and linked their fingers together. "Thank you for being here."

"I couldn't imagine being anywhere else right now," she told him.

And they walked into the exam room together, still hand in hand.

The doctors concluded that Tilda's recent fainting spells were caused by an electrolyte imbalance and low blood sugar resulting from extended periods of fasting. Two days later, after consultations with various professionals, she was home.

Andrew invited Sarah to his daughter's homecoming dinner, but she declined, not wanting his eldest daughter to feel as if there was one more person at the table to watch her eat. She did stop by later that evening, though, to see for herself that Tilda was doing okay and to ensure that Andrew didn't think his overture had been rejected.

After Sarah chatted for a few minutes with each of the girls, he opened a bottle of wine and the adults took it outside to sit under the stars where they could talk without worrying their conversation might be overheard.

"She looks good," Sarah commented, accepting the glass of pinot he offered to her.

"They pumped her full of electrolytes in the hospital. They also made her undergo a psychiatric evaluation."

"Standard procedure," she said.

"You seem to know a lot about standard procedure," he noted.

"I told you that I had some experience with eating disorders," she reminded him.

"So you probably won't be surprised to learn that she's going to have regular appointments with a psychologist and a nutritionist. Oh, and she's got plans to go to out Friday night."

"The last part surprises me," Sarah said. "You're letting your fourteen-year-old daughter go on a date?"

"It's not a date—it's a movie with some friends."

"Have you met these friends?"

"I know Warren."

"The boy next door," she mused.

"The others are members of his D&D group."

"Really?"

He nodded. "She's been hanging out with them at the library on Wednesdays."

"She must really be bored."

"That's what I thought, but she seems to be enjoying it," he said. "I also talked to Miranda today. She's agreed to participate in family counseling via Zoom."

"That's good news," Sarah remarked.

"The counselor said it's important for Tilda to know that we're all here to support her."

"And Lilah? How's she doing?"

"She's okay. I know what happened with Tilda freaked her out and that she felt guilty, because she saw what Tilda was doing and didn't say anything."

"It's a tough spot for a sibling—especially a younger sibling—to be in," Sarah noted. "Wanting to keep her sister's confidence and, at the same time, knowing she shouldn't."

"You're not just thinking about Lilah now but your own sister," Andrew guessed.

She nodded.

"Did she keep your confidence?" he asked.

"Jenna didn't tell my parents, but she told Zack. He then told my parents."

"Were you mad?"

"Furious," she admitted. "Also relieved and grateful. Sometimes, when everything in your life seems out of your control, you look for any little thing that you can control. Such as the food you put in your mouth—or don't put in your mouth.

"Eventually I realized that it was the number on the scale that was in control, not me. But it was a long process," she warned. "Tilda's not going to have counseling for a few weeks and suddenly be cured."

"That's exactly what her counselor told us at the first session," he confided. "That this is going to be a long—possibly lifelong—journey."

She nodded again. "At least Tilda knows that it's not a journey she has to undertake on her own—that you and her mom and Lilah are all going to be there with her, supporting her and offering a hand when she stumbles."

"Do you think it's expecting too much of Lilah—asking her to be part of that?"

"On the contrary, I think it's essential to her well-being to know that she's part of the process. Otherwise she might feel as if she's being shoved into the background while the spotlight shines on her sister."

"She said something a few weeks back that startled me," Andrew admitted.

"What's that?"

"She said that Tilda always gets what she wants."

"Does she?"

"I hope not," he said. "But the truth is, I think maybe I do indulge Tilda a little more because I don't want to give her a reason to ever think that I love her less."

"Every kid with a sibling thinks the sibling is the favorite," Sarah noted.

"And every parent with more than one child will tell you that they don't have a favorite," he assured her. "And I don't, but I worry the day will come that Tilda won't believe it. That she won't trust I could love her as much as I love Lilah…because she's not my biological child."

"I did not see *that* coming," Sarah admitted, as Andrew lifted the bottle to top off their glasses.

"Miranda wasn't the love of my life," he confided to her now. "We met because we were working at the same restaurant—she was the sommelier and I was the pastry chef. We were attracted to one another and our shifts sometimes overlapped, so we started hanging out—and hooking up—because it was easy.

"We were together for almost a year, but then our relationship started to fizzle and we decided to go our separate ways. Not long after we broke up, Miranda started dating someone else. A few weeks later, I did, too. And then, a few weeks after that, Miranda showed up at my apartment and told me she was pregnant.

"So we got married, because even if she wasn't the love of my life, the moment she told me that she was having my baby, I wanted to be there for her and our child, every step of the way. But she assured me that she could handle all the routine doctor's appointments, she just wanted me there for prenatal classes and the birth.

"I was a little concerned about the milestones throughout her pregnancy. According to the books I'd read—because yes, I was *that* expectant dad, the one who read everything he could get his hands on in preparation for the birth of his child—she should have felt movement around twenty weeks, and she claimed that she did. Four to eight weeks after that, I should have been able to feel the baby's movements, but it was nearly ten weeks before I did.

"Of course, the numbers are only guidelines, and all the books and online resources assured me that every pregnancy is different and so long as the doctor wasn't worried, I shouldn't worry, either.

"Anyway, her due date came and went, but the baby gave no indication of wanting to be born. We knew she was a girl by this point, and I teased Miranda that our daughter was already taking after her mom in being late for everything.

"Miranda reminded me that babies came when they were ready, and I tried to be patient, but I worried that she was more than a week past her due date. Then it was two weeks.

"Finally, she went into labor. Twenty-two hours later, Tilda came into the world weighing six pounds ten ounces and measuring eighteen inches. The doctor said she was a good size for a baby born at thirty-eight weeks."

Sarah blew out a slow breath.

"And that's when I knew the baby girl that I held in my arms wasn't actually my baby," he confided. "And when I looked at Miranda, I realized it wasn't a revelation to her.

"But we didn't talk about it until they came home from the hospital. I certainly didn't want the doctors and nurses who'd taken such good care of my wife and baby to know that she'd duped me into marrying her and taking responsibility for another man's child."

"I can't imagine she tried to deny it, at that point," Sarah said.

"She didn't," he confirmed. "But she insisted that, at the beginning of her pregnancy anyway, she really believed the baby was mine. It was only at her first ultrasound, when she discovered she wasn't as far along as she thought, that she realized the truth herself."

"Did you believe her?"

"I wanted to," he said. "In any event, I let her maintain the charade, because we were married and parents to a newborn— and I loved Tilda with my whole heart.

"But I felt guilty, too. Because I was experiencing the joy

of being a dad to another man's child. I certainly didn't want to lose Tilda, but I felt strongly that Miranda should let the biological father know he had a child. I thought he at least deserved the chance to be part of her life, even if it would make things a lot more complicated for us.

"Miranda then confessed that she'd gone to Nigel when she realized she was having his baby, and he assured her that he had no interest in being a father."

Sarah swallowed another mouthful of wine.

"But after all of her deceptions, I couldn't be sure Miranda was telling the truth about that, so I tracked him down. Anyway, long story short, he already had two kids with two different women and didn't spend much time with either of them, so he was glad that this one had a better father than he would ever be.

"I felt sorry for him, that he couldn't appreciate the opportunity he'd been given to be a dad, but mostly I was relieved that he had no interest in Tilda, that my family would remain intact—at least for a while longer.

"But juggling the responsibilities of our jobs and our family wasn't always easy, and we inevitably went through some rough patches. During one of those patches, Miranda decided that having another baby would solve all our problems. Again, though, we didn't talk about it—she just decided to go off birth control and hope for the best. Nine months later, Lilah came along, so while I wasn't too happy with her machinations, I was overjoyed with the result.

"But, of course, there were more rough patches to come. And when we finally decided that living separate and apart was the best solution for everyone, she was surprised that I asked for joint custody of both our daughters—as if I'd feel less of a connection to Tilda because we didn't share DNA.

"Surprised and relieved, I think. Because as much as she loved her daughters, her work schedule wasn't particularly conducive to handling the day-to-day demands of parenthood, and she was happy to let me take on those responsibilities."

"Tilda doesn't know any of this?"

He shook his head. "I'm kind of dreading when she does that genetics unit in high school science where students chart Mom and Dad's eye color and figure out what options there are for baby—because blue is not an option with a brown-eyed father."

"So long as there's a grandparent with blue eyes, there's a twenty-five percent chance of a blue-eyed child," she pointed out, proving that she'd paid attention during science class.

"You're saying that she might not need to know the truth?" he asked dubiously.

"I'm saying she shouldn't find out in high school science class," Sarah clarified. "That you should tell her yourself before she starts asking the tough questions."

"I'm not sure that's a good idea. Especially not when she's dealing with so much other stuff already."

"The timing might not be ideal," she acknowledged. "But secrets have a way of coming out—and usually at the worst possible moment. The only way to ensure that doesn't happen is to tell her the truth on your terms."

Andrew found himself thinking about Sarah's advice long after she'd gone. He'd refused to heed her concerns about Tilda's eating habits—to his daughter's detriment—forcing him to acknowledge that being a parent didn't give him an inside track on making the right decisions.

Friday afternoon, determined not to make the same mistake again, he knocked on Tilda's partially open door.

"Come in," she invited.

He stepped over the threshold. "Are you busy?"

"Just checking my course schedule for September."

"How's it look?"

"First term I've got English, science, US history and phys ed. Second term is math, music, Spanish and computer science."

"Music? I thought you wanted to take art."

She shrugged. "Warren told me that the band gets to go on some cool trips, so I thought I'd give music a try."

"Cool trips?" he said dubiously.

"A couple years ago, they went to Disneyland."

"Sign me up for band," he said.

That earned him a small smile.

"The teachers aren't listed for second-term courses yet, but I've got Mrs. Channing for science first term, and Heidi says that she's the best, so I'm happy about that."

And Andrew was happy that Tilda finally seemed to be looking forward to the start of a new school year.

"There's a downloadable checklist of required school supplies on the website," she continued. "Do you think we could go shopping this weekend?"

"Sure," he agreed. "But can we talk about something else for a sec?"

"Okay," she said cautiously, spinning in her chair to face him as he perched on the edge of her mattress.

"I'm sorry I didn't see what you were doing. A parent always wants what's best for their child, and it's scary to admit that you had a problem I wasn't equipped to help you deal with."

"This is what you want to talk about?" She made a face. "Can't we save this for therapy?"

"We can talk about it again there," he told her. "But I want you to know that you can talk to me about anything at any time."

"Okay."

"Because secrets can eat away at us…" He inwardly cringed over his use of the word *eat* but maybe he was being overly sensitive, because it didn't seem to faze her.

"You think I'm keeping something else from you?" she guessed.

"No," he immediately replied, aware that he was bungling it. "I'm saying that you can talk to me about anything. And that sometimes parents keep secrets from their kids, too. Either because they feel the child is too young to understand or to deal with the truth."

"Like when you said that you and Mom grew apart instead of telling us that she had a boyfriend?"

"That's a good example," he admitted. "How did you know she had a boyfriend?"

"She moved out of our house and moved into his."

He nodded. "And sometimes parents keep secrets from one another—like when your mom didn't tell me that you fainted when you visited her in California."

"I asked her not to tell you," Tilda admitted. "I was afraid you'd freak out."

"And you were right—I would have freaked out," he confirmed. "I *did* freak out when the same thing happened here. Because there is absolutely nothing more terrifying for a parent than being unable to help their sick or injured child.

"But your mom and I promised one another that there would be no more secrets between us—at least not when it comes to you and Lilah. But there is something that we've both been keeping from you," he confided. "And, to be honest, I don't want to tell you now, but I've realized that if I expect you to be honest with me, then I need to be honest with you."

"Okay," she said again.

"You already know that your mom was pregnant when we got married."

"Yeah, because I can count."

"What you might not know is that your mom and I dated for a while and then spent some time apart before we got back together and decided to get married."

She looked wary. "Maybe there are some things that a kid doesn't need to know."

No doubt that was true.

But what Sarah said was also true—secrets had a way of coming out. Usually at the most inopportune times.

If he told Tilda, he could maintain control of the narrative. If she found out in some other way, she might jump to all kinds of wrong conclusions.

"The most important thing you need to know is that I love you and your sister more than anything else in the world."

"You're starting to freak me out a little here," Tilda said.

"There's no reason for you to freak out," he hastened to assure her. "It's just not easy for me to find the words…"

"Rip off the Band-Aid, Dad," she suggested.

"Okay." He nodded. "Your mom and I weren't together when she got pregnant."

For a long minute, Tilda was silent.

"You're saying that you're not my dad," she realized.

"No," he immediately denied. "I'm not saying that at all. Because I *am* your dad in every way that counts…just not biologically."

She fell silent again, for even longer this time.

"And now you're not saying anything," he noted.

"I'm…processing."

He nodded. "That's fair."

"I think it's going to take some time."

"Okay." He rose to his feet. "I'm going back to the bakery. But whenever you're ready to talk, I'm here. Whatever questions you might have, I'll answer them as best I can."

"One question," she said. "Can we have pizza for dinner?"

"You bet." He dipped his head to kiss her forehead. "I love you, Tilly."

She only nodded.

And when he came home with pizza a few hours later, she was gone.

Chapter Twenty

Since walking out of her job at Blake Mining, Sarah's life had proceeded according to *her* plan. And even if it wasn't a flawless plan, at least she went to work every day with joy in her heart, happy to be doing something that mattered and happier still to be doing it alongside her best friend.

Maybe choosing to be a rancher wasn't going to change the world, but it had changed *her* world—giving her a sense of purpose and personal happiness. Meeting and falling in love with Andrew Morrow was the icing on the cake. (An appropriate analogy, she thought.) And after their tête-à-tête on Wednesday, she honestly believed that their relationship wasn't just back on track but on a better track.

And so, when her phone rang Friday afternoon and she saw his name on the display, she didn't even try to hold back the smile that curved her lips.

The smile immediately slipped when he responded to her greeting by saying, "Tilda's missing."

"What do you mean *missing*?"

"I mean that I came home with dinner and she wasn't here."

"Did you try texting or calling?"

"I tried texting *and* calling. And before you ask about the tracking app, that's not going to help because wherever she went, she didn't take her phone with her."

Now Sarah understood the panic in his tone. Because teenagers were rarely more than two feet away from their smartphones, and if Tilda had purposely left hers behind, it was because she didn't want to be contacted.

"I'm calling you because I wondered if you'd seen or heard from her."

"No, I haven't," she admitted. "But if she left her phone, I'm sure she didn't go far."

"Are you sure?" he challenged. "Like you were sure it would be a good idea to tell her about her parentage? Because I did that earlier today."

She reeled at the anger in his tone.

"So this is my fault?" she guessed. "Because I recommended that you be honest with your daughter rather than continue to perpetuate a lie?"

"Because I took your advice and now she's gone," he said.

Sarah sucked in a breath, unable to deny the apparent cause and effect. And she felt not only guilty but sick with worry. "I was trying to help."

"And now my fourteen-year-old daughter is only-God-knows where."

"We'll find her," she said confidently, needing it to be true.

"No," he said. "There's no *we* here."

And suddenly she saw that the new track their relationship was on had come to a dead end—the broken rails hanging over a bottomless chasm.

"*I* need to focus on my family right now."

And, as he'd made clear not even a week earlier, Sarah wasn't part of his family.

Even after everything they'd been through in that week, she remained on the outside looking in.

Though the realization made her heart ache, that was something to be dealt with later. Right now, the only thing that mattered was finding Tilda.

"I'm here," she said. "Whatever you need. I can call the

sheriff. I can call everyone I know. I'm at Twilight Valley, but I can come back to town, drive around the neighborhood, knock on doors."

"Thanks," he said. "But I think you've done enough."

And then the line went dead.

Sarah tucked her phone back in her pocket and resumed her chores, because so long as the world continued to turn, there were animals that needed to be tended to.

Ordinarily the evening feeding was something that Claire handled, but Devin had taken his wife to an appointment with their ob-gyn and Sarah offered to hang around until they returned.

As she went through the motions, she tried to make sense of recent events. Had Tilda been so upset to learn Andrew wasn't her biological father that she'd run away? And if so, where would she go?

She was tempted to reach out to Warren, to ask if the neighbor might have seen her, but no doubt Andrew had already done so.

Her next thought was to call the sheriff, but it wasn't her place to report Tilda missing and the girl's dad had likely covered that base, too.

Instead, Sarah finished with the horses, but when she started to close up the barn, Ed sat down smack in the middle of the open doorway, deliberately impeding her efforts and refusing to move.

"What's the matter, buddy? Are you feeling neglected because Claire and Devin went into Battle Mountain for an appointment with the baby doctor?" she asked.

He whined, a low and plaintive sound from deep in his throat.

"That sounds like more than feeling neglected," she noted,

crouching in front of him. "Did you get caught in something? Are you hurt?"

As soon as she reached for him, to examine him for bumps or cuts, he backed away.

So she straightened up again and he barked.

"I'm sorry, but I don't understand what you're trying to tell me."

He tilted his head, as if to communicate that he was having the same problem.

"You know I love you, Eduardo, but I don't have time to play games," she said. "So why don't we head up to the house now to get your dinner?"

He barked at her again.

"I still don't speak dog," she told him.

He turned and trotted away, and she followed, because it seemed as if that was what he wanted her to do.

He made his way to the far end of the barn, where there was a ladder to the hayloft.

"If there are rats up here, I'm going to scream," she warned, as she started to climb.

It took a minute for her eyes to adjust to the dim lighting and another several seconds to scan the mostly open space and spot a pair of sneakers peeking out from behind a stack of hay bales.

She recognized the bright pink Converses immediately, and nearly collapsed with relief. "Tilda."

The teen wiped at the streaks of tears on her cheeks. "That dog is a worse tattletale than Lilah."

"And thank God for that," Sarah said, lowering herself to the floor beside Andrew's daughter. "How did you get all the way out here?"

"Warren gave me a lift," she admitted.

"I didn't see anyone drive up."

"He was going to see his friend Matt, who lives a little

farther down the road, so I told him to drop me off at the end of the lane."

"But you didn't tell your dad where you were going—and you left your phone at home."

Tilda sniffed. "He's not my dad."

"Is that what this is about?"

The girl's eyes narrowed. "You're not surprised."

"No." If Andrew had decided to be honest with his daughter, she was going to do the same. "He told me a few days ago."

"That must be when Mom told him," Tilda realized. "And why he finally decided to tell me."

"You think your dad just found out that you're not his biological child?"

"Well, yeah. Obviously. And now that he knows, he doesn't have to be responsible for me and he's probably going to send me to California to live with Mom, but she doesn't want me, either."

"I can't speak for your mom, but I can assure you that's not true about your dad," Sarah told her. "He would do absolutely anything for you—including tell you a truth he would prefer to deny."

"Then why did he tell me? Why now?"

"Maybe because he was trying to be honest with you, so that you would know that you can be honest with him."

"How long do you think he's known?"

"Since you were born," Sarah said gently.

Tilda seemed puzzled by that. "If that's true—why did he stay with my mom? Did he love her that much?"

"He loved *you* that much."

The teen sniffled. "Do you really think so?"

"I know so," Sarah promised.

"Even after everything I've put him through these past few months?"

"I'm not saying he's loved everything you've said and done,

but I promise that he loves you. And right now, he's worried sick about you, so you need to call him and let him know that you're safe."

"He's going to be mad," Tilda noted.

"First he's going to thrilled to hear your voice," Sarah said. "Then relieved to know you're okay. The mad will probably come after that."

"He's going to ground me *forever*."

"Quite possibly," she agreed. "Because that's what parents do to make sure their kids understand that actions have consequences."

"Maybe you could call him for me," Tilda suggested.

"I could," Sarah allowed. "And I definitely will if you don't. But if you want your dad to stop treating you like a child, you have to stop acting like a child and take responsibility for your actions."

Tilda wiped her eyes again, then she took a deep breath and nodded. "I'll call him."

Andrew snatched up the phone on the first ring, before he even saw Sarah's name on the display. "Have you heard anything?"

"Dad, it's…me."

"Tilda." Relief turned his knees to jelly. He slid to the floor, clutching the phone like a lifeline. "Where are you? Are you okay?"

"I'm fine," she said. "I'm at Twilight Valley."

Of all the places he'd imagined she might go, that wasn't one of them.

He knew his eldest daughter wasn't a big fan of Sarah, though when he'd shared his concerns about her attitude with Rachel, his sister assured him that Tilda wasn't likely to be a fan of any woman he dated in the beginning. She'd also assured him that Tilda would come around—but even if she didn't, he couldn't give his teenage daughter a veto over his love life.

But right now, it didn't matter why she'd gone to Twilight Valley—all that mattered was that she was safe.

"You're sure you're okay?"

"I'm fine. And... I'm sorry," she said. "For leaving without telling you where I was going—though I didn't know myself when I walked out the door—and for making you worry."

"Are you ready to come home now?"

"Yeah."

"Don't go anywhere. I'll be there in twenty minutes."

While Tilda was on the phone with her dad, Sarah went to the house to get her a snack and a drink. When she came back, it seemed as if the weight of the world had been lifted off the girl's shoulders and she was throwing a ball for Ed, laughing when he returned to drop it, wet with doggy drool, at her feet.

Though Tilda had only been gone a few hours, Sarah knew those hours must have felt like an eternity to Andrew, because they'd felt the same to her as she'd desperately tried not to think about all the horrible things that could happen to a teenage girl on her own.

Ed halted abruptly in pursuit of the ball Tilda had thrown for him, his ears twitching back and forth for a moment before he barked, obviously hearing a vehicle on the laneway before it came into view.

As soon as Andrew climbed out of his SUV, Tilda ran into his arms and they clung to one another for a long time.

Sarah held back—letting Andrew have his reunion with his daughter. When he finally released Tilda from his embrace, she raced over to Sarah to give her a quick hug before returning to the passenger side of her dad's vehicle.

Andrew made his way to Sarah more slowly.

"Thank you for finding Tilda," he said, his tone a little stiff and a lot distant.

"It was actually Ed who found her," Sarah told him. "I've promised him extra treats every day for the rest of his life."

"I'm sure he appreciated that."

"Or he would, if he had any idea what I was saying."

He nodded slowly, and with every second of terse silence that passed between them, so did Sarah's hope of a happy resolution for their relationship.

Her ominous feeling was confirmed when he said, "Anyway, it's been a chaotic couple of weeks and the next few won't be any better with the girls both starting school soon."

She took a moment, not because any effort was required to read between the lines, because she needed the time to absorb the impact of the words she knew were intended as the knockout punch to their fledgling relationship. Then she lifted her chin and met his gaze evenly. "Could you at least be as honest with me as you were with your daughter and admit that you're dumping me?"

"I'm sorry," he said, and to his credit, he did sound regretful. "But I have to focus on what's important. My family needs to be my priority."

Because he was a dad, and implicit in the parental role was a willingness to always put your child's needs ahead of your own. Perhaps she hadn't realized that before, because she hadn't grown up witnessing that kind of selfless love, but that was the kind of parent Andrew was.

Her actions had been motivated by love for his daughters, too. But obviously he couldn't see that, or maybe it didn't matter. Because she was, as always, on the outside looking in.

And when their relationship hit a bump in the road, his response was to bail. Just like every other man she'd ever loved, starting at the very beginning with Zack. Maybe it hadn't been his choice to move to Seattle when he was released from juvie, but he'd gone, anyway, and she'd been alone.

Just like she was alone now.

But she didn't say any of that to Andrew.

She didn't say anything at all, because she couldn't speak around the lump in her throat.

"So... I'll see you in town, I guess," he said, his tone somewhat wooden.

She simply nodded and stood there with her heart breaking into a thousand pieces while he walked away.

When Tilda got home from Twilight Valley, she found Lilah standing in the doorway of her bedroom, her eyes red-rimmed and swollen from crying. Tilda immediately knew that she was responsible for her sister's tears, and the realization that she'd caused Lilah so much distress made her stomach cramp—like it sometimes did when she wouldn't eat.

"Tilly!" Lilah called out her sister's childhood nickname as she ran to her, wrapping her arms around her middle and sobbing as she held her tight.

And Tilda found herself crying again as she hugged Lilah back.

After several minutes passed, Lilah finally let go and took a step back. "Why'd you run away?"

Tilda stuffed her hands into the front pockets of her shorts. "I didn't really run away. I just needed some time to think about some stuff."

"What kind of stuff?"

Tilda hesitated. But Dad was right about secrets eating way at a person—and she'd been sick about this one since February. And maybe it didn't affect Lilah directly, but she deserved to know.

"Like the fact that Dad's not really my dad," she said. "I mean, he's not my biological father."

"I don't understand," Lilah said.

"Mom got pregnant by someone else before she married Dad."

Lilah's cheeks turned pink. "Oh."

Obviously the idea of their mom having sex with a man who wasn't their father was a little disconcerting—to both of them. (Although Tilda didn't really want to think about Mom having sex with Dad, either.)

"But you're still my sister," Lilah said.

"Yeah, I'm still your sister." She hugged her again. "I'll always be your sister."

"I'm glad you're home," Lilah said.

"I thought maybe you'd be glad that I was gone," Tilda admitted.

"Why would you think that?"

"Because I've been a horrible sister."

Lilah sniffed. "I'd be happier if you weren't a horrible sister, but I never wanted you to go away."

She could barely speak around the lump in her throat. "I'm sorry, Lilah."

"For leaving?"

"For everything."

"I'll forgive you if you promise to try to be nicer from now on."

"I promise to try," she said. "Maybe we can start by walking to The Trading Post to get some cherry blasters?"

"I don't know that Dad's going to let you leave the house for the next month," Lilah warned.

"Let's find out."

After confirming that they each had their phones, Andrew did let them leave the house. And though the events of the day had scraped his emotions raw, he realized he was happy to see them go off together. How long their newfound understanding of one another would last was yet to be seen, but he was taking it as a win for now.

While the girls were out, he called his sister to let her know that Tilda was home and safe—because of course she'd been one of the first calls he'd made when he'd realized his daughter was missing.

When they were back home and tucked into bed, he collapsed on the sofa, physically and emotionally exhausted. His eyes had just started to drift shut when he heard footsteps on the stairs.

He patted the sofa beside him, a silent invitation, and Tilda sat down.

"We said no more secrets, right?" Tilda said.

"That's right," he confirmed.

"Then you should know I didn't leave because I was upset to learn that you weren't my dad," she admitted. "I've known that since February."

"Since *February*?" Andrew was stunned. "How did you find out?"

"I heard Mom talking to Daphne," she said, naming a longtime friend of Miranda's in Beaumont.

Secrets have a way of coming out.

And he could only imagine how distressing it must have been for Tilda to learn about this one, and his heart ached for her.

"Does your mom know that you overheard her conversation?" he asked her now.

She shook her head. "No."

"Why didn't you say anything?"

"Because I was afraid that if you knew, you wouldn't want me."

"Oh, honey. I would *never* not want you."

"But... You're not even my dad."

"Just because we don't share DNA doesn't mean I'm not your dad."

"That's what Sarah said," Tilda confided. "She also said that I should know that I can always talk to you, because you'll always be on my side."

"Did she have anything else to say?" he asked, feeling more than a slight twinge of guilt to realize that while Sarah was working to mend the fractures in his relationship with his daughter, he was resolving to end his with her.

"She said that if you grounded me for life it was only because you were so worried about me—because you love me."

"She's right about that, too," he noted.

"Am I grounded?"

"It's my job as a parent to ensure you know there are consequences to your actions."

She sighed. "That sounds like a yes."

"On the other hand, while I'm certainly not happy you snuck out, I'm glad you went somewhere you felt safe."

"So… Maybe I'm not grounded?" she said hopefully.

He managed a smile. "I think I need to sleep on this one."

"Okay." After another minute she said, "I'm sorry I gave you a hard time about Sarah. I was afraid that if you fell in love, like Mom and Perry, you wouldn't want me and Lilah around, either."

"I promise, even if I fell in love a hundred times, no one would ever take the place of you and Lilah in my heart."

"Nobody falls in love a hundred times," she scoffed.

"Probably not," he acknowledged with another smile. "And even though things didn't work out between me and your mom, I'll always be grateful I fell in love with her because she gave me you and Lilah."

"But you love Sarah now, don't you?"

"Yeah," he admitted, only now acknowledging the truth to himself. "But I messed things up there."

"Because of me?" Tilda asked worriedly.

"No. Because of me. Because it's been the three of us—me and you and your sister—for so long that I forgot how to let anyone else in. Or maybe I didn't want to let anyone else in."

And he'd been so terrified for Tilda that the fear had pushed everything else—including Sarah—aside.

"But you can fix it, right?" she asked him now.

"A relationship isn't like a broken appliance," he said. "You can't just order a replacement part and expect it to work like new."

She considered that for a minute. "So maybe it's like an egg," she decided. "Once you crack the shell, you have to make it into something else—something better. Like an omelet."

"That's a pretty good analogy," he mused.

"A lot of life's lessons are learned in the kitchen. My dad taught me that."

"He must be a pretty smart guy."

Tilda tipped her head against his shoulder. "He's the best."

Chapter Twenty-One

Andrew had spoken to his sister several times over the past few weeks in an effort to keep her up-to-date on all that had been happening. And even when they didn't talk, she checked in almost daily via text message.

Two days after Tilda went missing (his daughter still maintained that she'd only needed some time and distance to think and had *not* been running away), Rachel called while he was finishing up a batch of cream puffs for a bridal shower. He put her on speaker so he could continue to pipe filling while they talked.

After the usual exchange of pleasantries, she asked, "Have you got a bed for the spare room yet?"

"A bed and a dresser plus a wingback chair and reading lamp," he told her. "When are you coming for a visit?"

"Rob and I want to make the trip for Thanksgiving."

"You usually go north to spend the holiday with his family," he recalled.

"That was when we saw you and the girls all the time. Now that you don't live ten minutes away, we miss you."

"We miss you, too."

"So… Thanksgiving?" she prompted.

"That would be great," he said.

"I suspect you're going to be busy at the bakery, so I'd be happy to handle the shopping and cooking for the big meal— assuming I wouldn't be stepping on any toes."

"My toes will be at the bakery," he confirmed.

"I was referring to Sarah's toes."

"Thanksgiving is more than three months away. I have no idea where her toes are going to be by then."

"If that's true, then you're not half as smart as I've always given you credit for being," she said.

"Sarah understands that my focus needs to be on Tilda and Lilah right now."

His sister sighed with obvious exasperation. "You're my brother and I love you, but you really are an idiot sometimes."

"I love you, too," he said, deliberately ignoring the latter part of her remark.

"Sarah cared enough to see what was going on with Tilda, to draw your attention to her behavior, to forgive you for challenging her observations and to be there for all of you when the situation hit a crisis point. She was also the one that Tilda ran to when her world was turned upside down, and you responded by pushing her out of your life?"

"Tilda didn't run to Sarah," he denied. "She went to Twilight Valley."

"Because she knew Sarah would be there."

"And maybe Tilda wouldn't have felt the need for time and space if I hadn't followed Sarah's advice and told her the truth about her parentage."

"It was the right thing to do. Tilda had a right to know."

"When you have kids of your own, I'll come to you for parenting advice," he said.

"I'll bet that's what you said to Sarah, too," she retorted. "And if you did, then I hope *she* dumped *your* ass."

"I've got cream puffs to box up," he told her.

"I'll let you get to it," she said, and disconnected the call.

A few minutes later, after the cream puffs were on their way to the bridal shower, his phone chimed with a text message.

We're still coming for Thanksgiving. Hopefully you'll have your act—and your family—together by then.

When Andrew pulled up outside Claire and Devin's house—only a week after he'd raced to Twilight Valley to find his daughter—he took a minute to appreciate the ecstatic greeting he got from Ed, because he suspected the dog's owner wouldn't be nearly as happy to see him.

"Did you take a wrong turn somewhere?" Claire asked, both the question and the distinct chill in her tone confirming his suspicion. "Because that's the only reason I can think of that you'd be at my door."

He straightened up slowly to face her. "I did take a wrong turn. And I made a lot of other mistakes, too. Which is why I need to find Sarah to make things right, because there's a big empty hole in my life without her."

He could tell his admission surprised her, but Claire's tone remained guarded when she replied, "Well, she's not here."

"But you know where she is," he guessed.

"I do," she confirmed.

"Will you tell me?" He offered her the box of chocolate caramel nut cupcakes in his hand. "Please?"

"Are you really trying to bribe me?" Her tone was colder now than the inside of his flash freezer.

"They're not a bribe," he denied. "They're a *thank-you*."

"A *thank-you* for the information you want me to give you?" she guessed.

"No, a *thank-you* for being the one person Sarah can always count on."

She accepted the offering then and responded in a tone only slightly less chilly. "Sarah went to Las Vegas for Jenna and Harrison's wedding."

"I didn't know they'd set a date."

"Now you do."

"And now I know why her phone's turned off," he realized.

"It might be turned off," she allowed. "Or she might have blocked your number."

"Another possibility," he acknowledged.

"Was there anything else?" she asked, when he continued to linger.

"I know I screwed up," he told her.

"That's something we agree on."

"I was worried about Tilda—panicked—and I took it out on Sarah."

"She was worried, too. And you responded to her efforts to help by telling her that you were done."

He winced. "She really doesn't have any secrets from you, does she?"

"We're best friends," Claire reminded him.

"It wasn't one of my finest moments," he acknowledged.

"And yet, it was no less than what Sarah expected."

"What do you mean?"

She gave an exasperated sigh, the breath escaping her lungs like air bubbles from a soufflé. "Throughout her life, whenever the going has gotten tough, instead of standing by her—as people who care about you are supposed to do—the men in her life have walked away. And so did you."

"It wasn't like that," he denied.

Except it was exactly like that, and the blatantly skeptical expression on Claire's face told him she wasn't fooled for a minute.

"Okay, I can see why it might look that way," he allowed. "And I know I'm going to need to prove myself to get her back."

"Do you have any reason to believe that she'd want you back?"

"She told me that she loves me."

"And she'll be the first to admit that she falls in love too easily, and always with the wrong men." Claire glanced at her watch. "She's been in Vegas for almost thirty-six hours—by now, she's probably fallen in love with someone else there."

"You don't pull any punches, do you?"

"Not when it comes to my best friend," she agreed.

And he knew that Sarah was lucky to have Claire in her corner. That when the going got tough, this woman at least had always stood by her.

"When is she coming back?" he asked now.

"I don't know."

"I thought she told you everything."

"And you expect me to prove that she does by sharing that information with you?" she challenged.

He shrugged. "It was worth a shot."

After a brief hesitation, she said, "She said she'd be at work on Monday. I told her there was no reason to rush back and suggested that she should take a few extra days to have some fun."

"But she'll keep you in the loop about her plans," he realized.

"Of course."

"Will you let me know when she's on her way?"

"No. But I'll tell you that she went on a private charter out of Battle Mountain."

"Thank you."

"I won't say you're welcome, but I'll wish you luck. You're going to need it."

Whoever said it was better to have loved and lost was obviously a masochist, Sarah thought, as she gave the hand-tied bouquet of creamy white roses to her sister in preparation for her walk down the aisle.

It was better—far better—to love and be loved in return, as Jenna and Harrison obviously loved one another.

"I can't tell you how much it means to me that you could be here," Jenna said to her after the formalities were concluded.

"There was no way I was going to miss my little sister marrying the man of her dreams."

"I never dreamed of anyone like Harrison," Jenna confided. "And I've never loved anyone more."

"Be happy," Sarah said. "Always."

"I will be."

When the bride released Sarah from her embrace, the groom moved in to hug his new sister-in-law. "Thank you for celebrating with us this weekend, but especially for letting Jenna have Han. She told me the story, and if you'd taken the puppy, she and I might never have met, and my life would have been forever incomplete."

Those words echoed in Sarah's mind throughout her flight back to Battle Mountain the next day. Maybe it had been destiny that Jenna and Harrison met at the dog park—and maybe she was destined to be alone.

Not that she was ready to give up on love just yet, but she was finally considering the possibility that her life was meant to follow a different path. That she'd find her happiness in the job she loved and the friends and family who enriched her life in countless ways.

But still her heart ached, because there was a great big Andrew-Tilda-Lilah-shaped hole in it.

Because he was on her mind, as he always seemed to be these days, when Sarah saw him standing beside her SUV in the airport parking lot, she felt certain he must be an illusion. She blinked a few times, but every time she opened her eyes, he was still there. Looking every bit like the man she suspected she would always love, even if he wasn't capable of loving her back.

And then she saw that he had something in his hands.

Oversized cue cards, she realized, and her heart did a slow somersault inside her chest.

SOMETIMES I STRUGGLE TO FIND THE RIGHT WORDS

SO I'M GOING TO TRY IT THIS WAY INSTEAD

"I'd rather you didn't," she said.
His only response was to turn to the next card.

TO TELL YOU THAT I'M SORRY I EVER BLAMED YOU

AND THAT I WAS WRONG

She really didn't want to do this, but she couldn't seem to make her feet move to walk away.

MY DAUGHTERS ARE THE CENTER OF MY WORLD

BUT WITHOUT YOU—IT SEEMS AS IF THERE'S NOTHING ELSE

She felt a lump rise in her throat, because she knew exactly what he meant. It had only been nine days, but she'd missed him unbearably.

SO PLEASE SAY YOU'LL GIVE ME ANOTHER CHANCE

TO PROVE HOW MUCH I LOVE YOU

AND WANT YOU TO BE PART OF OUR LIVES

He lowered the last card and waited, obviously for some kind of response.
But how could she agree to give him another chance—even

if that was what she desperately wanted to do—when her heart was still battered and bruised from the last one?

"Who told you that *Love Actually* is my favorite movie?" she asked instead. "Because I know it wasn't Claire."

There was no way her friend, understanding how much he'd hurt Sarah, would give him an inside track.

"It wasn't Claire," he confirmed. "She said that her loyalty would always be to you and if I couldn't figure out how to make things right on my own, I didn't deserve you."

"So who told you?"

"Zack," he confessed, a little sheepishly.

"Zack?" She frowned. "You mean Zack Kruger?"

"Yeah."

"How do you know him?"

"I don't know him, but I called him."

"You called Zack?" She was struggling to wrap her head around what he was telling her.

He nodded. "And let me tell you, I'm glad your first boyfriend wasn't named John Smith, because I'd probably still be making phone calls in an effort to track him down. Thankfully my search for Zack Kruger only turned up thirty-nine people by that name in the whole country. Two of them residing in Washington State and only one of those a lawyer."

"Okay, so you get an A in your efforts to track him down," she said. "But the real question is, *why*?"

"Because I knew I needed an edge if I was going to have any hope of winning you back and Claire had already made it clear that she wasn't going to be any help. To be honest, Zack wasn't too keen on the idea at first, either, and it took a lot of fast talking to convince him that I'd finally realized you were the best thing that ever happened to me and now needed to convince you that I knew it. In the end, he agreed to talk to me so long as I agreed that he could kick my ass if I ever hurt you again."

"And you agreed to that?" she said dubiously.

"If I ever hurt you again, I will absolutely deserve to have my ass kicked."

"If I let you back into my life, you will hurt me again," she said, both saddened by and resigned to the fact. "Because I want—I *need*—to be an equal partner in a relationship and you don't know how to let anyone in."

"I know I've been overly protective of my daughters—and myself," he admitted. "Perhaps because it's just been the three of us for so long and because Miranda's decision to abandon our family left some pretty deep scars."

"I can empathize with what you've been through," she told him. "But we've all been hurt. And while that's a risk you take when you open your heart, it's a risk I can't take with you again, because I know it will only end with more hurt."

"You said you loved me," he reminded her.

"And I do," she confirmed. "But love isn't always enough."

"Don't say that," he pleaded.

"How many times have you seen *Love Actually*?" she asked him now.

"Once," he admitted.

"So maybe you didn't realize that while Mark's grand gesture with the cue cards is widely viewed as one of the most romantic scenes in the movie, he doesn't get the girl in the end."

Andrew frowned. "That doesn't seem right."

"But it's realistic," she told him. "Not everyone gets a happily-ever-after in life."

"Maybe because they give up too soon."

"Or maybe because life doesn't follow a movie script."

"I'm not giving up on us, Sarah." He rifled through the

cards until he found the one that said "to prove how much I love you" and held it up again.

It took every ounce of willpower she had to turn and walk away.

"Five days," Claire said to Sarah, as they moved the horses into their stalls the following Friday afternoon.

Sarah looked at her blankly.

"It's been five days since the hottie baker channeled the most romantic scene in the most romantic Christmas movie ever for my best friend, and I had to hear about it not second-hand but—" she counted silently on her fingers "—fifth hand."

"How did you hear about it?" Sarah wondered, giving Jezebel's cheek a rub as she latched the mare's door.

"Nat told Kevin who told Jason who told Devin who told me."

Nat was Natalya Dawson, who'd flown the charter from Las Vegas, Kevin was her husband, Jason was his best friend and colleague as well as being a cousin of Devin—and also of Sarah.

"I didn't realize Nat saw anything," she said now.

"She was parked not too far from you at the airport, which isn't the point and not how this friendship thing works," Claire admonished. "You're supposed to tell me these things. And when they happen, not five days later."

"Are you saying I should have pulled out my phone and sent you a text while he was going through his cards?"

"Maybe not right then," her friend allowed. "Although if you'd pulled out your phone, you could have snapped a picture. I would have paid good money to see that."

"I'm sorry I didn't tell you. I'm even sorrier that you had to hear it from Devin who heard it from Jason, et cetera."

"I'm your best friend. I would have been there for you."

"Aren't you tired of being there for me?" Sarah asked wearily.

"Never."

"Well, maybe I'm tired of needing someone to be there for me and trying to stand on my own two feet for a change," she said, offering a slice of apple to Dumbledore when the usually shy gelding put his nose over his gate to greet her.

"Which is admirable," Claire said. "But even standing on your own two feet, how did you resist throwing yourself in his arms?"

"By reminding myself that his gesture was nothing more than blatant emotional manipulation and that I didn't have time for that."

"Was it emotional manipulation?" her friend asked gently. "Or was it finally opening up his heart to tell you how he feels?"

"Maybe it was how he felt in that moment," Sarah allowed. "Because it's easy for Andrew to be sweet and charming when all is right in his world. But the minute there's any kind of crisis, he shuts me out."

"He's been a single dad for a number of years—he's probably grown accustomed to having to deal with everything on his own."

"And now he can continue doing so," Sarah said.

"That's it? You're over him? Poof, like magic?"

"It's a process," she acknowledged, as they exited the barn. "But I feel good about the fact that I've taken the first step."

She tipped the brim of her hat to better shield her eyes from the bright afternoon sunlight—and gasped softly when she saw Andrew was there.

Not just Andrew, she realized, but Tilda and Lilah, too. And the girls had cue cards in their hands.

Aware that she'd been set up, she sent her friend a look.

"I missed the first grand gesture," Claire said with a shrug. "No way was I missing this one."

"What are you doing here?" Sarah asked Andrew.

"I thought about what you said," he told her. "Then I watched the movie again. And I realized that the reason Mark doesn't get the girl is because he lets her go, because she's happy with Peter, and he wants her to be happy. Because when you love someone, you want them to be happy.

"And if you tell me you're in love with someone else—and that you're happy without me—then I'll let you go, too. But if you're even still a tiny bit in love with me, then there's no way I'm giving up on you—on us."

Behind him, Tilda and Lilah cleared their throats. Loudly.

Andrew stepped aside then so that Sarah could focus on his daughters and their cue cards.

Tilda: APOLOGIES FOR OUR DAD

Lilah: WHO DESPITE HAVING TWO DAUGHTERS

Tilda: CAN BE A LITTLE CLUELESS SOMETIMES

Lilah: IN HIS RELATIONSHIPS WITH WOMEN

Tilda: NOT THAT THERE HAVE BEEN A LOT OF OTHER WOMEN

Lilah: TRUTHFULLY, HE'S HARDLY DATED AT ALL

Andrew: YOU CAN PROBABLY GUESS THAT THEY SCRIPTED THEIR OWN CARDS

Tilda: WHICH IS WHY IT TOOK US SO LONG

Lilah: (AND TOOK HIM EVEN LONGER)

Tilda: TO REALIZE HE WAS IN LOVE WITH YOU

Andrew: AND MAYBE LOVE ISN'T ALWAYS ENOUGH TO GUARANTEE A HAPPY

ENDING
BUT ISN'T LOVE EVERYTHING YOU NEED
TO TAKE THE FIRST STEP
TOWARD A HAPPY BEGINNING?

"Now would be a good time to throw yourself in his arms," Claire said to her friend in a stage whisper.

When he'd shown up at the airport with his cue cards, Sarah had been wary of a gesture obviously designed to weaken her resolve—and very nearly succeeding. And while, at first glance, what he'd done today wasn't all that dissimilar, his willingness to enlist his daughters' help—and their willingness to give it—proved to her that he was finally ready to let her into not only his heart but also his family.

And that was an offer she couldn't refuse.

Andrew handed his cards to Tilda and stepped forward.

"What do you say?" he asked Sarah. "Is love enough to at least get us started?"

"Maybe love and…fresh beignets every Sunday morning?" she suggested, with a smile in her eyes and love in her heart.

"Whatever you want," he promised, drawing her into his embrace.

Lilah: (KISS)

But Andrew's lips were already on Sarah's.

Then Claire and Devin, who'd come out of the house to stand beside his wife, started clapping even before Tilda had a chance to show her last card.

(APPLAUSE)

And Ed barked happily as he danced around the kissing couple.

Epilogue

Ten months later

Andrew decided to mark the one-year anniversary of Sugar & Spice with free cupcakes for the first one hundred customers through the door. Sarah didn't understand why he felt the need to give samples away when the success of his business proved people were willing to pay for his delectable treats, but she did understand his desire to share the milestone with his loyal customers.

And she was happy to join the party and reflect on how much they had to celebrate—most notably how well his daughters were thriving in Haven. Tilda continued to have regular sessions with her counselor and was maintaining a healthy lifestyle that included daily walks with the dog Lilah had finally convinced Andrew to adopt—along with two cats—from the local shelter. In addition, the girls were enjoying regular visits with Miranda and Perry, who (according to Tilda) still talked too much about wine but absolutely doted on his stepdaughters.

Warren was researching colleges in advance of his senior year, had a part-time job stocking shelves at The Trading Post, continued to volunteer at Twilight Valley and somehow still found time to play D&D with his geeky friends—a group of which Tilda now declared herself a proud member.

The previous fall, Sarah had been surprised to get an invitation to Zack and Imani's wedding—addressed to "Sarah and Andrew"—and even more so when he voted to go to the wedding so that he could thank Zack in person (and maybe prove that he didn't deserve to get his ass kicked).

A few weeks after that, they were in attendance when Gramps exchanged vows with Helen. And after the ceremony, the octogenarian groom expressed sincere pleasure that Sarah had finally managed to find a man worthy of her—even if that man hadn't given him a discount on the cake.

At the end of February, Claire had given birth to a baby girl, and Sarah was currently making the rounds of the bakery with four-month-old Everleigh on her hip while the new mom chatted with Jenna, who'd recently announced that she and Harrison were expecting their first child before Christmas.

But they were the only ones expanding their families. Rachel and Rob had shared similar happy news when they visited at Easter and now, at six months, the mom-to-be was absolutely glowing. Sarah had been a little surprised when Rachel and Rob said they were making the trip to Haven again for Sugar & Spice's anniversary party, but she was always happy to see them, as were Tilda and Lilah.

Feeling a slight tug on her skirt now, Sarah glanced down at Elijah, Nat and Kevin's three-year-old foster child. The little boy had been in their care since the previous Thanksgiving and, if all went according to plan, they would officially be his parents by Thanksgiving this year.

"Cupcake?" Elijah said hopefully.

She squatted beside the boy, the baby still on her hip, so that she was at his eye level. "What kind do you like?"

He pointed to a vanilla cupcake with a swirl of multicolored icing in the display case—Tilda's handiwork, no doubt—and Sarah ducked behind the counter to snag his treat, not worried that the last of the freebie cupcakes had been distributed hours earlier.

"That's his second one today," Nat said, shaking her head when she saw the little boy with the cupcake in hand and smears of red and blue and yellow icing on his face.

"Whoops," Sarah said.

"Not your fault," the other woman assured her. "I can never say no to him, either."

"I swear there are more people here today than there were on opening day," Erin Landry remarked, sidling up beside Sarah when Nat moved away.

"The really odd part is that people keep coming in but no one seems to be leaving."

"Has it happened yet? Did I miss it?" Kyle asked, joining his wife.

Erin sighed. "You didn't miss it, but you might have blown it."

He spotted Sarah then and winced.

Before she could respond, Devin swooped in.

"Mine," he said, and stole back his baby.

Over the quiet murmur of voices, someone cleared their throat. Loudly.

Then Andrew made his way to the center of the room.

"I want to take a minute to thank you all for being here today to celebrate the anniversary of Sugar & Spice, but also and especially for your support over the past twelve months without which we wouldn't be celebrating this milestone.

"I will admit to having some reservations when I moved from Texas to Nevada to start my own business here. It's hard to start over, especially in a place where you know only two people. But soon I knew three people and then four and five and—"

"Most of us here can count," Rob interrupted his brother-in-law.

"My point is that, very quickly, the residents of Haven showed me and my family what it means to be part of a community. And one particular member of that community has become an integral part of our family—offering her love and support through sickness and in health, good times and bad, for better and for worse."

Rachel stepped forward to elbow her brother. "I think you're getting a little ahead of yourself and treading on the actual vows there."

He met Sarah's gaze then and shrugged.

Tilda came to her dad's rescue, handing him some cue cards.

I SOMETIMES STRUGGLE TO FIND THE RIGHT WORDS TO KNOW WHAT TO SAY

SO I'M GOING TO TRY IT THIS WAY INSTEAD

"Really? You're going to do this again?" she asked. But she was smiling, her love for him and his whole family shining in her eyes.

"Just one more card this time," he promised, and turned it around so she could see the words he'd written.

WILL YOU MARRY ME?

Sarah lifted a hand to her chest, where her heart was suddenly so full it felt as if it might burst out of her chest. The crowd around her was silent, waiting, as she blinked away the happy tears that blurred her vision to accept the Sharpie Lilah offered.

Still smiling, and holding Andrew's gaze the whole way, Sarah breached the distance between them, uncapped the marker and wrote her response.

Of course, it was YES.

And the crowd of family and friends gathered around erupted in applause without any prompting.

* * * * *

Don't miss the first installment in
Brenda Harlen's new miniseries

The Cowboys of Whispering Canyon
The Rancher's Temptation

On sale July 2025, wherever
Harlequin books and ebooks are sold.